COMING HOME
by
Becky Haydock

Chapter One

Beginning Over

"For goodness sake Miranda, open the window, I'm getting soaked here!" Steve banged furiously on the car window making Miranda jump. She frowned and wound down the glass as Steve hastily pushed a damp brown envelope through the tiny gap. Miranda grabbed it quickly, placing it on her lap. "Thanks Steve, you're an angel." she said. "I'll see you in a few days. Take care of yourself." Steve smiled at her, rain dripping down his face. "Okay my lovely. Don't forget to say hi to your sister from me!" he chirped back as he ran hastily to the front door of the house trying to avoid the huge raindrops that dripped off the porch roof.

Miranda White sloped back in her seat, tutted in irritation and bit her lip. She wasn't sure if she was more annoyed about forgetting the brown envelope or her husband's sarcastic little farewell quip. She knew how much he disliked her sister Dahli; her lifestyle, her demeanour and her complete ambivalence towards him. Steve, always the dependable, hardworking, loyal husband had put up with lots these last few years and she started to feel a little sorry for him. She pulled off her wet brown leather coat, throwing it on the backseat of the car and placed the envelope on the passenger seat, slowly moving her fingers across its damp surface. She paused for a moment to read the writing scrawled in her mother's hand, "To my darling Dahli, love your dearest Mother". A sudden and rather unexpected sadness filled Miranda's mind and she grimaced. "This is no time to get sentimental." she thought and quickly fastened her seatbelt, started the ignition and checked the mirrors. A long journey across the country in search of her errant sister was about to begin and she was not looking forward to it one bit.

Four and a half hours later and the rain was still not easing. This was not normal September weather Miranda thought as it pounded on the soft top of her Audi convertible and made visibility tedious and trying. There had been roadworks after roadworks on the motorway and she was feeling weary from the concentration. Finally she pulled into the hotel car park in the small market town called Flockinton just north of the New Forest where she was staying for a couple of nights, and grabbed her overnight bag. "At last."

she thought. "Rest and relax before heading out again in search of darling Dahli". They'd been so close as children, spending every waking moment together in an idyllic childhood in the Cheshire countryside with their two parents, Ian and Mathilde Rosenberg. Their father was a solicitor working out of an office in Knutsford and their mother owned a craft shop called, "Crafty Creations" also in the town. Dahli was two years older at thirty eight though Mother always used to call them the twins due to their closeness but then things changed. Dahli suddenly grew into a distant and uncommunicative teenager and left home at sixteen to study in France. Miranda put it down to adolescence and Mother and Father seemed more than keen to pay for her to study at a private French college in Lyon. She had become incredibly belligerent and especially towards Father, but she had a passion for France that absolutely no-one could ever fathom why and no-one dared to ask.

The hotel room was basic and sterile; a typical budget chain thought Miranda. She opened the drab brown blackout curtains and looked down at a small paved courtyard scattered with a few brightly painted metal chairs and tables. A couple of staff members were on their break, smoking and laughing. Miranda was used to high class hotels and she looked around the room with dismay. She flopped down on the end of the big double bed, resigned to her situation and took out her phone, gave it a wipe and unlocked the screen. She clicked onto Facebook and searched for her sister's profile. There she was - Dahli Patricia Rosenberg. Miranda stared intently at the tiny profile photo and then scrolled down to Dahli's last post - a photo of her looking very happy and maybe a little drunk, with her arm slung around three other women also looking very happy and maybe also rather worse for wear. They all looked so very cheerful, with big smiles on their faces and glasses of wine in hand. A pang of jealousy shot through Miranda like a bolt of lightning. When had she last had a good night out with girl friends? Months. She was annoyed at yet again feeling jealous of Dahli. She had secretly grown ever more resentful of her sister's eclectic lifestyle and the freedom that it brought yet her although she was herself a successful woman with a multi-million pound cosmetics business started when she was just twenty-one with her husband, and two beautiful seventeen year old twin girls, one at finishing school in France and one at agricultural college in

Cirencester. The family home was a modern five bedroomed detached house in a desirable neighbourhood of Didsbury with nice cars on the drive and her and Steve were always draped in designer clothes and jewellery and many exotic holidays. Steve and Miranda had been together since sixth form college where they met in a business studies class, married at twenty and built their lives together. Perhaps it was all becoming too predictable or was Miranda just having an early mid-life crisis? Whatever it was, it pained her.

Chapter Two
The Funeral

Miranda closed her eyes and laid back on the bed, her thoughts wandering back to Dahli and the day their relationship faltered in dramatic style. Having drifted apart in their teens with Dahli going through her adolescent pains, they became close again in their twenties and early thirties, Miranda following Dahli's extensive global travels on social media, sending each other postcards and letters frequently, and meeting up once a year or so to celebrate another year round the sun with copious amounts of partying and alcohol. But then their father died suddenly from a heart attack, three years ago at the age of seventy-two. Dahli had been travelling in Australia in a rented campervan at the time and begrudgingly returned. Dahli and Miranda had not seen each other for about a year, and at their father's funeral there were initially lots of hugs, kisses and good sentiments.

The funeral was a formal affair with many of their father's acquaintances coming to say their final farewells. The chair of the local golf club and his wife attended plus representatives of the local solicitors guild, the local Catholic church, and the Conservative Party of which their father was an active committee member right up to his untimely death. Dahli looked at them with resentment and repugnance as she had always despised her father's friends' often rightist lifestyles, and in particular their annoying sycophantic hero worshipping of her father which was subsequently overplayed at the funeral. The wake was held at their mother's home, a sprawling old house in the countryside and the venue for many a lively social function over the years. Inside people stood around nibbling politely on egg and cress sandwiches and drinking orange juice out of cut glass tumblers whilst quietly lamenting her father's demise and remembering him fondly.

Dahli chose to be alone, standing in the kitchen, leaning on the work top and drinking back her father's best rum which she had taken off the shelf. "Thanks Dad!" she said sarcastically to herself and reached for some more. She hadn't eaten all day, and started to sway slightly from the effects of the alcohol. She was all by herself, feeling emotional and tension started to rise up inside her. "If only these people knew what he was really like." She groaned and carrying the bottle of rum in her hand she careered into the lounge where people were sitting with her mother and looking at family photos. Dahli started to feel increasingly unsettled; everything was too nice, too sweet, too loving she thought. Suddenly she raised the bottle above her head to everyone's alarm, "Here's to my wonderful father, my wonderful kind father." She uttered sarcastically, slurring and swaying, her eyes opening and closing in a drunken haze. "Dahli, darling, please come and sit down." said her mother insistently, standing up and walking toward her, with her arms open, embarrassed and apprehensive.

Dahli waved the bottle again. "Nooo, I am not sitting down with you, any of you." She said, pointing at everyone. "I have only one thing to say." She swayed a little more and took another swig of the rum from the bottle. "You see this man here," she said pointing at a photo of her father displayed on the mantelpiece. "Well this man. He was a shit. A shit of the highest order." She laughed slightly hysterically and her mother took her arm. "Please sit down Dahli, you are embarrassing yourself." said her concerned mother looking at the guests, her eyes fearful and desperate. "Oh mother, you are so ridiculous." continued Dahli oblivious to her mother's increasing upset, and by this time people had started to quietly gather from the other room to find out what the commotion was. "Father? Some father he was. He was having an affair with Aunt Jude - that woman standing over there. For God's sake. They've been at it like rabbits and when I confronted him, he blackmailed me. His own daughter! Yes, blackmailed! What have you got to say now?" She said looking directly at the Catholic priest who lowered his eyes. "You all think he was so pious, so respectful, so dutiful. Aunt Jude, For ten years. Right under your noses. Deceiving you all. Preaching all that religious nonsense. A shit of the highest order. Why don't you all fuck off and go back to your silly little pretentious lives. " Aunt Jude held her hand up to her mouth, gasped, put her glass down and ran out of the room. "Yeah goodbye and good riddance to you Judy darling." shouted Dahli after her, laughing like a drain. By this time Miranda had appeared, grabbing Dahli by the arms before she could say any more, forcibly dragging her out of the lounge into the kitchen. Their mother was now sitting on the chair crying with people consoling her.

The atmosphere in the room grew awkward, people shuffling uncomfortably and looking into their glasses. "How could you, Dahli, how could you? I don't know what you're playing at but seriously?! It's a wake, our father's fucking wake!" screamed Miranda. "Get out of here, go on, take your stuff and don't come back! I hate you Dahli!" Dahli laughed in her face, put the bottle of rum down, grabbed her bag and coat and staggered out of the house, down the path and stood against the wall at the bottom of the drive fumbling for her phone. She vomited impressively against the holly bush and wiped her mouth with her sleeve, then called a taxi and booked into a local hotel for the night.

Back in the house people were starting to leave prematurely. "Please don't go." pleaded mother. "Stay and have another drink. There's lots more food too." but one-by-one people, embarrassed by what they had just encountered and minds troubled, made their excuses and left, and within half an hour the house was eerily empty except for mother, Miranda and Steve. Mother sat on the chair, clutching her photos and crying heavy salty tears. Miranda consoled her whilst Steve started on the clearing up. "I'm so sorry mum. I don't know what came over her. How dare she." Miranda said, still reeling and angry. "Don't worry my dear. She must've had her reasons and she's never been able to take her drink. Not like you my darling, not like you. Thank you." Her mother smiled grateful for her daughter's company, and Miranda put her arm around her and they sat in silence. The next day Miranda left the house, swearing never to contact her sister again and for three years they were estranged, their relationship once again in tatters.

The day after the funeral Dahli arrived back at her mother's house. She stopped on the doorstep and paused before ringing the bell. She could remember very little about the day before except she had told the world about her father's behaviour but more importantly knew that she had hurt her mother's feelings. The door opened and there stood her mother, looking tired and pale. "You'd best come in dear." She said wearily and Dahli followed her into the lounge closing the door behind her. They sat together, Dahli holding on to the arms of the sofa, nervously eyeing the room. She turned to her mother who was sitting quietly, her fists clenched. "I'm sorry mum that I upset you but I meant what I said and if you can't live with it then I'm sorry." There was a pause then mother said, "I knew

Dahli, I knew and I never had the courage to say anything to your father. I let them both make a fool of me. You had that courage, perhaps not at the right time." she laughed "but you had the courage that I never had. Your father was controlling, all his life. I feared him. I hated him."

Her mother stopped talking and burst into tears, of sadness, of relief and Dahli was taken aback. She instinctively put her arm around her mother and hugged her. "Mum, it's okay. We are okay. Nothing else matters." said Dahli trying to alleviate her mother's anguish. "Yes" said mother composing herself, "but I don't think Miranda feels this way. She's taken it very hard." Dahli's blood suddenly ran cold. Miranda, she'd forgotten all about her irate sister. "Don't worry about Miranda, I will speak to her." replied Dahli but that moment never came, there never seemed to be the right time, and Dahli went back to Australia.

Back in her hotel room Miranda closed her eyes, laid back on the bed and shuddered thinking about the whole experience and its subsequent fallout. The last time she had seen Dahli was from afar at their mother's funeral some three months ago. Miranda checked the location of the pub that Dahli was last tagged on Facebook less than a week ago; The Cock and Ferret. Yes she definitely had the right pub. Not having an up-to-date mobile number she had tried messaging her on Facebook but the reply came back unanswered. It might be a long shot but tomorrow she would go in search of the pub and with some super sleuthing hopefully track down her elusive sister to deliver the mysterious brown envelope, then go back home and that would be the end of it.

Chapter Three

The next morning Miranda woke late to her annoyance being an early riser, washed and dressed and quickly put on a slick of lipstick and mascara. She avoided the lift for fear of germs and careered down the cold dusty staircase in her high heels, in search of the hotel's restaurant. Breakfast was a semi self service affair. She sipped weak coffee and chewed on flavourless toast whilst observing a group of suited and booted young men sitting at the table opposite. One of them was shovelling scrambled eggs into his gaping mouth whilst guffawing loudly about some work nonsense. His bravado sickened Miranda. It was the last thing she wanted to see and hear today. How she hated the affected charisma of young professionals. It had been different in her day where modesty and ambition went hand in hand. Hark at her sounding like an old person - she was only thirty six! She turned away feeling suddenly old, got through breakfast and rushed back up to her room for a few hours to work on the laptop before heading out.

It was a bright and sunny day. and the roads were quiet. The route seemed quite ordinary; head west on the A31 for three miles before turning into Hathaway Crescent. "Sounds very romantic," thought Miranda; however Hathaway Crescent turned out to be a long, nondescript road with what seemed like a hundred smaller uninteresting roads adjoining it. Miranda had unexpectedly found herself in the middle of a huge 1950s style council estate, turning left, then right, then right again, then left. It was confusing and to make it worse it had started raining again. "Where's this blinking pub?" she asked herself crossly. "Got to be here somewhere!". The streets looked pretty deserted, just rows and rows of terraced houses and parked cars. She drove past a small playground where a few mums were playing with their children. She stopped the car beside the railings and shouted out, "Can anyone tell me where the Cock and Ferret pub is please? It's around here somewhere." She must have sounded exasperated as two mums came running, waving their arms. "Just over there, love. You can just see the sign. See it?" Miranda craned her neck and caught a glimpse of a rather battered looking pub sign hanging on a pole in the distance. "Ah yes, thanks so much.". "No probs me love" came the answer back. The two women darted back to their children and Miranda drove on despondently.

The pub looked like an oversized concrete toilet block; grey, ugly and neglected. Miranda's dreamy vision of a quaint stone country pub in the countryside with beautiful hanging baskets was well and truly quashed. She groaned loudly with disappointment. Its flat concrete roof, grubby looking windows and 70's style panelled door were uninviting, and she really wished she had done her research a little more thoroughly. Then to make things worse the car park was completely empty and her Audi convertible stuck out like a sore thumb. She reluctantly parked up, grabbed her coat and bag and got out of the car. The car lights comfortingly flashed at her as it locked and she walked up to the front door of the pub. She pushed it slightly and it scraped along the floor and then stiffened. "Damn," she thought. "Why is nothing straightforward?". She heard a loud male voice inside shout, "Give it good push, love," and with that she flung the door open careering clumsily into a man, upsetting his pint. "You okay, love?" he asked, standing up to help her as she collected herself ,"Yes I think so. Thanks." she replied deeply embarrassed and avoiding any eye contact. The man wiped his wet trousers, sat down and quickly went back to playing cards with his friend and supping what was left of his pint as if this was an everyday occurrence.

She looked up and saw that the bar was empty except for the two men playing cards. It was vast and cold, and needed a good lick of paint and new carpets and it was a far cry from the wine bars that her and Steve often frequented in Manchester. She felt alone, slightly nauseous from eating an indigestible breakfast, and somewhat out of her depth. She could see a man wearing Bermuda shorts and a band t-shirt standing behind the bar cleaning glasses with a tea towel so she approached him. "You made quite an entrance there", said the man in a friendly manner. "What can I get you?" Miranda smiled weakly. "Hello. Yes I'm a bit of an idiot. Just a half of lager please. Are you doing food?" Food? What was she thinking? The pub didn't exactly look like The Ivy. It's too late now. The man looked down at his watch, "Ah yes it's midday now so we are open for food. You go and sit down and I will bring your drink and the food menu over. There's also the specials boards at the end of the bar. I'm sorry that the door jammed. Must get it looked at." he said nonchalantly though it was doubtful it would ever get fixed and she reckoned it had been like it for years.

Miranda acknowledged his kindness, paid for her drink and found a seat at a table by the window where she could keep an eye on her car. She looked at the man again in his strange garb and wondered if it was some sort of fancy dress or joke. She decided he was just a bit wacky but it just added to the surrealness of her whole day. The man brought the lager and menu over and placed them on the table in front of her. "Enjoy!" he said as he turned around to go back to cleaning glasses, and she sipped it eagerly. It was cold and refreshing. She placed her bag on the seat next to her, briefly browsed the menu deciding she would skip eating, and got out her phone instead. She double checked the pub from the photo on Dahli's Facebook page. Yes it was definitely the right pub. Miranda finished off her lager and took the glass back to the bar. She waited for the barman to reappear from the back, and as he walked towards her, she started to talk. "Excuse, this might sound a bit odd, but do you know this woman by any chance? She was in here less than a week ago with some other women." Miranda lifted up her phone and showed the man the photo of her sibling. "Her name is Dahli, and she's my sister." He peered at the screen and frowned slightly. He looked up at Miranda then grabbed the phone and walked over to the two men. Miranda was a little surprised at his roughness but followed him dutifully. "'Ere Bob, do you remember this girl? Her name's Dahli."

The man put his pint down and squinted at the screen but said nothing. He passed the phone to his drinking pal and the two men ummed and ahhed for a little while. "Yep, that's Dahli" said the other man, passing the phone back to the barman and returning to his card game. Miranda walked over to the two men relieved that someone had recognised her sister and she hadn't wasted her journey from Didsbury. "Do you know where she might be living?" asked Miranda. The two men looked up at Miranda, seemingly a little annoyed to be disturbed again. "She lives at the campsite, down by the quarry in a van. I think it's called White Stones. I gave her lift there once." huffed Bob's mate immediately looking back down. "Thanks for your help." said Miranda a little helplessly before returning to the bar. She put her phone away and looked at the barman again. "Can you tell me where I might find this quarry please?" The barman smiled and wrote the directions down on a bit of paper. "I hope you find her but hope to see you in here again." he said softly, and Miranda smiled at him before leaving to get in her car, hoping that she didn't have to ever set foot in this place again.

Miranda looked at the bit of paper to memorise as much as possible the directions. She found a postcode on her phone and plumbed the address into her satnav. She was feeling suddenly hungry so decided to head back into town for a bite to eat. It was still early in the day. The town was quiet, the midweek slump thought Miranda. She found a cafe and ordered a hot bowl of tomato soup, followed by a piece of fruit cake and hot chocolate. She was relieved that she had never had to worry about her weight, being a tiny five foot two and a constant eight stone, the opposite to Dahli, who towered above her, with her strong, sturdy bone structure and crazily long legs. She left the cafe and walked along the high street, avidly looking in the many shops. She loved shopping and in particular buying clothes and shoes. She had a walk-in wardrobe at home which was probably the size of Dahli's campervan alone. This was the opposite to Dahli who hated consumerism with a passion. How could two sisters be so different? She bought a few pairs of jeans, probably not needed but satisfied her craving for something new and headed back to the car. Time to go and find Dahli but at least it had stopped raining.

Miranda got back in the car and turned on the Satnav. The old quarry was not far away, just down the main road then onto a little road called Crispin Lane but she had a change of heart and decided to head back to the hotel to drop off her new clothes and have a short rest. She was still feeling a little drained from the long journey yesterday and thought a rest would do her good. Just an hour or so she thought would make all the difference. She opened the hotel room door and dropped her bags by the table and flopped back on the bed. She pulled off her shoes and coat and yawned and fell sound asleep on the large welcoming bed. Three hours later she awoke with a jolt and then panicked. What time was it? "Oh heck, 6.30pm." she cried, she had overslept. Why are these hotel beds so comfortable? She jumped up, straightened her hair, grabbed her coat and rushed out of the hotel into the semi darkness. She felt disoriented but soon she was driving to the campsite near the quarry. Crispin Lane was a narrow country lane surrounded by thick woods, isolated and now getting darker by the minute to Miranda's despair. The lane suddenly came to an opening and there in front of her was a small gravel car park. Miranda stopped the car momentarily leaving the engine running and lights on, and looked around. She couldn't see a campsite or any sign for one so she decided to get out and walk around the car park for a closer look.

She stepped out of the car straight into a great big puddle. "Damn!" she said, shaking her foot aggressively and putting her feet down again, being careful not to get more wet. She walked around the car park slowly and pedantically but still couldn't see a sign for the campsite. She started to feel a little hopeless but just as she was getting back in the car she heard a noise behind her. "Hello, can I help you?" said the shrill voice of the young woman. Miranda jumped and clutched her chest, "Ooh, sorry, you made me jump!" she laughed and the woman smiled at her. Miranda composed herself and continued. "Yes, hello, I'm looking for someone called Dahli. I'm her sister. She's staying at a campsite called White Stones I think." The woman smiled again and looked over to her left whilst pointing. "Ah Dahli. Yes, she does live at the campsite. It's just through that gate over there. Best to stay parked up here, go through the gate and walk down the path. It's only a few minutes down the lane. I'd come with you to show you but I am already late for my Pilates class. Do you know what her van looks like? My parents own the campsite by the way. Well it's not really a campsite, more a place where travellers come and meet up. We provide electric, basic toilets and running water and they pay us a nominal amount. It works pretty well on the whole and we've met some great people."

Miranda didn't like to think of her sister as a traveller. In Miranda's eyes travellers were nomadic, scruffy types scrounging off the government and basically being a nuisance. She smiled and thanked the young woman, put on her coat, grabbed her bag and headed towards the path. She had seen a photo of Dahli's camper van on Facebook and was hoping she still owned the same one, otherwise her task to find the van could be a more tricky one and especially in the dark.. The path was muddy from the recent rainfall and Miranda was wishing she had worn more appropriate shoes as she slipped under foot. Too late now, she steady herself and carried on trying to avoid the bigger puddles. It was now much darker, especially under the trees, and she felt a little afraid, not being used to the darkness, being a city girl. She took her phone out of her pocket and fiddled with the touchscreen to try and turn on the torch, almost losing grip of it with her cold hands, shone the light in front of her, and made her way slowly towards a group of vans a little further ahead. As she got nearer she noticed a few lights and before her she saw Dahli's white van, recognisable by the purple stripes transfer stuck rather amateurishly on the side of it. She suddenly felt relieved but nervous about meeting her sister after such a long time. She walked up to the van and peered through the windows but it was all in darkness. She knocked on the van door but no one answered. She knocked again louder but again no one answered. She felt disappointed. "How dare she be out!" she thought impatiently and wondered where her sister could be. Resigned to not finding her on this occasion she rummaged in her bag and brought out a ballpoint pen and a bit of note paper. She scrawled a short note and her mobile phone number on the paper and stuck it through a crack in the van door. She hoped that Dahli would find it and get in touch soon as she really needed to head back to Didsbury soon.

Miranda started to head back along the muddy path when she heard a distant, faltering voice. "Rann... Rann... is that you?" Miranda's heart skipped a beat. Only one person called her Rann; it was Dahli. She slowly turned around and could just about make out the silhouette of her sister against the trees. A tall, athletic figure wearing dark clothing in tight fitting jeans, leather jacket and biker boots with arms akimbo and her trademark pixie hair. Her sister hadn't changed. The two women started walking towards each other slowly, the only sound of mud underneath her shoes. The air was still and cool against the skin and Miranda trembled slightly with the cold. Then they were standing opposite each other, motionless and staring in the half light. Seeing Miranda's frowning face Dahli spoke first with apprehension. "Miranda, why are you here? What's happened? Sorry I was just getting some fresh water when you knocked. You okay?" Miranda wasn't expecting Dahli to sound so concerned and it threw her off track but she stuttered on with rehearsed words, "I have something for you. Something important from our mother."

Dahli stood for a moment then replied. "Okay. You'd best come inside." She pointed at her campervan down the lane and they walked in silence, side by side then Dahli opened the van door and ushered Miranda inside out of the cold. The pungent smell of burnt incense, cigarettes and stale cooking made Miranda gag slightly. Miranda sighed a tired sigh, took off her muddy shoes and sat on the seat by the window, and Dahli put the kettle on. "Tea?" said Dahli. "Yes OK." said Miranda. Tea was always Dahli's answer to everything, she remembered. Miranda placed the crumpled brown envelope on the table and pushed it towards Dahli who looked down at it with some indifference and turned it round to read the writing on the front. She read the words in silence. Miranda spoke. "We've been trying to track you down for a few months now. Mother left strict instructions in her will for us to not open the envelope but hand it to you personally. It's been difficult, Dahli." Dahli said nothing and pushed the envelope away from her. "I'll open it later." she said dismissively without even a thank you. She was inwardly pensive of what might be in the envelope, didn't want to again experience the grief of losing her mother that opening the envelope might bring, and was embarrassed to have caused so much annoyance to her already obviously irritated sister. Outwardly she appeared rude and offhand.

Miranda frowned. She couldn't stand the developing tension and decided the best thing to do for both of them was to leave. She heaved herself off the cushioned seat and started to rummage for her car keys in her bag. "You're not going already?" said Dahli with a slightly pained look on her face. Miranda could hear the disappointment in Dahli's voice and she stood and looked at her for a moment then reluctantly sat down again. "No, I was just making sure I had my keys for later," she lied so as not to offend Dahli. She was astonished that she had instinctively felt sorry for sister. Dahli reached up and lifted a bottle of Jack Daniel's off the shelf above Miranda's head, poured a couple of glasses and said cheers ceremoniously lifting her glass to her sister's. Miranda had little choice but to join in the faux ceremony and decided that one small drink would be okay to drive on. One turned into two, and then three, and the conversation began to flow more naturally as they drank some more. They relaxed a little and talked about their mother; how they missed her, her smile, her laugh, her passion for life. How her life was cut far too short and how they so wished they could still spend time with her, talking, laughing, doing all the silly things.

It was more comfortable to talk about mother than to talk about each other. Each other, Miranda was thinking. Coincidentally Dahli was thinking the same too and almost at the same time they both blurted out, "What about us?". Miranda smiled a little tipsily "Yes let's talk about us, Dahli. You know it's been three years." Dahli looked up and felt awkward; after all she had been the sole cause of all the distress and the ensuing fall out. "I'm sorry, Miranda but I had to do it." It wasn't an apology but an explanation and before Dahli could get another word in Miranda drunkenly raised her voice - "But why then Dahli? Why then?" she slurred. The Jack Daniels had loosened Miranda's inhibitions. "You really picked your moment, didn't you?" she sharply quipped and took another slug of her Bourbon not really wanting a reply. Miranda started to feel the old anger bubbling up.

There had been three years of unresolved anger and only her patient husband Steve had experienced her fluctuating moods and brooding silences caused by that day's events. The two sisters sat yet again in silence until Dahli stood up. She opened her mouth and waited for the words to fall out but she was dumbstruck. She needed more alcohol so she took yet another swig. She knew she had to say something but what? Nothing could account for what had occurred all those years ago. Then suddenly she started to speak, slowly at first but subsequently nothing could stop her. "So you want to know? Here is my story Miranda, the whole truth..." and on she went.

Chapter Five

Dahli had been 14 years old. A sweet, loving, intelligent, happy young girl with her whole life ahead of her. Then her life changed; in a split second it changed forever. A stupid drunken teenage night and she found herself pregnant. Her parents were devout Catholics, the church they frequented very much against abortion, so they agreed a quick and discreet termination at a private clinic in Manchester and no one would ever know especially her sister, Miranda. Dahli and Miranda had always shared everything but not now. Not ever again. That sweet pubescent relationship that they so cherished was gone forever. Dahli had experienced adulthood rapidly and in dramatic fashion and she now knew things that Miranda would never understand at the tender age of twelve. Their rock solid bond was broken. Dahli's guilt was insurmountable. Dahli became a different person literally overnight. She started dressing differently to hide her shame, all baggy black clothes, drinking heavily and became distant and evasive. The church couldn't save her and counsellors couldn't help her. She had betrayed her loving, kind, sweet sister but had sworn an oath to say nothing to anybody. Miranda didn't understand and soon found other friends as they drifted apart. Dahli was anguished but relieved. Ten years went by Dahli and Miranda slowly became friends again. There had been enough time passed for Dahli to feel the need not to mention the situation of ten years ago. Then at a family party Dahli happened across her father with another woman, kissing in the kitchen and to make it worse the other woman was Aunt Jude, mother's sister. "If you dare tell anyone, I will tell everyone about your abortion, even your precious little sister, you little slut." screamed her Father. Dahli was startled by his name calling. How could her own father be so cruel? Dahli paused and stared Rann in the face, "And that's why I spoke out, Rann. Maybe not in the right way, but I'd had enough of him. I don't regret saying it, but do regret upsetting you and mother. Can you forgive me?"

Miranda sat back, reeling from the admissions, perplexed and confused. She couldn't believe that her sister had kept this from all for all these years and a huge part of their life as a family had been a lie. "I'm so sorry Dahli. I don't know what to say." Miranda and Dahli looked visibly upset. "I hope we can get past this, Rann... honestly I don't want you to be too sad by it all." She poured another glass of Bourbon and swigged it back.

Miranda reached for the bottle and poured one for herself too. She needed it. She sat back, sighed heavily and responded. "It's a bit late for that, Dahli. How did you think I would react?" Miranda's response had been sharp but not unexpected. The two women sat in silence for a while and Miranda thought on. There had been signs, she thought with much attrition. I should've known, she contemplated, reprimanding herself. Oh how she wished Dahli could've told her, but then their father had always seemed to have a hold over her, cold and authoritarian. It was all so plain to see now. Miranda stood up and hugged her sister, squeezing her tightly as a way of an apology for her outburst. Dahli smiled. "I'm so very sorry, Please can we start again?"

All evening and much into the early hours they talked it out, acknowledging the difficult circumstances and their father's controlling behaviour. It had felt good for both women, cathartic and cleansing. They had come a long way in a few hours, and sure, there was more talking to do, more emotions to unravel, but this was a good start. Miranda passed out on the van seat and Dahli lifted her legs and laid her down, pulling a sleeping bag over her and gently pushing a small pillow underneath her head. "Sleep tight, little sister." she whispered and kissed her on her forehead. She then went to sleep in the bunk above.

The next morning Dahli opened the small curtain above her head and let the light shine in. "Ouch!" she cried as the bright sun pierced her eyes. Her head throbbed and she rubbed her eyes and leant forward, vaguely remembering that Rann had stayed the night before. She peered down to see a neatly stacked pile of bedding but no Rann. Where was she? The whiskey glasses had been washed up and the van tidied. Dahli felt exasperated. "She's gone. Again. Always runs away when the going gets too tough for her!" she thought and lifted her heavy aching body off the bed and jumped down carefully from the bunk. She clumsily made her way to the van door, opened it and squinted in the bright sunshine. It was warm and sunny with not a cloud in the sky and she looked down the track but couldn't see Rann's car. She resigned herself to an inevitable outcome and went back inside, sitting down to roll a cigarette and considered going back to bed as it was still only 9am. She sat back and sighed, feeling nauseous and tired. The previous night's conversation was now turning uncontrollably round and round in her head. If only she hadn't told Rann the truth then her sister might still be here. She should have known that Rann would bolt. "She has never been able to deal with her emotions or difficult situations. ``Damn, damn, damn", she thought, feeling a rush of enormous guilt.

Dahli went outside again, leant up against the van and lit the cigarette. She breathed in the smoke deeply and with some satisfaction, and sat down on a camping chair taking in the sun's rays. She poured a glass of water and was swigging a mouthful when she heard a car, its engine low and thrumming and its tyres kicking up the gravel. She stood up promptly as it was unusual to have vehicles driving down the lane, and took a look. Was it Rann? A blue convertible promptly pulled up beside her and Rann jumped out with a brown paper bag in her left hand and a couple of thermos cups on a tray in the other. "Breakfast!" she cried exuberantly and beamed at Dahli. Dahli felt terrible for mistrusting her and couldn't believe she didn't have the mother of all hangovers but still managed a weak smile. "Thanks Rann. You're a star." she replied, grabbing the coffees before Rann dropped them, and Rann slammed the car door shut. The two sisters sat together on camping chairs and Dahli dusted off an old table, placing it by the chairs as they both sipped on the hot fresh black coffee. Rann opened the brown paper bag excitedly. "Don't you just love French baking?" she said in a squealing voice. "Croissants, pain aux chocolat and chocolate eclairs. Hope you're hungry. Great patisserie in town, you must know it - the one with the pretty yellow canopy?" Dahli smiled at her. "Yes I know it, I work there. Well maybe I don't bake the cakes but I do at least serve them."

They both laughed and Rann tucked into a pain au chocolat with vigour. Dahli took a croissant and broke it in her hands, lifting it to her mouth and tasting the warm. sweet buttery pastry. It was delicious. She didn't often get the chance to taste the produce at the bakery cafe and it took her back to her college days in Lyon when she had been packed off to France to study. Father had longed to see the back of her but she loved her time in Lyon and never regretted the move. After a few moments had passed Rann wiped her mouthed with a tissue and took another glug of coffee. "What now then, Dahli?" Dahli screwed up her face and scratched the side of her face with her forefinger. "Uhm, perhaps I should open the envelope from mother?" she said. Rann almost choked on her pastry.

What a turn round of attitude from last night. She agreed nervously and Dahli went to fetch the envelope.

Dahli placed the envelope on the table, paused for a little while to look at it once again then ripped open the seal and upended it. Out fell a small bunch of keys on an old brass keyring, a small white envelope and a cheque. Dahli picked up the keys and inspected them before putting them down carefully on the table again. She then opened the envelope and took out a letter, placing it under her nose; Mum's favourite rose scent she thought and smiled. She then began to read the letter aloud.

"Dear Dahli, my dearest darling girl. I hope that this letter finally finds its way to you. Go seek the truth and be happy. I wish you well. Remember I will always be with you. Your darling Mother. Xxx".

A short, sweet letter that was all mother, all mystery and all love. There wasn't a day go by when Dahli didn't think of her mother. She missed her with all her heart and regretted not spending more time at home to be near her over the years. She can still hear her mother's voice though saying, "Be yourself Dahli my darling. Take the world as you like it, and make the most of your time because one day you will not be here." What ironic words, Dahli thought and put the letter down and picked up the cheque; it was for £20,000. She was taken aback; she had never seen so much money. Rann butted in, "I had £20,000 too Dahli. What about the keys?" Rann looked at Dahli waiting for her to look at the keys but Dahli hadn't finished thinking about the cheque yet. She knew that Rann would never need for money and perhaps £20k wasn't very much to her but to Dahli it was an incredible amount of money and she had no idea what to do with it. She finally put the cheque down and picked the keyring up. looking at it closely. It was difficult to read, worn and rough in appearance. I think it says "'Bijou', Rue Edward, Port de Vacquelin. It's very old". Dahli looked at Rann confused. What the heck Rann?" Dahli laughed incredulously. "Why would Mother leave me a bunch of keys in her will? I don't get it, Rann. Where did she get these? They must've meant something to her." There was no answer as Rann was also at a loss as to what to think.

Dahli instinctively reached for her phone and opened Google Maps. Port de Vacquelin, Normandy. A seaside village on the north coast of Normandy. There were some lovely photos; it looked very quaint. Dahli put the keys, the cheque and the envelope back in the bigger envelope and got up. "What are you going to do now Dahli?" said Rann, following her with her eyes as she walked towards the van door. "Well there is only one thing for it, Rann. I need to go to this Port de Vacquelin place as soon as possible, and and find out more." Dahli would too, being the impulsive crazy sister, thought Rann. "But first we need tea." she said and stepped into the van, grabbing the kettle. Rann looked despondent as she knew she couldn't go with her sister as she had far too many things to do back home. Well that was her excuse anyway, and anyway Dahli hadn't yet asked her to go with her. Dahli was hoping that Rann would offer to come with her but she didn't so she continued making the tea, a little dispirited.

Chapter Six

It was time for Miranda to head home. She had stayed as long as she could but really had things she had to get on with back in the city. She was disappointed that her sister hadn't asked her to go to France with her but maybe it was something Dahli just needed to do on her own. Dahli had always been an independent person, choosing to spend her life mostly alone, without a steady partner or the need for children. Over the years she had travelled the world with just the backpack that Mother had bought her for her 21st birthday and a secondhand tent, winning and losing friends along the way, never staying in the one place longer than six months. She had sent Miranda many postcards from far flung places; many she had kept over the years. She'd chosen van life just before Father had passed away and it was the most settled she had been in years. She and Dahli were very different people. She waved goodbye to Dahli and sped up the gravel track on her way. She had promised to stay in touch and wished Dahli well on her quest to solve the puzzle that now lay ahead.

Dahli felt a little sad to say farewell to her sister. They had managed to rekindle some sort of relationship but they would now be apart once more and their lives on different paths again. Having thought that Miranda looked a little distant on the mention of a visit to Port de Vacquelin, Dahli thought her sister was disinterested in the whole story of the will and the bunch of keys. and that saddened her. How she would love to start on this journey of discovery with her sister by her side. Never mind, it was not meant to be. Rann had always been a little reserved when it came to taking risks, she thought. Everything in her life had to be planned to the finest detail and have purpose and resolve. How different could they be?

Over the next week Dahli booked the ferry and found a pitch on a local campsite, having persuaded her boss to give her some time off, and googled the internet endlessly, looking at photos of the area, the places, the people. If nothing else it looked perfect for a week's holiday especially as it was the end of the summer and the weather would still be good in France. She deserved a little sojourn she thought as it had been a busy summer in the cafe. She couldn't find out anything more about the mystery property itself though except that it still existed - a small old terraced cottage near the harbour. The day before leaving for France Dahli was packing her bags and checking the van over when her phone rang. It was Rann wishing her well. "And you'll be on the 6pm from Portsmouth, right? I'll be thinking of you." said Rann. "Yes that's right, Rann. Hope we can catch up when we get back?". It was a short conversation and Dahli had thought nothing of her sister's words except that she had the feeling that the sisters were drifting apart again. She was not in the mood for consolation though as she had too much to do before tomorrow.

Dahli drove the short journey from the New Forest to Portsmouth. It was a glorious day and perfect for a sea cruise. She didn't do rough weather as the movement of the boat made her nauseous. She arrived in good time, checked in and then boarded. Excitement started to bubble up inside her. She loved a journey and this one had potential to lead to much more. She had booked an overnight cabin too for a good night's sleep. She dropped her bags in the cabin and then wandered around the boat aimlessly in a happy stupor. It was a lovely feeling, moseying in the shops, grabbing a drink in the bar and booking a meal in the restaurant. Before it went dark she decided to head for the sundeck, to wave goodbye to England. The deck was busy with holidaymakers and Dahli found a seat next to a couple drinking wine out of plastic glasses and munching on peanuts. "Lovely evening, isn't it?" remarked the man, smiling at Dahli. "Oh yes, it certainly is!" replied Dahli peering at the vast calm sea hoping it would stay this way. They appreciated a shared joy and sat back to take in the last of the sun. It was warm on the deck. Dahli checked her watch and noticed it was almost time to go for dinner. She was hungry and looking forward to some French cuisine. As she grabbed her coat and bag she suddenly felt a hand rest on her shoulder, and she turned around surprised. "Oh my God, Rann!" she screamed. "What the f...?" Rann beamed at her and they hugged warmly. "Surprise!" shouted Rann. Dahli shrieked, "I can't believe you, you little devil! I'm just off to the restaurant, will you join me?" asked Dahli. "Mais oui!" replied Rann and off they trotted, arm in arm. The rest of the journey went by quickly. After a superb meal and a good night's sleep both women were refreshed and ready to face the journey to their new destination and possibly a new beginning.

Chapter Seven

December 1918

I've sat here many times before, looking out through the dirty, torn curtain in the coolness of the night and listening to the raised voices. The men are always shouting and arguing; it had become a regular occurrence but tonight it was different, more intense and threatening. I stood nearer the open window, head close to the glass to try and see who they were. One French. One Russian I thought but I could not see them clearly, just hear their endless rant, fierce and angry. They were arguing about money but exactly what was being said was difficult to tell; a mixture of Russian and French all spewing out in a vast angry growl. "You owe me money, you Russian scum! Sauvage Russe! Sauvage Russe!". I turned away to crawl into bed only to then hear what sounded like two gunshots, a woman scream and footsteps running urgently. I froze and grabbed my woollen blanket and curled it round my pale, frozen body, head pressed hard against the unforgiving pillow. My heart beat hard and fast, and my breath quickened. I was frightened but I couldn't dare to look at what might have occurred in the semi darkness of the alleyway outside. I swiftly closed the window to deafen the escalating din and drowsily watched as the moonlight drifted across the wooden floor boards landing on my little sister's sleeping face. Her ringlets softly fell around her cherubic cheeks and she breathed slowly and deeply, serenely asleep. I could cry for her. Just a child of nine years old in this unfathomable, chaotic world that we now lived in. Perhaps death would be easier for us now but no, God had other plans. Perhaps we had too good a life, Papa was too successful and wealthy, Mama too beautiful adorned with jewels and pearls, Lily too innocent and naive, and we are paying the price. We could not be let to die. Suddenly my thoughts were again drawn back to that dreadful day.

June 1918

I am Boris Ottakar Savin, better known as Otto. I live with my parents and little sister outside of Petrograd, Russia. I am 17 years old; not a child, not a man. My father is Gregoriy Savin and my mother is Anastasia Savin. My little sister is called Liliana, known to us as Lilly . We are a happy, quiet family. This is my story.

I sat on the stairs, my knees pulled tightly up to my chest and my palms resting on my cheeks quietly listening to the raised voices coming from the sitting room. The two stern-looking men who had earlier been let in by the butler suddenly appeared at the door, shook my Papa's hand and wished him well, their demeanour serious and tense. Through the gap I could see Mama sitting on the sofa holding her head in her hands. I screwed up my eyes to take a better look; she was clearly distressed. I got up and instinctively headed for the room to find out what was happening but Papa lightly grabbed my arm, "Not now, Otto. Please go to your room. " He hesitated then continued, "The Bolsheviks are coming, and they are coming for us", he whispered in a calm but determined voice. "Go pack a suitcase. Maurice will help you. We leave in the morning." and he disappeared into the sitting room and closed the door behind him without another word. This was not like our Papa but at 17 years old I was old enough to know what this meant. We had lived through two revolutions in less than a year.

My mind went back to early March 1917 and Mama, Papa and I had travelled into Petrograd on that day as we so often did together. Oh, the beauty of Petrograd, I pondered; the grandeur and glamour, its gawdy palaces and lavish churches. It was as if it had something to prove to the rest of the world. Papa went to his office, and Mama and I had visited our tailor as I was in need of a new suit for a family wedding. Our journey into Petrograd was normally a mundane affair but today as we entered the city we could see masses of people gathering on the streets. "What's happening Papa?" I asked innocently, excited but a little afraid. "The workers are not happy with our new government, Otto."said Papa matter of factly. They have no food and the men have no work." The chauffeur avoided our usual route and dropped us in a back street to circumvent the marching crowds. Mama rushed us into our tailors; she was visibly shaken at what we had already encountered. Mr Volkov, our tailor, welcomed us in and noticed my Mama's shaking hands, and sat us down at the back of the shop away from the windows. "You are safe in here, darlings" he said in a gentle voice and ordered his assistant to make tea. Then we heard the noise. Hordes of people were on the move, chanting, waving banners and marching, like a tidal wave moving ever forward, foreboding and brooding.

There must've been 10,000 people on the street on that day, synchronous in intent, pounding the street in their dirty heavy work boots, men, women and children, a black sea of penury. Mama put her hands to her ears as they passed the window, and uttered a little shriek. Papa had told us of the months of public restlessness due to the people's hatred of Russia's involvement in the First World War with its subsequent loss of thousands of young peasant men, the Machiavellian Rasputin with his fatalistic hold over the Tsar and his family had damaged their reputation almost beyond repair, and the lack of available food in the cities was causing a crisis beyond measure with the new government and the Tsar being entirely blamed. Papa had recently witnessed women queuing for bread for hours in the streets in zero temperatures. "What is the government thinking and where is Nicky? Gone to the front but he's needed here!" Papa had said angrily one evening referring to the Tsar with sudden exasperation. "It won't be long," said a man sitting in the tailors, peering over the top of his newspaper directly at us, completely unruffled and nonplussed by the increasingly agitated situation outside. I look at him, puzzled. "Revolution, young man. They won't stand for much more, mark my words. It's coming. The change is coming." He then went back to reading his paper. Mama glanced at him with fear and then she stood forward and started to make her way towards the front door. "Mama, where are you going?" I asked, unsettled by her sudden movements. Mr Volkov ran towards her. "Madame, please stay here. You might not be safe outside." he said but Mama kept going, opening the door with haste and rushed out before we could stop her. I held my hand up to my mouth as she disappeared into the vast moving crowd.

Anastasia pushed her way through the crowd, holding her long dress in her hand so as not to fall and caught the eye of a woman with her small children. "Excuse, miss, excuse me." she shouted insistently to the woman and the woman smiled at her and bowed her head, aware that she was talking to someone from the higher classes, noticing her lace frills and diamond necklace. "Yes, madame, how can I help you?" she uttered keeping tight hold of her two children. "Please tell me, why are you marching today? I do not know." said Mama. The woman saw my mother's concern and naivety, blindly unaware of the circumstances of the people in the crowd. "We march because we have families to feed and we are starving. We have moved our families into the city from the countryside because we were promised a better life but we are working in the factories where conditions are bad, we are poorly paid and now there is no food. We stand in queues for hours in the city for bread. Women have come out on strike and now we are followed by many of the men factory workers in the city too. We are making a peaceful stance. We march to the government building as we want them to help us." She looked Anastasia up and down and then faced her squarely. "I hope you never find yourself like us." she said, looking knowingly at Mama, her final sentence indeed cutting, and wondering what she was doing here in the first place. Mama was shocked and angry. She thanked the woman and walked back down the street pushing her way back through the crowd, then returning to the tailor's. "Mama, are you okay? What were you thinking?" I hugged her and she felt cold. "Come inside and warm up." I said but Mama did not smile. "Let's call the chauffeur and go home. I have seen enough today." She replied, passing me my coat, saying a brief farewell to the shocked tailor and walking hastily to the door.

Gregoriiy stood at the window in his architect's office and stared down at the sea of people on the streets below him. He put his hand to his head, feeling apprehensive and uneasy when his colleague, Ivan, entered the room and they both watched as the crowds walked slowly past, carrying banners heralding slogans like "Land and Freedom" and "Feed the children of the defenders of the motherland" and singing songs. "They're certainly making their point. They seem fairly buoyant." said Ivan but Gregoriiy was not so sure. "This isn't good, Ivan. Something is terribly wrong. These strikes will escalate. " and he sat forward on the edge of his desk, rapping his fingers on the polished wood. Ivan sat down on his leather bound chair and fiddled with a pen. "You worried, then?" he said unperturbed and Gregoriiy wiped his brow with his handkerchief before putting it back in his trouser pocket. "Yes," he answered gravely. Both Gregoriiy and Ivan had been born into modest surroundings but had excelled at their studies and entered the profession of architectural design not long after leaving university. "We've both worked very hard for ourselves and our families. We've reaped the rewards of our labours; nice houses, nice lifestyles, working for the Romanovs and such like but, Ivan, we're caught up in a tug of war. Can't you see it? The Duma is losing control and our alliances will go against us. I'm afraid that our close associate, Nicholas, has become a thorn in our side." Gregoriiy did not fear for their lives at this stage but he felt growing impatience for the bourgeoisie from the Soviet government and peasantry which did not bode well.

The world knows how the events of that week played out. The peaceful protest turned to bloodshed and many innocent people were killed in the days following the first strikes. A new government led by Volodymyr Zelensky was installed but at what cost? Then a few months later overthrown by Vladimir Lenin and the Bolshevik regime. Lenin, a quiet leader of the peasant man exiled for his policies, now appeared from nowhere to "save" Russia from three hundred years of Romanovs rule. I was confused and troubled. After the second revolution of October 1917 much was spoken in our house amongst the adults about the Bolsheviks intent on causing suffering to anyone who had an association with the Tsar, and an ominous and a terrible dread now hung over our heads. The new state wanted to divide all land and estates belonging to the nobility between the people, and Papa envisaged that this would undoubtedly include our house, assets and land too. Over the last ten years Papa had been called on many occasions to do business with the Romanov family, as a successful architect, drawing up plans for the constant renovations taking place at various palaces, but now our alliance with the Tsar threatened our wellbeing.

We lived a comfortable life in a country manor house fifteen miles outside of Petrograd. Papa worked very hard to give us everything we could need. We had ten housemaids, a butler and a chauffeur, and me and my little sister Lilly were home tutored by Anton, a larger than life and rather rambunctious man from Paris. We had been to Paris many times on holiday, Mama and Papa spoke the language perfectly and we delighted in everything French. Worryingly though, Papa had already lost much work due to the First World War and we had already said our sad goodbyes to most of the loyal household.

Chapter Eight

After watching my Papa close the sitting room door I dashed upstairs and flung open my bedroom door. Maurice, our manservant, appeared and put a reassuring arm around my shoulder, an unlikely gesture for someone of his status but perhaps fitting at this moment. "Come now, Otto, let us pack together" and we did just that, quickly and quietly. Clothes, books, some rubles I had saved up, a few photos of the family, my camera, a bar of soap and a comb. That was it. My whole life in a small suitcase. I stood up and looked around the room, and my eyes fell upon my accordion sitting on the chair in the corner. Although I hadn't played it for some years I still felt very attached to it. I scratched my head and thought for a while but there was no way it could come with me. Maurice saw my frustration. "Perhaps your Papa could buy you a new one in Paris?" and he smiled reassuringly. That was comforting enough for now then Maurice said goodnight and left the room.

The next morning we rose early after a fitful sleep and Papa called the chauffeur. It was a grey day and the cold rain would not hold off. We stood on the doorstep watching it bounce dismally off the gravel driveway. The car came around to the front of the building and we calmly got in and took our usual places. Lilly always sat between Mama and Papa on our day trips out. She would be giggling and excited, jumping up and down on the soft leather seats and playing with her soft curly pigtails. Today she was silent and pale, her parents' bodies stiff, their hands clenched, and their faces solemn. Mama put her arm around Lilly and comforted her, her eyes were dark and her gaze terrified, angry and bewildered. I had never before seen Mama like this and it frightened me. She was so ageless and beautiful with a huge gleaming smile, dark brown eyes and black hair, often swept back in a delicate bun. She wore glamorous clothes, gems and jewels of much worth, and dainty gloves made of the finest lace. She was always happy and joyful. Today I felt bereft of this memory.

We drove slowly down the driveway as the fierce rain battered the car, and I pressed my face hard against the cold glass window to take one last look at our home. We drove like a solemn funeral cortege with the only mourners, the overgrown hedgerows and pretty flowers, heavily battered by the rain, hanging their saddened heads. Goodbye beautiful home. In darkness she stood magnificent, proud and brave. What would become of her in our absence? There was talk that houses like ours were being looted and razed, as the Bolshevik Red reign of terror advanced and the revolutionaries gained more control. What had we ever done to them? We were quiet, hardworking, genteel folk, kind to our neighbours and not in any way interested in their politics. I felt a heavy sickness in the pit of my stomach and turned back round. I looked down and wanted to cry and heave and shout and scream but we were not a family of hysterics so I sat back and looked across at my Papa for answers. "Papa, where are we going to stay?" I asked, a little amazed by my forwardness. My Papa, surprised, broke a slight smile and cleared his throat, "We are going to the sixteenth arrondissement, Otto." he stuttered slightly. "Do you remember Madame Zhakarov?" His voice then brightened. "She has found us an apartment to live in whilst we wait to return to Petrograd once the troubles are over. We will be safe there. I have found work as an architect and Mama will home tutor you and Lilly. Think of it as a bit of a holiday, Otto." Mama and Papa both grinned but Papa's words had not been convincing enough, and I watched him shuffle side to side, tapping his foot awkwardly on the floor. I thought of my grandparents; we would be leaving them behind. Would they be safe? I looked over at my Papa. Did he feel that he had somehow failed us? Knowing my Papa he would be feeling for his family. I wondered many things in those few moments and none of them were good. There was silence until we reached the station.

After saying our final farewell to the chauffeur we walked into Petrograd station. It was as I remember it, beautifully decorative, lofty and regal but today it was echoing with tumultuous sounds from the vast disorderly crowds that had gathered hoping to get on a train out of the city. Papa momentarily paused to check the platform location and I noticed beside me a young child lying on the floor wearing a beautiful red coat. She held a dolly in her small chubby hands and spoke softly to it, smiling as she did so. She then placed it next to her and pretended to fall asleep beside it, closing her eyes and placing her hand on her dolly's fragile body. Her naivety of the chaos around us grieved me. Meanwhile her parents were arguing bitterly above her, totally overwrought and exhausted it seemed. Her father waved his hands around above his head angrily whilst her mother screamed, gathered their bags and started to walk off without both of them. The father then roughly wrenched the little girl off the floor causing her to bellow and drop her dolly. He sprinted after the mother, still shouting madly. The dolly lay on the floor forlorn and I picked it up and placed it in my pocket in the hope I would see the girl again. There was nothing else I could do but hope. This was no ordinary day. "Come, Otto, we're heading on," said Papa hurriedly and we rushed along the platform where we observed the train to Odessa in all its magnificence waiting for us.

There was much noise, much more so than usual today. I could see further down the platform a scene of mayhem and confusion. Many people were trying to board the train in third class. Men, women with suitcases and bags, children crying, dogs barking; absolute chaos, pushing and shoving, shouting and screaming in a desperate attempt to get on the train. A young pregnant woman fell to the floor. People trod on her as she bawled, her bags strewn and her arms and legs splayed. There was no humanity or dignity present today; just gross disregard and fear. The train guard blew his whistle, waved his flag, and the final passengers scrambled onto the train, doors open, some with legs hanging over the tracks, with many left behind on the platform, distraught, bewildered and resigned to another day waiting for passage out of Petrograd. Everybody seemed to want to get out of Russia today. In comparison we calmly boarded the first class sleeper carriage to Odessa and the huge train slowly and painstakingly heaved its way out of the station. Papa said if we were going to have to leave our homeland we would do it in style. Mama pulled down the blinds to stifle the evolving outside noise and chaos. "We mustn't worry ourselves with other people's worry" she calmly said, and on that ironic note for three days and three nights we stayed in that sleeper only to venture out to the bathroom or take tea.

Chapter Nine

Odessa was a madness of people. It was mid evening, pleasantly warm and we left the station and walked to the boarding house that Papa had booked us into for one night. Papa had reserved us a family room so we would have some quiet and rest before our long journey across the sea to Constantinople by ship. On arrival at the boarding house there were many weary looking people sitting across the entrance, with their belongings strewn everywhere. We pushed our way through them and stood in the entrance hall looking around for some assistance. A young, dishevelled woman appeared, her face contorted with anxiety. "Can I help you?" she said impatiently, obviously distracted by the noise of men shouting coming from across the hallway. Papa stood forward and smiled, "Good evening, we have booked a family room for one night under the name Savin." The girl smirked rudely and shouted upstairs, "Mrs Oborin, four more arrived." The girl, without a word, then disappeared into a far room and Papa looked perplexed. Then from the upstairs appeared Mrs Oborin, a feisty, thick set older woman wearing a bright red dress and wrinkly stockings. "Good evening, sir. Please follow me to your room." She said as she walked downstairs, pleasant and courteous, and Papa relaxed slightly as we followed her to our room. We were looking forward to a good night's sleep. Mrs Oborin opened a door and walked into a large, semi lit room. We peered into the darkened room curiously. There were two bunk beds that were already occupied by sleeping children, and sitting on the floor were two families, making their beds for the night and sorting their belongings. In the corner of the room by the door was an old man smoking a cigarette and drinking beer from a green bottle, the smell of alcohol drifting across the room. He acknowledged us and went back to drinking. Papa was mortified. "There must be some mistake. I booked a private family room for me and my family." Mrs Oborin looked at him dismissively and with much arrogance exclaimed, "We have no family rooms here. This is what you have. Either take it or leave. I have other families wanting a room." Papa shouted back, "But I paid for a family room. I paid you. We spoke on the telephone." but Mrs Oborin had already disappeared down the corridor, waving her arms behind her. Dejected, Papa reluctantly passed by the other families sitting on the floor and led us to a space near the back window. "I am very sorry," he said, looking at Mama, "This is the best I can do." realising that there would be no other vacant rooms in the city that night.

For the first time in my life I felt sorry for Papa. He had been deceived by a rude and greedy woman and I can guarantee that he would have paid a good price for a family room too. Mama put the bags down on the cold floor, and the young woman who we met earlier threw four blankets and four pillows over to us but missed. They landed in disarray on the floor. "Thank you." Mama said sarcastically, picking them up and we placed our coats in a tidy pile and made our beds. It was only 8pm but the room being in semi-darkness and people already sleeping meant we had no choice but to settle down and try and get some sleep. However Papa was in no mood for sleeping so he made his apologies and stepped out into the chaotic night. Mama let him go without questioning his reasons, for she must have felt, like me, that he needed some time alone, to compose and forgive himself.

The next morning we rose early and folded our blankets. "Otto, Otto!" whispered Papa. "Shhh! Put the blanket in your suitcase. Be careful so no one sees you. It'll keep you warm on the ship. I have one for your Mama too." I obeyed without question as my Papa was always right, and he did the same. Papa never stole or would condone such actions but he was a desperate man at this point and was thinking only for his family's welfare. As we left the room the young woman from the night before pointed at a large laundry bag and was shouting gruffly. "Blankets and pillows in there." and along with everyone else we placed our remaining blankets and pillows in the bag and smiled gleefully as we slowly shuffled out of the boarding house, passing her, and across to the port. It was a hot summer's day and the sun was beating down but the atmosphere was worse than icy. There were scenes of confusion and disorder as crowds and crowds of people hell bent on getting on a ship to take them to Constantinople to start their new unknown lives were aggressively pushing forward. We waited patiently for many hours for our turn to board the ship and little Lilly slept in Mama's arms and Papa held onto the suitcases tightly. I took off my coat as I was hot but Papa wore his wool coat buttoned to the collar despite sweating profusely. "Papa, are you not hot in your coat?" I asked him and he came closer to me and opened his coat surreptitiously. "Look Otto, look inside quickly," and there inside the lining of his coat were sewn what seemed like a thousand jewels, red, green and white. "Wow, Papa, that's amazing." He smiled knowingly. "These will keep us in food for some time, Otto." he joked and we both laughed.

Little was said after that for a while; we were deep in our own thoughts, thinking back to our happier lives, focussing on keeping upright in this precarious mass and agonising about an uncertain future. We suddenly surged forward and found ourselves, to much relief, about to board. People around cheered and Mama smiled relieved however, much to our dismay, a burly man abruptly put his hand out, "Stop! The boat is full! No more people today." He turned his huge back on us but Papa shouted in anguish."We have paid to be on this ship. Look, look at our tickets!" and he waved our tickets frantically at the man but he was not letting us through. In desperation Papa opened his coat pocket and pulled out a huge wad of cash and put it up to the man's face. "Take, take!" he cried, despair etched on his face. Papa had learnt over the years that Russian officials liked bribes. He must've thought it was worth a punt. The man looked around furtively then grabbed the money and quickly pushed it into his jacket pocket. He looked down almost ashamedly, grunted and quickly waved us on to the boat without saying not a word. Papa smiled and the relief was palpable. We pushed our way forward and Mama started to head for the back of the boat but Papa shouted, "No, head upstairs to the deck, my darling. You hear those people coughing? They are ill my dear. Typhus. Keep far away from anyone coughing. They won't get better and they will spread their germs to us." Mama struggled to turn round in the tightly packed crowd but eventually made her way up the wrought iron steps. I looked back to glance at the burly man taking more money from desperate Russians. "Huh, the boat wasn't full after all. " I thought. I was sickened and couldn't believe that my Papa, my strong brave Papa, had yet again been duped by some lowlife.

Mama was holding Lilly tightly who had now woken and was mesmerised by the people, the sights and the sounds, her eyes wide and her mouth gaping. The top deck was crammed with people but the air was cleaner and smelled much better however the silence was noticeable. As we got upstairs I saw the sadness and regret in the eyes of the people here. Some were sitting on the floor, holding their heads or holding hands, praying or weeping. Others were staring out to sea leaning over the side of the heavily listing and immensely crowded ship silently saying their woeful goodbyes to the motherland. I noticed a proud White soldier stood upright, decked in his finest uniform, holding onto his loved ones and hoping for better days ahead, possibly feeling a certain level of guilt for leaving his battalion and his country. The wretchedness felt beyond comparison but what did the future hold for any of us? For many it would be a simple matter of survival in Europe, having lost everything to the state. And our homeland, what would become of her? Stripped of her finest medics, lawyers, soldiers, priests, academics, artists and businessmen, the country would be a much poorer place now we feared.

A large tarpaulin had been secured across part of the deck, held together with a few thin ropes. I didn't fancy its chances as we headed out onto the ocean but it was all we had to protect us from the elements. God help anyone making this same journey during the colder months. For four days and four nights we sat or slept on the deck, huddled together in a corner below the huge stinking, steaming funnel, covered only by the thin blankets that we had taken from the hostelry. Our bones ached from lack of sleep and our conversations became stilted and monosyllabic. Mama had bought provisions on the harbour in Odessa from unscrupulous vendors, inflating the prices, yet naively we had eaten far too much in the first few days and almost ran out of food, leaving us with just a small loaf and three pieces of ham between the three of us.

The morning of day three I awoke early, stretched and looked around. The sun was trying to show its face from behind wispy clouds; it wouldn't be long before it was beating down on the deck. I stood up and tiptoed carefully around sleeping, snoring passengers, making my way below deck to the dismal toilets on the lower deck. It was never an enjoyable experience but essential. I started to make my way downstairs when in my peripheral vision I glimpsed a red coat. Instinctively I turned around and there, sleeping curled up on the floor, was the little girl from Petrograd station. I could not believe my luck. I was ecstatic; I had found her. I slid my hand into my pocket and could feel her dolly's little legs between my fingers. Her parents were fast asleep next to her, the father's arms draped across the mother's, her hair all a mess. I did my business and made my way back up to the deck. The family had awoken by now and were chatting and smiling, sitting upright in the sunshine, eating big chunks of bread and cheese and drinking water from a flask; they looked so different to when I had seen them exhausted in the station in Petrograd. I picked my way through the people and stood opposite them, dolly in hand. "Excuse. Hello. I was at Petrograd station when your daughter dropped her dolly. I picked it up and not knowing what to do with it, put it in my pocket. I am so glad to have found you." The mother laughed happily. "Oh my dear boy, thank you so much. Please, come and sit with us for a while. Would you like a bite to eat or some vodka?" Her invitation was warm and inviting, and I took a seat next to the family, taking hold of a piece of cheese and swigging on the hip flask offered to me. The liquor hit the back of my throat hard and I gasped. It was delicious. We spoke at length. The father was an engineer who had just left the army and they were heading for Constantinople as the mother had family there who they could live with whilst they settled into their new lives. I wished them well and stood up to make my way back to Mama and Papa when the mother spoke, "If you ever find yourselves in Constantinople, please come and see us, or maybe write?" she said, pushing a piece of paper with her address on it into my hand. I felt like I had made some true friends amongst this complicated situation.

Talk on deck had now turned increasingly sour, with the men raging arguments about politics and religion, almost coming to blows on occasion. People were bored and impatient. The wind blew each night and the sea cursed us ever more. Finally we sighted Constantinople in all its glory, its Byzantine walls splendid in the sunlight. There was much conversation now and people were gathering their belongings, wide eyed, excited yet still afraid. I thought about my new friends and what Constantinople might bring them.

From Constantinople we travelled by steamer to Marseilles then onwards by train, changing four times before we finally arrived in Paris. It was another wretched week of constant fatigue and hunger. Mama looked particularly exhausted and Papa held her gently for most of the journey, kissing her forehead and talking to her gently. We arrived at Gare du Nord late afternoon. The station looked like a refugee camp, people scattered everywhere, sitting and standing, some lying down exhausted, looking bewildered and lost, gravitating towards men with clipboards and papers, helping them find accommodation. There was an unpleasant stench in the air of body odour and strong tobacco which caused me to heave. Our friend Mrs Zhakarov pulled up outside the station in her gleaming new Renault Coupe. It was a welcome sight to see after almost two weeks of constant misery. Sofia Zhakarov was a voluptuous woman in her late forties bountiful in both size and character, her hips swaying as she sidestepped out of the car, her bleached blonde hair piled up in the shape of a beehive. Sofia and Mama had been friends for many years in Petrograd but Sofia had chosen her home as Paris as it suited her eccentric lifestyle and eclectic fashion sense. She had never worked a day in her life, having been married to a very wealthy businessman who had left her for a younger woman but had left her with a very healthy bank balance. She embraced my father warmly and guffawed with happiness. "Tis wonderful to see you again my dear man. Welcome back to Paris." Papa hugged her back meekly.

We fell back into the seats of the car, drained emotionally and physically. Mrs Zhakarov started the car and pulled off, jabbering incessantly, words falling out of her mouth like rain, excited and agitated. She gesticulated wildly, frequently taking her hands off the wheel making the journey hair raising. "What is Sofia talking about, Mama?" I sleepily asked Mama who turned to me and sighed. "I am not really listening, Otto". We were shattered and we both giggled quietly. The journey to our new home took about thirty minutes from the station. We were some of the lucky ones. We would be living in the 16th Arrondissement in a grand apartment on a leafy avenue. Papa had secured work with Grand Duke Sarkozy, resdesigning his palatial house in Bois de Boulogne. Papa and Sarkozy had been trusted, loyal friends for many years whilst in Petrograd. It was good, profitable work and as Papa said, "Will see us through until we return to our homeland". I could see Paris out of the car window in all its glory - the Eiffel Tower, Parc Monceau, the Arc de Triomphe and Bois de Boulogne. Not long after I must have drifted off as I was awoken abruptly by Mama's voice, "Hurrah, we've arrived!".

We stood on the roadside looking up at the tall building with bewilderment. There were many small windows, rows and rows of them. I had never seen so many small windows on one building and bright little wooden shutters. Madame Zhakarov pointed upwards, "Third floor. It's okay, my dears. You'll be happy here." then she said her goodbyes and drove off at speed. The huge front door swung open and a little old man casually dressed in an open shirt and loose brown trousers showed us in, more of an escort than a welcome. He handed Papa a small bunch of keys, uttered something in French which only Papa understood, and then helped us with our bags to the front door of the apartment up three flights of winding stairs; if nothing else I would get fit in Paris. It turned out that the old man lived on the floor below us, and Madame Zhakarov had paid him to help us. Father also tipped him generously as was his kind nature but after that we seldom saw him, just the odd "Bonjour" every now and again. I think he was suspicious of us, being Russian, his eyes always narrowed when he saw us, always quick to make an exit; were we really that alien?

Chapter Nine

The apartment was warm and bright though much smaller than we had become accustomed to back in Russia. "More like a butler's quarters." Mama remarked with slight repugnance as she looked around. My Mama wasn't a snob, just used to higher standards. There was a lounge, small kitchen, two bedrooms and a bathroom, with perfunctory furniture and rather mundane decor. It was not quite the grand residence that I had imagined but it was functional. We soon discovered that Madame Zhakarov had left a hamper of freshly baked bread for us, plus the fridge was full of French patisseries, milk, meats and cheeses. The first little bit of kindness after weeks of desperation and selfishness. Papa had employed a part time cook and housemaid who would prepare dinner each night and keep the apartment clean. We spent the next three days in the apartment, recovering from our arduous journey from Russia. Mama had particularly suffered and had picked up a nasty cough which frightened us all. Thankfully it turned out to be no more than a heavy cold and within the week she had recovered fully.

I soon found that the 16th Arrondissement was an elegant neighbourhood, with sweeping boulevards, large parks and gloriously golden buildings. We lived not far from the right bank of the Seine with its wonderful river walk, the Arc de Triomphe and the Bois de Boulogne where the wealthy French and Russians resided comfortably in their grand palaces, shuttered away from the rest of society. Our time living in the area was happy, spending our days picnicking in the parks in the warm sunshine, visiting the many museums and going for long walks along the banks of the Seine. We were absorbed in the culture of the city, enjoying visits to museums like the Russian Literature Library in Rue de Gobelins or the The Carnavalet-History of Paris Museum in the Marais. Papa purchased me a push bike so I was able to travel about the city with ease. The Parisians we met were as gay as described in the papers, with their flamboyant clothing and love of life. This was in marked contrast to the Russian people back home who never broke a smile, however I think Mama and Papa struggled with the contrasting emotions that Parisians evoked, finding them frivolous and fanciful although Lilly and I enjoyed the new way of life.

Whilst Papa worked, Mama, Lilly and I felt a certain amount of freedom that was gratiated upon the wealthier Russian emigres, like one long holiday, with little purpose or impetus. We were living in a kind of holding room, waiting for the return to Russia where I would continue my studies with Anton and eventually secure a place at university. That was my dream, to study and become an architect like my father. Papa and Mama frequently socialised with Russian high society and nobility and although Papa's grasp of French was exquisite from many holidays in the capital they preferred the company of Russians than the Parisians, enjoying many evenings at the theatre, ballet, restaurants or the jazz clubs of Montmartre. We were enjoying our own "Belle Epoque " immersing ourselves in the arts and culture of wartime Paris.

Madame Zharkarov made many visits to our home over the months, drinking tea and devouring our cook's best homemade cakes. She was a godsend for Mama who didn't know anyone in Paris apart from the aloof Duke Sarkozy and associates that Mama and Papa socialised with during the evenings but who rarely had time for us during the day unless it was for business. Though Mama and Mrs Zharkarov were very different people in manner and appearance they soon found that they enjoyed the same cultural interests and read the same books. They would sometimes go out in the car and drive around Paris at great speed that excited Mama, frequenting the odd museum or walking up and down the Champs Elysees visiting the couture shops. Madame Zhakarov introduced Mama to some other wealthy ladies and they would enjoy endless afternoons sitting in some of Paris's finest cafes passing the time of day. Their chatter was endless gossip, and Lilly and I loved listening to them when they visited us on a weekly basis, sitting on our sofa conversing like a gaggle of old geese.

Chapte Ten

Igor

Days in Paris gradually became a little monotonous and I missed my friends back in Petrograd. Papa had sensed my increasing sadness and so one day in September he invited me to join him on a business trip to Duke Sarkozy's palace in Bois de Boulogne. I was delighted at the idea, having always enjoyed the long walks around the park and the sense of freedom that it gave, and now the opportunity to visit a palace too. We walked to the Duke's residence, taking in the fresh Autumn air, discussing the Duke's architectural plans and the Duke's son, Igor who Papa explained had been unwell recently, unable to leave house and would benefit from some company. On arrival at the palace we were requested by the butler to sit in a side room whilst we waited for the Duke to walk downstairs and greet us. The atmosphere was decidedly formal and antiquated but I relished the chance to be away from home and our daily patterns that had become progressively lonely and tedious. We entered a large sitting room and there sat a young boy, arms crossed, chin tucked into his chest, frowning and looking rather uncomfortable. He was as thin as a rake with legs like a sparrow's, and painfully pale. I was starting to regret my coming out of the house this morning; was I here as a friend or as a nurse I wondered? The Duke spoke, "Welcome Otto. This is my son, Igor. We will leave you now for a few hours whilst we work." and on that note Papa and the Duke exited the room, closed the door and I felt my heart sink.

I slowly walked over to the huge green leather sofa that Igor was perched on, and sat down beside him. The room was vast and lofty with large panelled walls, huge old paintings on the wall and a collection of antique vases and other ceramic items staged on tall wooden plinths. A manservant stood in the far corner of the room, still and silent, awaiting instructions. Igor turned towards me and put out his hand, shook my hand limply and spoke, "Hello Otto. Thank you for coming to visit me. Would you like tea and cakes? Our cook makes the best cakes." Igor was a polite young man and the thought of cake excited me, so if nothing else I would at least feast on some glorious pastries before going home. The manservant left the room and we sat in silence again until Igor spoke again, sensing my awkwardness. "Do you like playing chess, Otto? Perhaps you would care to play a game with me?" I nodded my head in agreement knowing full well that my game was below amateur and that Igor would be embarrassed by my lack of skill.

The chess board, a fine piece of furniture with marble pieces, was set up on a table in the bay window overlooking beautiful sweeping gardens, filled with flowers and huge ornamental trees. I momentarily looked out of the window and it chillingly reminded me of our home in Petrograd. I wished to be back there right now, playing football with my friends but instead I was indoors with an infirm sixteen year old boy about to play a game I was useless at and wishing I was anywhere else. At that moment the door opened and the manservant strode over and placed a tray of tea and cakes down beside us. I felt relieved that our chess game would be temporarily halted as we took elevenses. We sat again in silence, eating and drinking with haste. "I have to admit to not being very good at chess, Igor. Will you show me how to improve?" I said to Igor, a little ashamedly, with a mouthful of sponge cake. Igor smiled widely. "But of course Otto."

We finished off the cakes gleefully then took our places at the chessboard. Igor patiently taught me an array of moves and tactics and I was completely absorbed by his gentle style and keen mind and eye for the game. I couldn't believe that I was soon finding the game interesting and then suddenly at the door stood the Duke and my Papa. Was it really that time already, I thought? "Come on, Otto, time to go. Same time next week?" I nodded eagerly and said my goodbyes to Igor and The Duke. Igor looked flushed and alive, his face animated; I had been much more than a nurse and he had been much more than a friend.

The following weeks we regularly returned to the palace and my relationship with Igor developed into a close friendship as we chatted endlessly about our lives, our passions and our families back home in Petrograd. We shared the same reflective emotions, the same sadness for leaving our country and our friends, and a keenness to return. Igor was also a proficient singer with his stunning tenor voice, and I would accompany him on the piano, we played cards and illicitly gambled, and made model planes, giggling like children. Igor grew in strength and I decided that it was now time to take him outside for a short walk around the gardens. He was nervous, "My parents won't like it." he said with some reluctance. "But Igor you need fresh air and exercise. You will waste away!" I replied and he ordered the manservant to fetch our coats, hats, scarves and gloves and we sneaked outside like two naughty schoolboys into the Autumn sunshine and started down the stone steps to the gardens. I looked back with some trepidation and glimpsed Igor's mother watching us from an upstairs window, her face expressionless. I felt her anxiety as she had already almost lost her one and only precious son to pneumonia, however she stayed there almost frozen to the spot, her eyes fixed on Igor. I sensed consent, and carried on down the steps with Igor. We walked around the garden, threw leaves at each other, hopped across the flower beds and swung on the branches of the large oak tree. We felt alive. "Same time next week, Igor?" I shouted and for the next month we continued to play, talk and learn more about each other. I had made a genuine friend in Igor and hoped we could continue our friendship on our return to Petrograd.

"Are you ready yet, Otto?" Papa shouted as he headed for the door, "We cannot keep the Duke waiting." "Yes Papa. The Duke has bought Igor a push bike so we are going for a ride today." I said excitedly, wheeling my push bike out of the apartment, down the winding staircase and looking forward to taking Igor along the banks of the Seine. "Not too far, Otto, you know Duke won't be best pleased." said Papa. "Yes, I know." I said, slightly irritated, having full confidence in Igor's increasing abilities. We arrived at the front steps of the formidable palace and I propped my push bike up against the wall. I followed Papa up the steps and he knocked on the door. The butler opened the door and looked surprised at our presence. "Oh, yes, good morning Mr Savin." He stammered and opened the door fully to let us in. "Duke Sarkozy will be with you promptly." he continued and disappeared down a corridor. We were left a little perplexed and I wondered where Igor might be. We waited patiently and the Duke appeared at the top of the stairs and walked slowly towards us. His face was grey and he looked a little unkempt. "Hello, please come this way" and he signalled for us to follow him which we did so, concerned at his unexpected manner.

He sat us down in the sitting room where I had first met Igor and then sat awkwardly opposite us, and for a moment closed his eyes then reopened them with purpose. "Thank you for coming to see us today." he said, then paused for a little while and wiped his brow. "I am very sorry to announce that our dear Igor passed away yesterday." He stopped and cleared his throat, his voice now faltering. " I felt my blood run cold, put my hand to my mouth and gave a little gasp. "Igor collapsed shortly after lunch and although a medic was called, no one could save him. We are yet to find out the cause." The next few minutes went by with a blur.; I wanted to run away, my heart pounded and felt hot tears prick my eyes. I had lost my best friend; just like that; taken away from me. The Duke said his apologies trying to stop the tears that had started to flow from his bloodshot eyes, and we left the palace, appalled and grieving.

The next few weeks were sad beyond belief. Igor's face haunted me each and every day; his smile, his laugh, beautiful singing voice and his quick wit. He was a good friend to me in those short few months, and I had lost him at a time when we needed each other most; two strangers in a foreign country, living without sense or reason. We soon learnt that he had died from a fatal asthma attack aggravated by the lasting effects of the pneumonia. We attended his funeral, a small affair with only a few friends present and we cried as they lowered his coffin into the ground and I thought angrily, what a waste of life. I had never lost a friend before and it hurt me gravely. Oh the fragility of life.

Over the next few months Papa made many frequent visits to the Duke's residence however he would often return home disillusioned. "The Duke is unwell again." he would tell us but I knew the Duke was not unwell. Reports were that he had started drinking heavily and gambling since the death of poor Igor, often to be found in the gambling dens of Paris until the early hours with equally like-minded souls. Papa had taken to spending time with the Duchess Sarkozy and although his Russian countenance made the showing of emotion difficult he could always afford the poor woman some empathy. In the mornings Papa would take tea with her whilst waiting for the Duke to awake. She would sit and cry, talk about Igor and thank my Papa for his time. Papa did not enjoy these moments but felt it necessary to avoid any breakdown of relationship with the Duke.

Chapter Eleven

For a few months we enjoyed our new life very much then one day late November 1918 Papa came home from work early. I will always remember it. Mama. Lilly and I were sitting in the lounge reading and drinking tea having just returned from a brisk walk in the park when in walked Papa unexpectedly. "Hello, Gregoriiy my dear, you are home early?" Mama said. "Is everything okay?" She looked concerned when he didn't answer but instead put down his briefcase, and took off his hat and coat, placing them neatly on the table. "Otto, Lilly, please go and finish your tea in your room, I need to talk with Mama." His voice was low and serious so I did as I was told without question, holding Lilly's delicate little hand and disappearing into the bedroom next door. I put my ear to the wall but it was almost impossible to hear clearly what was being said but the tone of Papa's voice, although muffled, was grave. Perhaps he had had bad news from back home? Perhaps someone close to us had died? That's all I could think of. Eventually we were called to return to the living room where Mama and Papa sat calmly on the sofa and ushered us to sit down. I squeezed Lilly's hand tightly with slight trepidation. Papa eventually spoke, "Children, I no longer have work with Duke Sarkozy as his plans have changed." He paused then continued. "From tomorrow I will be looking for work elsewhere, maybe somewhere local so I can spend more time with you. You do not need to worry. We will manage and maybe Mama will look for a job, too". Mama looked at us reassuringly but I could sense some intrepidation from the slight quiver of her lips. Mama had never worked. Never needed to. Papa had always provided for us entirely. I knew things were disagreeable if Mama now had to work too. What would she do? She had no qualifications, no experience, and who would look after us? What about my studies? This was not looking good.

Duke Sarkozy had mysteriously decided to move to his country house near Nice, selling his palace in Bois de Boulogne and destroying any hope of Papa's architectural designs coming to fruition. Papa had been paid for the conclusion of his work and sent on his way with many other Russian emigres that the Duke had employed. Nothing seemed as it was though and Papa soon discovered that the Duke, who had become a known heavy gambler and drinker since the death of his beloved Igor, had been involved in a drunken card game that went disastrously wrong and had lost a vast amount of money. Without his Russian wealth from the homeland, the state having seized most of his assets, he had stupidly borrowed money from the French mob called the "Milieu", but couldn't pay it back on time and had been forced to sell his palace in Paris to pay them back with huge interest. It was a disaster for us. One man's tragedy then stupidity would change our lives forever.

There was plenty of work in Paris as the First World War had left a deficit of men in menial employment like working in factories, in the bars and clubs waiting on, labouring, working in the kitchens of fancy restaurants or cleaning the streets. Papa didn't have trouble acquiring jobs, and for a few months worked three jobs a day - road sweeping in the morning, kitchen porter and barman each afternoon and evening in the more affluent 16th Arrondissement. It was such a come down for our father. Jobs weren't paid well with long hours and poor conditions, and Papa had to deal with daily ignorance, fear and prejudice from the local Parisians and, due to his middle class countenance which was hard to disguise, harassment and bullying from the working class Russians who seem to take pleasure in ostracising him on every possible occasion. Attitudinal isolation and the lack of intellectual and academic stimulation took its toll on Papa and he was frequently exhausted.

After a month or so it became noticeably evident that Papa could no longer afford the rent on the apartment in the 16th Arrondissement. The cook had to be let go, then the housekeeper and finally the size of our meals reduced to almost a pittance. Whilst people were celebrating the end of the war on the boulevards of the arrondissement we were reluctantly moving downtown to the 8th Arrondissement, an area of the city lived in and frequented by many working class Russian emigres. It was a lively but on the whole deprived area, with a Russian community centre and a number of scruffy looking cafes tumbling out onto narrow cobbled streets, and its only remarkable feature the large and rather impressive Russian orthodox cathedral. There was tall gloomy building after building with little greenery or space and I felt claustrophobic, and the new apartment was markedly smaller than the previous one. We had two cramped rooms - a bedroom for me and Lilly, and a lounge and kitchenette that doubled as a second bedroom for Mama and Papa. We shared an often dirty and foul-smelling bathroom and toilet with three other Russian families living on the same floor. We could no longer afford a cook or housekeeper so Mama had to learn to cook which took some getting used to for all of us.

We had moved in during a cold snap, and the windows always rattled letting in a harsh draft of cold air every night, and we were often without hot water due to a faulty boiler. Mama would light the fire with wood collected from fallen branches along the Seine and boil water in a pan for us to drink and bathe. Good personal hygiene became a luxury and we started to look and probably smell unfortunate but Mama still managed to paint her face and wear her pretty pearl necklace. Many of the jewels that Papa had brought with him from Petrograd had been sold off at a modicum amount. We staved off malnutrition by collecting free fruit and vegetables from the community centre, discarded by local restaurants or donated by wealthy Parisians. The landlord, a brusque man from Nantes, grubby looking and always smoking, came for his rent every Friday without fail but had no interest in fixing the faults. "If you no like, go someplace else." was always his curt answer and then he would disappear until we saw him again the next Friday demanding his money. Papa knew we couldn't afford the rents in other arrondissements, and there were no other suitable places to rent in this area. We were stuck here, resigned to a more meagre way of living, maligned for having trusted the Duke and naively believing that the troubles in our country would soon be over.

Papa left the apartment block where they resided at 6.30am each morning and took the long walk past the Arc de Triomphe and through Bois de Boulogne to the 16th Arrondissement and the building where he was employed as a taxi driver, ironically just around the corner from our previous residence. He had managed to acquire a taxi licence meaning he could relinquish the three-jobs-a-day lifestyle and earn a little more money however any chance of him spending more time with his family were dashed as he needed to work twelve to fourteen hours a day to make ends meet. He always dressed well for a poor man; greased back hair, suit and tie, shoes polished. Always proud yet modest but I never looked too closely for I would see his suit threadbare, his shoes worn and his hair once gleaming black, now grey and thinning. I refused to feel sorry for my Papa as he was my father, my hero, my guide and salvation, not a poor man, not a man struggling with life with its hopelessness and melancholy but it was becoming ever difficult to look him in the eyes and see salvation, ambition and aspiration. He had changed. We had all changed. After almost one year the move back to Russia was now becoming less imaginable. The new government was stabilising and pushing forward to create a new unified Russia. The White Russian army was being defeated in every town and city with ever increasing blood shed and the Tsar and his family now dead. What would we have if we moved back? No home, no money, no belongings, no work, and our friends long left for Europe. At best we would be controlled and cruelly spurned by the new echelons of Russian society and at worst - I didn't want to even think about that. We found ourselves in between a rock and a hard place in a hopeless situation.

Papa drove the rich French to their workplaces and their soirees with all their brocade and facade of gay Paris. He would listen to them talk about their amusements, and their fanciful ways of life, and Papa was particularly popular with the women who would flirt endlessly with him, and with much overbearing audacity, and Papa being a quiet and sober man, found it endlessly embarrassing and uncomfortable. He would utter to Mama at night, quietly so that we could not hear, that he abhorred them and he cursed that they kept him and his family from starving. He took their fares and embarrassingly modest tips, and by 8pm he was walking back home with a pittance of a pay and a hunger in his belly.

It was a long and probably boring day for him, seven days a week. Mama greeted him every night with a warm kiss served with boiled beef with thin, watery gravy and one slice of black bread. Scarcely enough to feed a child yet just enough to satisfy a starving appetite. For an hour they conversed, then Papa would read and Mama often embroidered. Long into the night she would sew, under a light of the yellowing oil lamp. She worked long hours at home day after day, sewing the most intricate designs for the nearby Russian fashion house "Etiffee", as Slavic patterns were "de rigueur" at the moment with the sophisticated Parisian women. Her beauty was also much sought after as a mannequin and days modelling would delight her, bringing a little extra money into the household. To see her smile was rare but comforting that there was hope in this world of ours albeit brief. I too sought work, having to give up on my studies for now. I tramped the streets each day, working as a shoe shine on the Champs Elysees, and also selling newspapers. The work was hard. monotonous and non profitable but it meant a contribution of sorts to the family's income.

Chapter Twelve

Mama hated the poverty of the people that she saw and experienced every day. There was a lack of good housing for the working classes, healthy food, decent sanitation, quality schooling and as she often said, "Russians think they do religion well but even that won't save us." often pointing up at the huge Orthodox church that loomed over Rue Daru, an enduring reminder that God obviously wasn't saving our country. She particularly felt much empathy for the women living in this area who sacrificed much to try and keep their families safe and well. One day she walked over to the community centre and expressed an interest in setting up a group for women, to support them through this trying time. She admitted that she didn't have a clue what she was doing, had never until now lived in destitution but something inside her was urging her to do it. "You can meet here every Tuesday morning Anastasia." said the manager and so on one cold but sunny day in February 1919 Mama and a volunteer from the centre set up tables and chairs, providing cakes and tea, and sat and waited. They sat there, together, in silence but no one came. After an hour Mama was feeling dejected. "I'm sorry, I gave it a go." she said standing up and putting the cakes away in boxes, then a young woman peered through the door and coughed. Mama turned around surprised. "Hello, have you come for the group?" she asked and the young woman nodded, pulling open the door, pram and three children in tow. She didn't say much, sitting down but she drank tea with Mama and gave some cake to the children who delighted in the sweet treats and ran around the hall with much glee. The young woman told Mama about her life, her struggles and how she needed help with her housing. "The landlord has told us we must leave because he is moving. We are to be homeless in less than two weeks and I have the children to think of. My husband works at the car factory but we have little money." Mama was appalled and wanted to help but didn't know what to say or do so she sympathised and offered more cake and the woman eventually started to eat, having given most of it to her children then devouring it quickly as if Mama was going to snatch it away from her. "Thank you for your kindness today. I will tell my friends." she said, gratefully . She reached into her pocket and pulled out a few coins, offering them to Mama. "This is for the cake and tea." she said but Mama held her hand over the woman's. "No, please, they are on us." she said and the woman smiled gratefully. and then ushered her children out of the hall.

The next week the young woman, whose name was Polina, returned with a few friends. Again there was much talk of the strife of living on the bread line and it became clear to Anastasia that these women needed proper help, much more than what she could give them. She fretted later that evening, "Gregoriiy, you should see them. They shuffle into the building, worn down and exhausted, victims of a system that works against them. I'm at a loss as to what I can do. What I thought was a good idea is turning into something unmanageable, like a raging monster." She sat at the table and buried her head in her hands. Gregoriiy put his arm around her, and spoke. "You can do this, Anastasia. You're their greatest asset. Seek some support for yourself. Seek some advice." So the next day Anastasia rallied round a few volunteers at the centre, and poured out her woes. They empathised and together they devised a well meaning plan. They would be listeners and enablers, bringing the women together in solidarity, and invite people from the council, from the schools, and local government to speak to them, to help them, to reform the systems.

Over the next few months the numbers at the group swelled. The room had turned from one of reservation and hopelessness, to one of empowered compatriotism and action. Activities had been formed - needlecraft, budget management, cookery, French language classes and regular advice sessions with professional help with doctors, nurses, government representations and landlords attending on a regular basis. Mama arranged visits to local museums and exhibitions, giving most of the women their first taste of France and Russia's rich culture. Many of the women had joined as volunteers too, helping with the group, running classes and building a hub of support. Mama had come a long way since that first meeting.

One day Mama was busy serving tea with some of the women when she heard, above the chatter and laughter, a lone female voice, strong in its declaration and tone. A woman had stood up at the back of the room and started singing a Russian folk song. Slowly the hall quietened and then one by one the women stood up and sang with her. Still and powerful, their voices in unison, they sang passionately and with emotion. Louder and louder their voices resounded, and Mama stood there, humbled, immobile and shaken, the hairs standing up on the back of her neck. She had never experienced anything like it; women standing strong together, indestructible and defiant. The folk song came to an end and the woman sat down, but the other women stayed on their feet applauding rapturously and Mama could only stand there crying.

Twice a day I would pass the local Russian restaurant "La Cantine Russe " on my way to work, cosily sitting between the butchers and a hardware shop, opposite the large and imposing Alexander Nevsky Cathedral and just one block down from our apartment. During the day it served as a bakery and cafe, emitting wonderful sugary sweet smells and was an unofficial social centre on our street where the working class would meet, eat lunch and enjoy each other's company. I was too poor to visit the cafe or the restaurant but would often stare through the big front windows and gaze at the food or just watch the many people. Then one day I caught sight of the most beautiful young woman I had ever seen. I peered through the windows and there she was, this goddess dressed in a black and white uniform, serving the many guests, flitting between tables. I knelt down, pretending to do up my shoelaces so I could gaze at her for a further few minutes before going on my way. I watched her, her smile as radiant as a summer's day and her hair tumbling across her shoulders, a dark, shining mane of gloriously soft locks. Her face was flushed and soft, and her lips pink and full. I longed to press my lips against hers and hold her body against mine.

Every day, twice a day, I would walk past the restaurant windows in vain hope that I would see her and on one bright winter's morning she was standing on the front steps of the restaurant adjusting her apron. "Hello there." she said. "I see you every day walking past here. My name is Svetlana. Nice to meet you." She was so friendly, speaking fluent Russian, beaming the most stunning smile, about the same age as me and I blushed, said hello quickly, then looked down at my feet with embarrassment. I hurried on, not looking back in case she was staring at me, wondering why I acted so ridiculously. She must have seen me blush and noticed my awkwardness. For the next few days I crossed over the road to avoid walking past the restaurant so she did not see me. Why was I acting this way? Of course I knew; I was besotted, infatuated, swept off my feet by a woman I hadn't even passed the time of day with. Has she really seen me every day? Was she watching me too? Many thoughts ran through my mind.

I had lived a sheltered life back in Petrograd; never had a girlfriend though my adolescent fervour had sometimes been stirred by the younger, prettier acquaintances that my Mama invited back for tea on occasion. I would watch them as they wafted in and out of the house, giggling and girly, with their pretty dresses and soft floral scents. I was younger then, a boy of maybe fourteen or fifteen, finding my juvenile zeal exciting and arousing. I was small for my age, short brown hair, small pointed nose and I didn't consider myself good looking, just very ordinary but I had feelings like any other boy. Now at eighteen these feelings for the opposite sex were changing; no longer just wanting flighty sexual desire I grew hungry for deeper, meaningful relationships. I wanted to get to know this young woman but where was I to start? I hadn't even spoken to a woman without the presence of my Mama or Papa. I cursed myself for being so naive. I saw the Parisian men of my age, hanging off women, kissing them in the street, laughing and bragging. I wanted to be more like them. I wished Igor was here. I would have told him about her and he would have laughed and teased me but then listened as he always did. He was a great listener. I could hear him saying, "Just get yourself into that cafe and speak to her." so I decided that's what I should do, and soon.

The following week I was happily surprised to see an advert go up in the window of the restaurant looking for an accordion player to entertain the customers on Fridays and Saturday nights as their current accordion player was moving away. I had learnt to play the accordion as a small child back in Petrograd, and had excelled at mastering its technique. Papa had entered me in many local competitions, often competing against adults and I had almost always won. However I chose to give up playing as a teenager and followed the trend for football instead, falling in with my peers. You never forget your first love though so when I saw the advert and being hard pressed to find any other work in the area I jumped at the chance to audition. I dashed home and announced to my family that I intended to audition for this job. Papa acquisitioned an accordion from an acquaintance and the very next morning I found myself tentatively walking through the doors of the restaurant with the accordion in my hand. It was cold in the restaurant and I shuddered a little, having forgotten to wear my wool coat. I looked around the room but no one was in sight and I was disappointed not to catch a glimpse of Svetlana but alas she was not here. A scruffy and rather surly man appeared from the back, and without saying hello, waved at me to sit down. "You play for me, young man. You need to be as good as me but I am leaving. I will tell you if you are good enough. " I was surprised by the man's offhand attitude as there was no need for it. "What would you like me to play, sir?" I replied being as polite as I could so as not to offend him. He looked at me and frowned as if I had said something disrespectful but nevertheless replied, "You play Russian folk music for me of course." I sat on the high stool, strapped the accordion to my body and blew on my fingers to warm them up. The man tutted slightly and I was aware that he wasn't in the mood for waiting. I closed my eyes and started playing a fast Russian folk tune, a little tentative at first then the notes tumbled from my fingers, fast and unfaltering, with passion and increasing in pace. I then segued into a folk song, this time sad and lamenting.

My love.
As white as snow, tender as the flower.
We will be together forever more.
Summer will be with us,
My love you need not weep
Summer will be with us forever more.

After a few minutes I came to the end of my performance and breathed a sigh of relief. The man sat still, a blank, expressionless look on his face, his mouth slightly open and I felt deflated. Had he not enjoyed my performance? Was I not good enough? I had been so used to congratulatory applause whenever and wherever I played that this response disarmed me. I started to step down off my stool when he suddenly came over to me and held out his hand, taking hold of mine and shaking it. "Thank you, young man. I am taken aback by your prowess. Of course you have the job. Start on Friday. " He smiled unexpectedly and we said goodbye then I ran back home, accordion bobbing up and down on my back, and I told my parents the good news. We celebrated with a few small cakes and Papa allowed me a glass of his best vodka bought before our fortunes turned sour. After some intense practice I was back to my old brilliance.

Chapter Thirteen

Mama continued to run her weekly women's group but to her surprise a few of the women approached her one morning. "We would like to start a choir, Anastasia. Some of us have a love of singing but we are not sure how to go about it." They looked upon my Mama as the leader of the group and yes she knew now that she could help them, she knew what to do. Within a few weeks the women gathered on a Thursday afternoon in the hall, a little unsure of themselves but Mama sat with them, encouraging them to sing together, letting the emotion drive them. They walked in, a little nervously, many children in tow who sat quietly on the floor with their books whilst their mothers took their places, forming a small circle in the centre of the room. A young woman called Sasha called everyone to order. "Good morning ladies, and thank you for coming today. We will start with the folk song Kalinka." And they all nodded, some smiling, some frowning slightly with apprehension and Mama was so proud. "First we will start with some scales, ladies." said Sasha. "I have read that this is a good way to warm our voices up." and they followed Sasha's instruction, running up and down scales effortlessly. They had song books which they browsed avidly, and within a few weeks they were an ensemble, learning harmonies and sounding harmonious. They found a pianist, a Russian man who often came to the centre to drink coffee with his friends who had many years ago trained as a concert pianist but had suffered health issues and had to give up on his dream. After being asked to accompany the group he dusted off the piano that sat forlorn in the hall for most of the week and could be heard rehearsing hour after hour, playing everything from Beethoven sonatas to jazz favourites. "I think you have made an old man very happy" said one of his friends to Mama one day. They had found their forte, and sang and played from their hearts to dull their sadnesses and pain.

"Mama, why doesn't your choir sing in the church? The local orchestra has a concert there in three weeks' time in the cathedral. Wouldn't that be wonderful? I could ask Yuri, the conductor of the orchestra, if the choir could sing some of their songs?" Mama looked at me and smiled with glee. "I think that would be wonderful my dear. I will ask them if they would like to partake." At the next choir practise Mama told the group and with excitement they agreed. The evening of the concert arrived too soon and the group found themselves seated together at the back of the cathedral waiting for their time to sing, nervous and restless. Some of the group looked around in awe of the enormity of the cathedral and as this was a free concert in aid of the Russian emigres it was crowded with locals. "You know Picasso got married here?" a girl said suddenly. "I learnt that from the visit to the Louvre. Amazing!" Her friend hugged her, loving her innocence. After a short performance from the orchestra the choir took their place at the front of the audience, their faces anxious and solemn, and they stood very still, each one wearing a white sash to represent their country, and concentrating on Sasha who spoke to the people waiting with anticipation.

There had been much talk in the local community about the new choir. It was the first time that women in the community had formed any sort of alliance, never mind a musical one. Sasha spoke calmly and with assertion, "Good evening to you all and thank you for inviting us to sing for you. We are the Russian Women's Choir. We formed two months ago and we meet every week at the community centre next door. We were all broken women, each of us with a story of suffering and misery. We joined the local women's group where we found our voices, as women and as singers, and we are now unified, an empowered collective of women making a difference to our lives. We have our wonderful leader, Anastasia, sitting over there, to thank for that." Sasha smiled and pointed over at Anastasia, who sat with myself and Lilly near the back of the cathedral. People turned around and there was a round of applause. Mama was embarrassed but grateful. Sasha continued, "We hope that you enjoy our performance." The cathedral hushed and she turned around and eyed each choir member, then smiled and raised her arms and with that signal the choir began to sing, their voices as sweet as honey and beautifully in tune. The audience were spellbound, mesmerised by the music, powerful both in sentiment and sound and each song told a story, from tragedy to love with the final song written by the group journeying their story from strife to salvation.

Мы тебя любим
Наша Родина
Мы будем любить друг друга

    Утешайте друг друга

    Пока мы не встретимся снова

(We love you
Our motherland
We will love each other
Comfort each other
Until we meet again)

With the performance ended Sasha put her arms down and lowered her eyes, shaking from emotion then there was a moment of silence before the audience erupted, cheering and clapping, standing up and shouting "Bravo! bravo!! The hall quietened and Yuri stood forward, shook Sasha's hand then turned to look at the choir "My dears, you are a credit to our community. Well done! That was a very special performance." The women hugged each other and some cried happy tears before leaving the stage and sitting down at the back of the cathedral. "We did it!" cried Sasha as the group left the hall at the end of the concert, arm in arm, and skipping a cheerful step. "We blooming well did it!".

Mama continued to run the group for many months until one day she gathered the group together, "I have done my work here." She said and many of the women looked confused so Mama explained herself. "You are strong enough to run this group yourselves now. You've grown in the months that I have known you. It was always my aim to hand it over to you." The women hugged Mama and many cried and thanked her for her help and with that she left the building for the very last time, happy in the knowledge that the women had changed, were surviving, if not thriving, and would be here for each other and others like them for many years to come. Later that year Mama received a civic award for her contribution to the community and it pleased her greatly

On Friday and Saturday evenings I donned my only suit, slung the old dusty battered accordion over my shoulders and walked with pace down the cobbled street to "La Cantine Russe" where I played in the evening for welcoming diners. After a day on the streets shining the shoes of the Parisian ``hommes" this was always uplifting and of course Svetlana was always there making my heart sing. One evening on my way to the restaurant I strolled past a young man half sitting, half lying on the pavement, moaning slightly, his face pale and drawn, his arms and legs turned outward and his belongings scattered across the dirty wet cobbles, bottle in hand. He was an appalling sight, lost to the blight of drink, despairing and hopeless. He was not an unusual sight in this area, with men sitting on most street corners, drinking or begging. They had once been part of a family, part of a community, part of society with probable jobs and a future. Now they were lost to another world, an alien world, given up, succumbed to depression and destitution. Though maybe not much older than me, I knew he didn't have long for this world. I turned away sickened and faced the restaurant, its bright lights spilled out onto the street and Alexei Sidorov, the restaurant owner, was sweeping the front steps with much verve. He was a short, portly ageing Russian who always wore a red checked neckerchief and had much enthusiasm for life, not unlike many of the established Parisian Russians who had melted comfortably into a western way of life.

He saw me walking down the street and shouted over , "My dear boy, come here and make me a happy man!" I appeared at the steps uplifted by his happiness and he hugged me, making the accordion dig into my shoulder just a little too hard. I winced but smiled so as not to offend Alexei. The two of us then stepped into the restaurant and I followed him to the back of the room where a glass of vodka and a bowl of hot borscht were waiting on the counter as well as my usual high chair. I was always hungry by the time I got there, having been on the streets all day often without a bite to eat, and was always so grateful for the food that Alexei prepared for me each evening. As a respectful man Alexei never said anything. There was just a light pat on my shoulder or a quick head nod of reassurance to acknowledge my growing tribulations.

During the day the restaurant was also a bustling bakery, the counter brimming with sweet cakes and savoury pastries - meringues, biscuits, cheesecakes, iced fancies, sponges, chocolate pastries, savoury buns and sandwiches as well as French favourites, all handcrafted by Otto's charming wife, Olezka, and her daughter, Svetlana. The cheesecake was a particular favourite of mine, with its creamy taste and delicious fruity topping. I would see local Russians gazing at the cakes on the counter and we would together share a nostalgic yearning for our homeland. How something as simple as a cake could evoke such strong emotions I really could not understand. A smell, a taste, rapidly giving way to something more powerful and tragic. The longer we gazed, the more distant we felt from Russia and its normalcy but similarly we felt comforted and included by Alexei and his kind family. Both day and night the restaurant was our little piece of home.

It was now 6.30pm and the restaurant would be open in half an hour. I knew that by 7.15pm the restaurant would be full of people. People from all walks of life frequented this restaurant and I loved them all, warts and all. Monsieur Blanchet and his charming yet eccentric wife, Elena, both Parisians, dined here each Friday night, always taking the same table by the window. They were of old Paris; she wore fine silk dresses covering her tiny feet, adorned with puffy sleeves and lace, and he a suit with checked trousers and highly polished leather shoes. They drank champagne and ate small dishes but many of them. They were both tiny and frail, maybe in their eighties, yet exquisite and refined, reflections of how life I assumed used to be in Paris. Then there were the old Russians as I liked to call them. The restaurant was full of them; most had emigrated to Paris back in the late 1800s and had become as Parisian as possible, wearing the latest fashions, speaking French at every possible opportunity and living the "bonne vie" but still enjoying the odd evening of Russian culture, patronising the restaurant often in large groups and filling the room with their noise and laughter. In contrast were the new Russian emigres; often working class, quiet and somewhat dour from years of cultural adversity, sitting on the edges of the room, stiff like frozen sausages, inspecting the menu like it was a work contract and talking in hushed voices. Their clothes and their demeanour were sombre and a little drab and sadness was often etched on their faces. I empathised with them as they were as near to my people as I would get these days. Saturday nights saw an influx of students from the finest universities that the city had to offer. They were young and boisterous yet good mannered.educated and full of fun. They would whoop, sing and dance and fall down from too much liquor. I was always thankful that Alexei knew had to handle them. Finally there were the non-European tourists, mainly Americans. Questionable manners and even more questionable taste in clothing, garish and loud, they would interrupt my playing, ask for non Russian songs that I had never heard of, then attempt to sing lousy American ballads, wildly gesticulating for me to join in. It was never enjoyable but they were often rich and gave great tips so we allowed them to revel in their soliloquies before sending them on their way.

Everyone adored Alexei's cooking but they had mostly come to see me playing, and of course Alexei knew this too. We would smile across the room at each other as people lined the streets at opening times to get a good table. If the restaurant was busy, tips were good for me. It was a cosy restaurant with small wooden tables covered with pristine starched white and blue checked table cloths, ashtrays and vases of real cut flowers. On the whitewashed walls were photographs of old Russia and of family members, Russian Orthodox paintings and souvenirs from Alexei's European visits - a picture of Buckingham Palace, a postcard from Italy, a flag from Germany and even a menu from a restaurant somewhere in America. I wasn't sure if he had been there or this was given to him. Alexei liked to also burn incense so the restaurant always reminded me of the Russian Orthodox cathedral across the road but without the worship.

Chapter Fourteen

Playing in the restaurant became the routine for the next few months, then one evening after the people had gone home and the restaurant had been tidied and cleaned, Alexei called to me to sit and drink some Mediterranean wine with him. It was unusual but I did as I was told because you never turned a man like Alexei down. "You like my daughter, yes?" Alexei enquired warmly. "Well yes, of course" I replied, keen not to offend. "No," chuckled Alexei. "I mean, really like?" He smiled cheekily. "I love my daughter for her beauty and as a daughter, my youngest of five girls. The apple of my eye, Otto but you can love her for other things." I was embarrassed at that remark and its innuendo, and felt my cheeks burn. Alexei always spoke openly and with emotion, and I had never heard anyone speak like this before. "Yes I do like Svetlana like that." I admitted. The honesty was liberating. "Then ask her out, dear boy. Go to the park for a picnic. Talk and laugh,and be young." I smiled at this and before I even had the chance to reply Alexei shouted to Svetlana who was washing up in the back room, "Come here, Svetlana. Come here now. Otto has something he wishes to say to you." Oh God, I thought, nothing like being put on the spot. "Hello daddy. What do you want, Otto? I have things to do here". She said sitting down next to me frowning and impatient, throwing her tea towel on the table. I hesitated and felt my throat constrict and my mouth go dry. Alexei and Svetlana sat there expectantly. My head was spinning and I felt a little dizzy. "Uhm, Svetlana, do you want to go out with me, for a picnic, this Sunday after church?". That was it. I had done it. She could either say yes and it was sorted, or she could say no and I could walk out with my head hanging low, feeling boyishly awkward and self-conscious. "Yeah sure, thank you. " she said nonchalantly and got up and went back to drying the pots. I don't think I have ever felt so relieved and excited.

Sunday came around and I didn't remember any of the sermon as I was so nervous. Svetlana was sitting in the row in front of me dressed in a tight red knee length skirt and white bow neck blouse. Her father had allowed her to wear some lipstick, and her hair was tied back in a slick ponytail. She wore dainty patent blue t-strap shoes and little white ankle socks. She turned around and beamed at me, then turned away before her father caught her. I felt flustered and sweaty. She was beautiful. We spent the warm, sunny afternoon walking along the banks of the Seine, chatting nervously and giggling like children. We picnicked under a great oak tree, sitting on a green checked blanket that Svetlana's mother had packed for us. We sipped lukewarm rose and ate ham and cheese baguettes heartily. I think it was the best time I had ever spent in Paris, and maybe ever. We had to head back to the restaurant by 5pm as Svetlana was working at 6pm and needed to get washed and changed. As we said our goodbyes, Svetlana stood on her tiptoes, leant over and kissed my cheek. I didn't know how to respond so I just smiled like a little child, and said goodnight. She smiled sweetly and went inside.

The next few months were bliss. Svetlana and I would meet every Sunday afternoon after church, going for romantic walks and picnics, cycling across the city, visiting museums and sometimes just sitting in the cafe, reading, talking and laughing. We laughed a lot and it was a great tonic for me after all the agony of leaving Russia. We would sometimes walk north to visit Cafe L'Opera; we would stand outside and watch the people drinking coffee. We couldn't afford to drink there but we hoped for a day when I was earning better money and could take care of my Svetlana. I was keen to know more about this sweet girl that had stolen my heart and I asked her about her family. Her parents were Alexei and Olezka Sidorov. They had met at a local dance one evening in the village where they lived and were married a few months later, and a year after they came to Paris with his parents in 1884. Her grandfather was a larger than life man, she told me, who owned a farm in a small village near Moscow. "But he had become disillusioned with the state of Russia and the treatment of the Asheknazi Jews in particular. He was gregarious and outgoing, and had always dreamed of a life in Paris so sold everything to start a new life with his family. They moved to Rue Daru and opened the restaurant. He promised that it would cater for the Russians and his friends the Jews, who had settled largely in a neighbourhood known as the Pletzel located in the Marais area of the fourth arrondissement. He was an amazing man." Svetlana oozed pride when talking about her grandfather. "When my grandfather got sick he handed the restaurant over to my papa. It's his fifteenth year of running the popular little restaurant." She looked a little sad and held my hand tightly. "My Grandpapa died in 1904 from cancer. My Grandmama only lasted another three months after that. It was very sad and we still miss them very much." She got up and made a hot drink and brought over some cakes before sitting back down and again holding my hand. She continued to tell me about her family.

She had four older sisters. Olga, Katerina, Alexandria and Anya. Katerine, Alexandria and Anya lived in France. Katerina lives in Rouen with her husband and four cats. "She's an odd fish. None of us see much of her." Svetlana scowled. "Then there's Alexandria who is a ballerina and dances with the Paris Opera Ballet. Mama is very proud of Alexi. She's a wonderful dancer. You must come with me one evening to see her dance. She lives with some friends in the 15th arrondissement. You'd love her!" Svetlana paused for a while and had a bite of her bun. "What about the other two sisters, Svetlana?" I enquired, hoping she would conclude the story. She chewed on her bun and waved her arms around."Yes." she said with bits of bun stuck in her teeth. "Katerina is a teacher in Bayeux. A teacher of politics and sociology. Very clever woman. I think she will eventually teach at some posh university. Papa always wonders where she gets her intelligence from!" laughed Svetlana.

I waited for her to continue telling me about her oldest sister, Olga but she seemed reluctant. "What about Olga? Where is she?" I suddenly wished I hadn't asked the question. Svetlana looked angry then her face turned to anguish. She gazed at me, breathing heavily and tears welled in her eyes. "Olga died three years ago. She was returning home one evening from a work trip to Reims from her home in Paris when the train she was travelling on crashed. Thirteen people died and she was one of them. They found her body crushed in the wreckage a few days later." She lowered her head, dabbing her wet cheeks delicately with her handkerchief. "I'm sorry if I appeared a little angry, Otto. I haven't spoken with anyone about her death for some time. It was such a shock. We are still grieving for poor Olga." I held her in my arms and hugged her gently. I was sorry for evoking such sadness, I thought of the shock of losing Igor and I shared her grief.

My French was still very poor so each Monday evening Svetlana would come over to our apartment and teach me. She was very patient as I was not a good student, often impatient and frustrated by my lack of concentration. I was always tired from a day on the streets and learning was hard. Sometimes Svetlana would get out her book of poems and read them to me. Svetlana wrote many poems; late at night she said she would find the motivation to scribble in her little notebook, poems about love, life and people. They were mostly fanciful and playful. "Why don't you come with me to the poetry meeting, Otto?" I knew Svetlana attended the poetry meeting at the community centre every Tuesday evening and I had dreaded her inviting me as although I enjoyed listening to her reading her own poems to me, her beautifully lyrical voice and sweet, seductive smile, the thought of sitting through other people's literary offerings made me cold but how could I refuse? I hesitated and then smiled at her. "Oh, okay Svetlana my dear." and that was that, I had committed.

Chapter Fifteen

We met outside the centre and held hands as we entered the building, Svetlana excited, pulling on my arm, and increasing her pace. There was an electric atmosphere in the hall as people filed in.; mostly men, but some families had come along, sitting at long wooden trestle tables in rows with small bottles of beer and baguettes wrapped in brown paper and smoking long French cigarettes. Mostly Russian emigres, for these people there was a social obligation to keep the real Russia alive, the Russia that they knew, the culture and the ideology of a lost homeland, a place they hope to return to one day. I could feel their purpose and their loyalty to keeping those traditions alive, through poetry, through religion, through culture but I had witnessed how they kept themselves to themselves, refusing to integrate into Parisian life, creating a little Russia within this great city, preserving their language and it worried me. I didn't mind but their resolve to protect the old was wearing my patience thin; I could see that eventually they would have to integrate, for the sake of their children if not themselves but we will always be Russian first, at least we all agreed on that. Svetlana talked of poets, energetically and with vigour. Names such as Bunin and Turgenev and I knew that it was her dream to meet them, maybe they would attend her poetry meeting?

The hall echoed with chatter, and Svetlana and I sat on a table with some others, their clothes shabby and drab, void of jewellery and other finery that our family had come accustomed to back in Russia. A number of people were pacing the room clutching bits of paper and I assumed that they would be reciting tonight, their faces slightly puckered with nerves. Everyone now wanted to talk to Svetlana. They hugged her, kissed her and shook her hand, talking endlessly about subjects I did not know or understand. How could one person be so popular? I felt a pang of jealousy as she conversed with many people, their eyes bright and shining, strangers, young and old. She lit up the room with her effervescent personality. I was so used to having her to myself; those perfect Sunday afternoons, holding hands, kissing. looking into each other's eyes as if nothing and no one else mattered. I sat back and waited for her to sit down and settle as I chastised myself for my feelings and smiled at her, trying to diffuse my angst. She flopped down and sighed, beaming with exhilaration. "I love it here, Otto! People are so much fun." She exclaimed innocently. I was pleased but wished that I too had more friends especially after the loss of my dear friend, Igor.

At precisely 6.30pm a young woman in a beautiful satin jade dress walked onto the stage and announced the commencement of the meeting. The audience hushed and the woman started to read off a piece of paper that she was holding tightly. "And tonight we have six poets for your delight. " I groaned to myself at the thought of having to sit through six poets for the next ninety minutes, though one of them would be Svetlana. The woman carried on, " We will hear three poets then there will be a break." Phew, I thought. I had some brought some beer and I opened a bottle and took a swig. "You okay, Otto?" asked Svetlana. She must have noticed my fraught demure. "Yes, my dear. I'm fine." and I smiled disgenuinely and squeezed her hand tightly, her smiling.

The woman stepped down off the stage and then a small, thin old man wandered to the front, papers in hand, and with some help, ascended the steps and placed himself in front of us on a wooden chair. He looked around, shuffled his papers and slowly took off his cap, resting it on the floor beside him. Perhaps he will start before 9pm, I hoped. People were starting to get restless, with some disquiet behind us. Eventually he began to recite his first poem and it was something about nature, his voice hesitant and broken. After a few minutes he finished and there was a ripple of applause, the audience subdued. He continued for two more poems, each time the audience lightly clapping in between chewing on huge chunks of baguette and swigging beer. The old man got up and the woman appeared, thanking him for his contribution. I hoped that the evening would increase in interest and even Svetlana was tapping her fingers impatiently on the table but then her name was called. She stood up with a start, grabbed her papers and rushed forward, almost falling over a small child in the aisle. People clapped more enthusiastically as she stepped on to the stage and she smiled her wide, beautiful smile. "My first poem is about the devastation of our motherland," and she cleared her throat and spoke clearly and loudly.

We are far from our land

Wasted from mental servitude
Tormented by the dust that we grasp at
Digging with our dirty bare hands
Searching for any remnants of our past life

We hide not to show our wounds
Deep and sore, ugly and without healing
We tend to them
But they open, every waking hour, they gape wide open,
Without respite, without love, who are we?

We pray for what God makes us proud
But pride has deserted us. Has deserted Russia
A land less welcome, cold and silent
We have come far, but not far enough
To return to our homeland. Our war is lost.

I sat, aghast by the emotion that her poem evoked. She had perfectly described the pain we, as emigres, suffered on a daily basis, being ripped from our country, and losing hope every day. How could Svetlana understand this? She had been born in Paris, and had never endured the sadness of leaving Russia. I suddenly saw her in a different light; empathic and intuitive, sensitive and compassionate. She read two more poems and then quietly sat down and placed her papers on the table and took a swig of beer. She turned to me and smiled contentedly, and I hugged and congratulated her. I felt so much love for this young woman, it frightened me. The rest of the evening went by quickly, and finally the meeting was over and again people came over and thanked Svetlana for her contribution but I needed the toilet so I walked away from the crowd that had gathered around her.

On the way back to the table I watched Svetlana. Most of the group had dissipated and she was talking with an older man, tall with thin pointed features, wearing a dark overcoat and large black hat. There was something I didn't like about him and they spoke seriously, and I suddenly felt concerned for Svetlana but I wasn't sure why. The man was talking fast with his face up too close to hers and then abruptly pushed a piece of paper into her hand, and she placed it quickly into her coat pocket. They acknowledged each other and he walked away towards the exit, head down, without looking or saying goodbye to anyone. Svetlana then reached for the piece of paper and read it for some time before again putting it back in her pocket. I felt uncomfortable at his presence; what had he said to my precious Svetlana that made her look so earnest, and what had he thrust into her hand so forcibly? I walked towards Svetlana and she smiled her usual smile, and I was unnerved by what I had just witnessed. "What was that all about, Svetlana?" I asked her. She bit her lip and looked over to her right, then answered. "Oh, just another poetry meeting he has set up. Thursday nights." and then she stopped and changed the subject. "We'd best be going home, Otto. Papa will be waiting up for me." I took her hand and walked with her back to the restaurant, said goodbye and took my time back to my front door, pondering on the mysterious man and the piece of paper.

Chapter Sixteen

For the first time I didn't trust Svetlana; she was hiding something and I needed to know what it was. That Thursday I waited around the corner from the restaurant, and watched as she left the building, crossed the road and disappeared out of view down a side street. I hurried my step, being careful not to be seen and cursing myself for my suspicious actions. I walked far behind her so as not to lose her, then she stopped at a doorway and knocked on the door. It was an old derelict school building, desolate and dark. There was a dim light on, and she went inside with the man who I recognised as the person she had met at the poetry meeting and this momentarily terrified me. I stood on the corner of the street, then walked up to the window, stood on tip toes and peered in, ensuring I wasn't seen by those inside. I could see a small group of people sitting around in a circle on chairs, talking quietly but with serious intent but there was definitely no poetry reading taking place. I put my ear to the window and listened in but it was impossible to hear anything, just muffled voices. I wasn't sure what to do; wait, knock on the door, bang on the window; go home? I decided to stay, kicking my heels as I idled on the street and pacing up and down.

After an hour the door opened and people filed out, saying their goodbyes and talking and I could hear the hushed words revolution, anti-Bolshevik and campaign mentioned and my blood ran cold. My worst fears were confirmed. What was Svetlana thinking, I thought. I dashed around the corner out of sight so that when she appeared I would not be seen. I was worried. I had recently read that poetry meetings had started to attract political activists in the city with a small number of extremists looking to brainwash young and sadly gullible people, like Svetlana, with their views of a new Russia; a new revolution to overthrow the Bolsheviks. To Svetlana it would herald a new cultural uprising, exciting and energising but to me it was filled with danger. Bolshevik spies were everywhere in the city and there had already been talk of assassination attempts on such factions as the one that Svetlana had joined. I felt afraid and ran back home, following a different route to Svetlana so to avoid her, watching her as she walked with her new found friends.

I laid awake that evening and felt for Svetlana's safety. The next day I went to the restaurant and in my desperation spoke to Alexei about the group. He looked concerned and angry but mostly frightened. He knew what this meant. "Thank you, Otto. I will sort this out." and he went back to his work. As usual I saw Svetlana the following Sunday and we walked around the city, visited a local park although Svetlana noticed my quiet demeanour but I said I was just tired. I tried to stay buoyant but I knew that the following Thursday Otto would certainly be taking a visit to the group's venue and a disagreement would almost definitely ensue, with the clash of Alexei's larger than life character and the passion of the strong-willed Svetlana.

I looked at my watch and noticed the time. 6.45pm. Alexei would be arriving at the venue very soon. I laid on my bed, studying the elaborate pattern on the wallpaper, and then screwed up my eyes. I felt sick but eventually fell asleep and was awoken the next morning by my Mama, calling me for breakfast. I ate very little and made my way down to the Champs Elysees for another day's work. Today was newspaper selling day and normally I would read the paper cover to cover but today I was distracted. The day dragged but eventually at 5pm I walked back to the apartment where I saw Svetlana standing on the restaurant steps, her arms folded and scowling. I couldn't avoid her and as I got nearer to her she pointed at me angrily. "How dare you, Otto! How dare you! You told Papa where I was going , didn't you? It had to be. You betrayed me!" I stood there, silent and afraid and I had never seen Svetlana so angry. "But I had to keep you safe Svetlana, don't you understand?" I pleaded with her, holding out my hands to her. "Safe? Safe? I can look after myself Otto. This is what I wanted and you have ruined it. Papa dragged me away from the group. He made me look like a fool in front of my friends. I don't want to see you again. Goodbye Otto. We're finished!"" and she went back inside the restaurant, slamming the door behind her and turning off the light. I was left, motionless, on the doorstep, frozen with grief and confused by her outburst. I inhaled deeply in and started to walk down the road quickly but then started to weep uncontrollably from the shock, like a baby, gasping and sobbing indiscriminately, feeling bereft, ignoring the people passing me on the street staring and frowning. Mama opened the door to the apartment and saw my face and I leant forward and cried on her shoulder, explaining the whole story. Mama was ever the realist. "But you did the right thing, Otto. You did it for Svetlana and if she doesn't understand then maybe you should be apart. Perhaps she has set herself a different path in life to you." But of course I wasn't listening. I had just lost the most important thing in my life; my beautiful, kind, funny, loving Svetlana.

The next few weeks and months were difficult, readjusting to single life, and yet still having to work in the restaurant on Friday and Saturday nights alongside Svetlana. Alexei had convinced me that she had stopped going to the group meetings but I wasn't so sure. She was aloof and cold but it saved having to make small talk. My evenings at the restaurant were tolerable but no longer as fun, however I couldn't leave and find other work as the money was good. The world had become a darker and sadder place during these past few months and everything reminded me of her but I had to carry on for the sake of my family.

One evening late at night there was a loud bang at the door, then another and then another. It was 11pm. I could hear Papa's voice, "Hello, who is it?" he said, a little worried. "It's Alexei, Gregoriiy. Please can you let me in. I need your help." I got up and watched Papa open the door and in rushed Alexei looking perturbed, his brow wet with sweat and his hands shaking. "It's Svetlana. She's not returned home. She went out with friends but she's not back. Have you seen her, Otto?" The poor man was desperate but I didn't know her whereabouts. Papa showed him in and he sat on the sofa. "Do you know who she went out with?" Alexei explained that he didn't know as she was often non committal to her whereabouts these days but I had a sickening feeling that I knew. "The meeting, Alexei. Is she at the meeting?". I said slowly. Alexei looked at me, fear darting across his eyes. "Oh, God, no. Please God no!"

He stood up and we shot out the door, the three of us knowing exactly our destination. Five minutes later we stood outside the venue, police everywhere, an ambulance parked up but no Svetlana. "What happened here?" I asked a police officer standing by the door. "Shooting, Tragic circumstances. Three men dead. Stinks of Bolsheviks." He stood aloof and unemotional but my gut told me that Svetlana had been here tonight and I felt panicked. We walked around frantically to find her but we eventually had to admit that there was no more we could do so we walked back to the restaurant. "If she was here, Alexei, she is not now, so we must wait." said my Papa and Alexei solemnly thanked us for our help and walked through the door, a lonely and sad figure. I didn't sleep well that night tossing from side to side, awake from my emotions and my deep yearning for Svetlana, had never died.

Chapter Seventeen

"Papa, papa, help me, please help!". It was 3am and Svetlana banged on the door of the restaurant furiously and her father appeared in his pyjamas, frantically trying to get the door open. "Oh, Svetlana, I have been so scared!" he cried. "Thank God you are home. Where have you been?" And without speaking a word Svetlana fell into her papa's arms and he caressed her face and wiped the tears from her swollen eyes. Her clothes were dirty and smattered in blood and she looked small and frightened. He led her upstairs, and her mother helped her undress and put her to bed. "In the morning we will ask her what happened but until then we will let her sleep and keep her safe."

The next morning Papa and I sat in silence at the table, eating our bread and jam and drinking black tea. No words could be spoken after the events of the previous evening, and Papa rose, said a brief goodbye and left the apartment, briefcase and coat in hand. I sat and stared at nothing, wondering what had happened to Svetlana. My first thought was to visit Alexei so I put on my coat and ventured out into the cold air, heading for the restaurant with intrepidation. Alexei was in the restaurant already, setting out the table cloths and vases of freshly cut flowers. He was stooped over looking unusually frail. I banged on the door and he turned around surprised then waved at me unsmiling. He opened the door and welcomed me in and before saying hello he spoke. "She is back, Otto. Early hours of the morning, scared and a mess. Thank God she's home. She's still asleep." He spoke softly from exhaustion, and I asked him if she had spoken and he said not yet but he was letting her rest. He mentioned the blood on her clothes and I was appalled. "Okay, Alexei, Send her my regards, and I will call again." I walked away, saddened but relieved, and carried on with my day.

Two days later Svetlana arrived at our door one morning, looking thin and pale. My Mama welcomed her in, slightly reserved in her embrace, and Svetlana sat down on the sofa, resting her tiny hands on her knees and looking at me afraid. "Hello Otto." she said and then quietened. I looked at her, not knowing how I felt. The last conversation we had was the bitter altercation on the restaurant steps many months ago but a lot had happened since then. Her group meeting had ended abruptly that terrible evening with Bolshevik sympathisers storming the building and killing the group leader and two of the group. Having witnessed the bloodshed, Svetlana had fled for her life with a couple of other group members, hiding in a warehouse around the corner for hours, laying low, cold and petrified. After a few hours they had carefully crept out of the building and seeing that the coast was clear, made their way home, drained of emotion. It was a horrific experience.

I sat beside her, but I felt unusually cold towards her. "What do you want me to say, Svetlana? I told you not to go. I need to go to work." And I stood up and made my way to the door. She looked embarrassed. "I just came to say that I am very sorry, Otto. That is all. I won't keep you any longer." She then hesitated before continuing. "And... and... I still love you, Otto. I am very sorry for the way I've behaved." She turned away. "Mama, please could you see Svetlana out. We are done here." I said and left the apartment feeling confused and a little guilty for treating her so.

I arrived home later that evening and Mama and Papa were sitting together at the table, playing cards. Mama looked up at me. "Go and see Svetlana, Otto. Go and sort your relationship out." she said sternly but I waved my hand at her dismissively as I wasn't in the mood for a serious discussion, tired from the last few days and troubled by the thought of conversing with Svetlana. Did I want to be with her again? Could I trust her? What about that terrible temper? I sighed, confusing thoughts blurring my mind, and sat down on the sofa. Tea was a simple chicken stew then I started to read my book but annoyed with my troubled thoughts and keen for a resolution reluctantly I rose and left the apartment to visit Svetlana. I knew that she would be sitting at home, her father allowing her a few days off to recover from her ordeal.

I found her quiet and forlorn. She looked like a little school girl doing her embroidery, and drinking orange juice, wearing a long, loose-fitting pinafore with her hair combed back in a tight bun. Olezka welcomed me in and I sat on the chair opposite Svetlana not knowing exactly what to say or do. "Would you like tea?" said Olezka, seeing my nervousness. "Yes, thank you, Olezka. That is very kind." Olezka was a quiet, older woman, always well mannered and measured in her gestures unlike her outgoing and unreserved husband though theirs was a marriage that worked well. She worked very hard each and every day and was equally successful in the business as Alexei. I was blessed to know such a calm and considerate woman.

I looked around the room that I had sat in many times before, simple in its style, wicker furniture, floral wallpaper and rustic textures, and a large signature patterned rug on the wooden floorboards. The room was stuck in the late 1800's not having been modernised in any way but it was homely and comforting. I smiled at Olezka and then my smile fell upon Svetlana, who glanced at me almost fearfully, and I sat beside her holding her small, delicate hand in mine. All thoughts of non forgiveness melted away. "Can we start again, Svetlana?" I said, rubbing the top of her hand gently with my fingers. "But you must promise that this group stuff is over." She looked at me sheepishly and spoke, "I will not go again or be involved again. I have learnt my lesson." She was emotionally drained and bearing a great mental weight from what she had encountered at the group. She was quiet and nervous, and I don't think that she had yet ventured outside. She rested her head against the back of the sofa and closed her eyes. She had witnessed something more terrible than anyone could imagine and most certainly more than I could ever conceive and she would need plenty of support over the next few weeks or months to help her make sense of her experiences. I hoped that my presence in her life would help her back to her old self. She fell forward slightly and I put my arm around her and we just sat, silently, motionless. I looked at her, gently cupped my hands around her face and kissed her slowly. How I had missed that taste and scent, the sweetness of her breath and the softness of her lips. Svetlana, my sweetheart, my love.

My days had again become monotonous. Although I loved my family, and Svetlana and her family, I still missed the closeness of friendship. One day I decided to wander into the grounds of the cathedral to ponder my life. I was feeling melancholy, a feeling that came over me more these days, often recollecting the happier times in my life and although meeting Svetlana had comforted me during darker times I was longing to meet new people, even if it was just a hello and a smile. I sat under the huge trees, just a priest walking past, acknowledging me from beneath his dark curly beard. It was a wintry day and I looked up at the cathedral, hoping for inspiration. I thought about Papa. He was a pious man, attending church every Sunday with Mama, Lilly and myself however my view of the church had changed considerably since moving to Paris. Until then we had forever put our confidence in Tsar Nicholas and Nicholas had ultimately put his faith in God entrusting his kingdom to the will of the Lord; a flawed philosophy if I ever knew one. Frankly, God doesn't exist in my mind anymore.

I stood up and looked up at the trees. I will only trust what I can see today and what I can also touch, feel and taste; what is real. I reflected and made my way over to the community centre, my mood having lifted slightly. I was accustomed to visiting the centre; to collect fruit and vegetables for Mama, to search for second hand clothes for the family, to attend the fateful poetry meeting and also to drop in for a hot drink on cold afternoons when I couldn't afford the restaurant prices. The volunteers were always kind and thoughtful and I felt welcomed every time. It was a Saturday morning and as I made my way through the door I could hear music coming from the hall. The sounds immediately made my heart sing; that familiar resonance and tone that spoke to me; live music played by real musicians! I eagerly opened the heavy door, being quiet so as not to disturb them. I pulled it back and the sun pierced my eyes as it shone brightly through the big rectangular windows, and I watched as the dust danced in its rays as if pirouetting to the sounds being created before me.

The hall was bright but cold with a strong smell of furniture polish and tobacco, and there were about twenty musicians sitting in rows playing an eclectic assortment of instruments; violins, cellos, clarinets, trumpets, trombones, an oboe and some percussion. It was a mismatch of sound, loud and brash, slightly out of tune but bursting with passion, with an older man conducting furiously, waving a wooden baton and tapping his foot in time with each beat. It was just glorious to watch and hearing it reminded me of the brass band concerts Papa and I used to go to back in Petrograd. I stood at the back of the hall taking in the atmosphere and watching the performers intently who were concentrating with their full might; I wondered who they might be and where they were from. From the look of their clothes they were mostly working class Russian emigres finding comfort in the playing of music from their homeland.

After ten minutes the conductor shouted "Time for tea!" and he put down his baton and turned around, setting his eyes upon me. He started to walk over, a big figure of a man, and I felt a little uneasy, not being good in social situations. It was Yuri, the conductor from the concert at the church. "Hello my dear boy, did you enjoy what you heard?" he said joyfully and shook my hand vigorously. "Oh, yes, sir, it was wonderful. " I exclaimed and he led me into the kitchen to meet the performers and have a cup of tea with them. I recognised some of them from the concert. I felt so nervous yet elated to be with like minded people and they enthusiastically threw a barrage of questions at me, and I told them about my accordion playing at the hotels in the city. "Why don't you come and join us, Otto?" one of the performers asked and I stuttered, "Well...yes...okay. Do you meet every Saturday morning?" They all nodded almost in unison, and continued to ask me many questions about my accordion playing and my musical likes and dislikes. After fifteen minutes they downed their cups of tea and resumed their places back behind their music stands and started playing a piece of romantic music, refreshed and engaged. The conductor resumed his place at the front of the orchestra and with serious intention, again waved his baton in time with music. I sat back on a chair and enjoyed the beautiful melodies they were creating, however I knew it was time to go home for lunch and Mama would be expecting me so I waved goodbye and some of the group waved back. "See you next week!" I shouted and left the building with much cheer, and excited at the thought of joining the orchestra.

Chapter Eighteen

Xmas Day 1918

Papa still wasn't earning very much so Christmas was quite different from previous years. Dinner was potato salad followed by roast pork, and then cookies and honey bread for dessert. Mama served sweet tea to me and Lilly, and sweet dessert wine to Papa. It was a quiet affair, ritualistic and almost undeserving. Lilly and I had presents - a new pair of shoes for me and a toy dog for Lilly wrapped in brown paper. Lilly loved dogs but we had to leave our loving dog, Stila, behind in Russia and Lilly bawled for a week. Her little face when she saw the soft little toy dog. She was so happy and grateful.

The next nine months were fraught with challenges. Since leaving the employment of Duke Sarkozy Mama and Papa's social invitations had slowly dropped off, one by one. Even Mrs Zharkarov had almost stopped dropping by, and Mama never saw any of her old friends who used to come once a week for afternoon tea. The move downtown had made them social pariahs. Mama said very little but Papa felt much sorrow for being cast out by his former friends and associates. "They were never really our friends! Only when there was money or they needed our help! Shallow bastards!" he cried one evening and shook his head in anguish. I was taken aback, having never heard Papa use such words. Mama and Papa now found themselves with few friends or acquaintances; they fell between the high classes and the working classes; no one, they thought, wanted them in their social circles; too poor for the rich people; too middle class for the poor people. To make things worse Papa got news of our house. It had been looted then set on fire and almost completely destroyed by the Bolsheviks. Mama grieved for what seemed like an eternity and Papa became afflicted with periods of insomnia and neuroses, battling the demons now looming constantly in his head. The torment dogged him for months and then one of Papa's colleagues introduced him to moonshine liquor, made out of the back of an old warehouse down the road from our apartment. "It will help calm your nerves, Gregoriiy." the man had assured. It was cheap to produce, cheap to buy and tasted harsh with a wonderful numbing effect, and a firm favourite with many of the working class in the area.

My Papa had never been a big drinker, only partaking at parties and never at home. At first we noticed very little change in our Papa when every evening he would bring home a small bottle of the liquor and drink it at tea time to settle his fraught nerves. He appeared happier and more jovial and we relished the evenings when he would joke and hug us, appearing carefree and well natured. Then slowly as the months progressed he began to drink more, often last thing at night and I would catch sight of him popping a bottle in his coat pocket when leaving for work. The mornings were worse; he would be tired, anxious and any little thing would irritate him. Him and Mama spoke very little each morning with Papa sitting at the table, staring angrily at his breakfast and often berating Mama for little or no reason. Lilly and I would avoid sitting with them both, preferring to eat breakfast once Papa had left for work. Our Mama would look at us sympathetically but say nothing.

The atmosphere in the apartment had changed. Gone was the playfulness, the hugs and the joviality, replaced by something sinister. I would dread the evenings, Papa and Mama arguing, and Lilly crying. "Mama, please get help for Papa." I would plead but she again did nothing. Why was she so afraid? In desperation, I turned to Alexei for help visiting him one evening after the restaurant had closed. "Alexei, I don't know what to do. The atmosphere at home is vile, and my Papa is drinking far too much. I am at a loss." Alexei looked at me, sucked his teeth and winced. "I have seen this many times before, Otto. We need to get your Papa away from the liquor and doing some positive things for himself and his community. First he needs to give up that dreadful job." I looked sad because Papa needed to work. Alexei continued. "He must come and work for me." I looked surprised. "Really, Alexei? Really? Doing what?" Alexei frowned slightly as it was obvious that he hadn't thought this through, and he scratched his head. "He can wait on, or help in the kitchen. The most important thing is that he will be surrounded by people that care for him." I felt incredibly relieved but how I convinced Papa would be another thing. "I suggest you send your Papa and Mama around here tomorrow evening for a chat." said Alexei and we kissed and said our good nights.

Papa and Mama left home at just after 7pm to visit Alexei. They were often invited for drinks at their apartment so this was not unusual and I watched them leave the apartment, dressed in their best clothes but looking exhausted. I crossed all my fingers for a good outcome, to help my Papa. At 8pm precisely the front door flung open and my Papa rushed in, arms flailing, his face flushed and angry. "I have never been so humiliated in all my life." he shouted loudly. "How dare you, Otto. How dare you speak to other people about our business. And to make out that I am a drunk and need pity. I am not anybody's charity case!" His eyes were dark and cold and he reached into the kitchen cupboard for a bottle of hard liquor, placed it on the table, unscrewed the lid and drank hastily from it before sitting down at the table. Mama creeped into the apartment behind him then disappeared into the bedroom. "I was trying to help, Papa. You are drinking too much. It is not good for your health." I said hesitantly but Papa was furious and my words only provoked him. He stood up and lunged at me throwing his fist towards my face but I caught his unsteady hand and with all my might pushed him back onto the bed where he laid for a few moments, shocked by my swift actions before getting up onto his elbows and looking at me. "I am ashamed of you, Otto. My only son. What have you turned out to be? No better than me? No better than the shoe shiners, the street scrubbers, the beggars. You are not my son." He fell back against the mattress and within minutes he was asleep. I covered him up the best I could and left him there.

His words hurt me. I knew he was drunk. I knew he was ill but the words cut me to my core. I sat down, feeling sick and lightheaded and Mama appeared by my side and put her hand on my shoulder. "What happened, Mama?" I asked her and she sat down and sighed. "Alexei offered him a job at the restaurant. What a kind man but your Papa blew up in his face, screamed and shouted. It was shameful. Alexei and Olezka tried to calm him but he wouldn't see sense. I am scared, Otto. He has become a monster."

I moved in with a friend temporarily to ease the atmosphere at home. Papa couldn't get past what I had done and he was increasingly morose and difficult to be around. I would meet Mama every few days at the restaurant where she would sit and cry, her face fearful and sad. Then one day I arrived at the apartment to pick up a few things when a police officer arrived unannounced to see Mama. "Madame Savin? I am sorry to tell you that your husband has been in an accident on the Champs Elysees." Mother sat down, shocked and pale. "He has broken bones but otherwise fine. I am afraid that we found him drunk and uncooperative at the scene. We had to arrest him." The police officer then left and we travelled to the hospital to visit him. We found him sitting up in bed, chatting and smiling at the nurses. When he saw us though his demeanour changed and he again looked aggrieved. "Hello Gregoriiy. How are you?" He refused to talk, got up and rearranged the bed covers before he sat back down and stared at us with hollow eyes. "You must talk to us, Papa. They are saying that you will lose your job then what will you do?" I said firmly. "I don't want to see your face. Go away Otto. " he replied, spitting the words through his teeth, and on that I walked out of the ward and sat on a chair waiting for Mama.

Later that week Papa lost his job. His employer had had enough of his drunkenness and unpleasant moods, and the standard of his driving had declined immeasurably. For weeks he sat at the kitchen table, often with vodka in hand, reading the paper or just gazing out into the coldness of the room. Then one day, having heard about his plight, Alexei came to visit. Me and Mama left the room and he sat with him at the table, made strong coffee because Papa was incapable and then spoke, "Gregoriiy my dear man, this is no way to live your life. You are so young and have so much to give. You are intelligent and charming and have your whole life ahead of you." Papa looked at him, his face crumpled and furrowed from the ongoing stress and the drink. "Come and work with me, Gregoriiy. We are a great team and you would be an asset to us. I beg of you to think about it." Alexei paused and waited for a turbulent response; however Gregoriiy sat back and sighed deliberately. "Thank you, Alexei. Thank you." Alexei rose to his feet and said goodbye. "You will let me know, Gregoriiy?" he said and Gregoriiy nodded heavily.

I met Mama as usual the next day and she skipped into the restaurant and I was taken aback by her change in manner. She sat down and held my hand. "Alexei has offered your Papa a job in the restaurant again. I am again taken aback by his kindness after the vile words that your Papa spouted at him. He has been so forgiving. Papa will start there next week." I smiled and breathed a heavy sigh of relief and then Papa appeared unexpectedly. He sat down wearily and looked me in the eye. I had become used to being afraid around my Papa so was expecting more anger, but he sat there staring and smiled slightly. "Alexei is a kind man and I misjudged the situation. I will be a better person for you, your Mama and Lilly. I am sorry Otto for letting you down." I held onto him and felt tears in my eyes, raw with emotion and relief and I hugged him close. "I am so happy for you, Papa." I said and closed my eyes. Papa pushed me away gently, embarrassed at such spontaneous affection, and sat down. Our roles had inexorably reversed; I was now the hero, the saviour, the adult and Papa in need of love and assistance. I stood there watching him, relieved but he was blighted by alcohol abuse; looking old and tired, his gait unsteady and his palour grey. What my Papa really needed was time at home to recover however we couldn't afford that. I hoped he would get better but I was not so sure he would ever recover.

Chapter Nineteen

The only brightness in a sea of gloom during those difficult months were the weekly orchestra meetings that I attended at the community centre. We met every Saturday morning with concerts nearly every week and to my delight Mama, Papa and Lilly had attended some of these. I was flush with pride when I spied them in the audience. I was finally making new friends and feeling part of the wider community; we were all in the same situation, having found ourselves awash and lost in a new country, with little money or prospects but music bound us together without the need for words or tears. My Mama was pleased to see me using my skills and looking happier. "Otto, you are a different person. You are a joy to be with." she said one evening but as we hugged lovingly I knew that her time spent with Papa was not as it used to be.

My relationship with Svetlana also deepened and I knew that my heart was set on being with her forever. I could not see my future without her and so I decided I wanted to marry her, and my nineteen years had been waiting for this moment. I just needed a ring for my beloved and fortunately my reputation as an accomplished accordionist had spread across the city and I picked up work in a couple of swanky hotels for four nights a week meaning that I could relinquish working on the streets each day. The pay was better and I loved performing. Papa was enjoying his time in the restaurant too, and sometimes I would join him, baking bread together in the mornings, or cleaning up late at night. It was a joy to work alongside my Papa, and see him happy and fulfilled. He had also started to make some new friends at the community centre where he volunteered helping with the accounts. It was good to see him using his skills at last. Sadly though, saving for the ring was taking a long time as I had my heart set on one particular ring in the jewellers just off the Champs Elysees; a small ruby and diamond gold ring that Svetlana had admired one day when we were shopping in the city. It was one week's pay and I put a small amount to one side each week. I had been with Svetlana for almost one year and I'm sure that she would be expecting some sort of proposal for sure. I just hoped she could wait a little longer.

Alexei grew impatient, stood up and paced the room. "Has he not asked to marry you yet,

Svetlana? What is he, a man or a mouse?". Alexei threw his arms up in the air with exasperation and sat down heavily. "Oh Papa, be patient. Otto will make his decision all in good time," replied Svetlana but her father's comments had troubled her and she went upstairs deep in thought. At that very moment I banged on the front door. "Ah, Otto!" shouted Alexei, pulling the door open with some force. "Come in! How can I be of help?" I stepped through the entrance and sat down with Alexei. "I need to see you tomorrow, Alexei. It's very important. Can I come to you after the restaurant closes, tomorrow?" I said, a little nervously. "Well, of course, young man." exclaimed Alexei, beaming knowingly, after all he had already had daughters married off to various men who had acted in the same fashion.

The next evening Alexei was waiting expectantly in the restaurant, apron on and cloth in hand, wiping down the tables for the last time before switching off the main lights and sitting under a small table lamp with his accounting books placed before him. It had been a busy day, Alexei was tired and didn't want to be kept waiting. He poured himself a small glass of vodka as I appeared at the door. "Good evening, Alexei," I called. The atmosphere was more formal tonight. "Drink?" said Alexei waving a shot glass at me as I sat down beside him. I accepted, took off my coat and hat, we said cheers, clinked glasses and glugged back the liquor. I wiped my mouth with the back of my hand and Alexei poured me another. We hadn't spoken more than a few words but now was the time. I cleared my throat, rehearsed the words silently for a short moment then spoke. "Alexei, from the moment I met your daughter I have been captivated by her charm and her beauty. I have fallen deeply in love with her. Would you allow me the honour of being her husband? I will care for her and look after her for as long as I live." I breathed, and Alexei sat back, eyes glued on mine, saying nothing for what seemed a very long time. I felt panic rising. Why was he is not answering me? I felt impatient and irritated but then suddenly a huge sweeping smile spread across his face. He stood up and grabbed me by the shoulders, lifting me out of my chair, shaking my hands fiercely and fast. "Yes, my boy, yes!". He kissed both my cheeks and I felt palpably relieved. We both fell back into our chairs and glugged back more vodka. "So you come around tomorrow lunchtime to ask for her hand?" Alexei was excited like a little child opening its presents on Christmas day so I agreed knowing that tomorrow was not a good day as I needed to earn some money to pay for the ring, but how could I say no to Alexei now?

The next morning I stood in the small jewellers and opened the little red velvet box and gently tugged at the delicate ring inside until it loosened and fell into my hands. It sparkled in the sunlight, tiny rubies and diamonds, and I felt happy and proud but also petrified. The sales assistant interrupted my thoughts. "Is this the one, sir?" he asked politely, looking intently into my eyes. I bit my lip. "Yes I think it is". I placed the ring back in the box, snapped it shut, handed over my money and pushed the box into my right coat pocket. It was mid November and the air was cool and the wind brusque and I walked out of the jewellers and pulled up my collar swiftly. I passed the goatherd standing on the street corner selling her deliciously warm milk to passers by. I could taste it now, tart and creamy. She had three beautiful young goats in tow, patiently standing by her, tied to a drainpipe.She acknowledged me, waving her black fingerless mittens and smiling. I hurried on knowingly that Svetlana would be at the restaurant with her parents, sharing lunch on one of the small wooden tables so I quickened my step not wanting to be late.

The restaurant was empty except for Alexei and Olezka who I could see were sitting at a table as expected with mugs of hot tea and biscuits but Svetlana was nowhere to be seen. I cupped my hand around the little red box in my pocket and stood on the doorstep, frozen for a moment whilst I took in the gravity of the situation before me. "Come in, come in." shouted Alexei warmly, ushering me to take a seat. Svetlana suddenly appeared at the door. "Svetlana, come here please. Otto has something to ask you." Svetlana appeared at the table and sat down, her little face looking a little tense but her mother held her hand and smiled at her. I straightened my hair nervously, then took the little red box out of my pocket and held it in my closed hand. "Svetlana." I said, "Will you do me the honour of becoming my wife?" Before she could respond I unclenched my hand, opened the box and presented the little ring to her. Her face softened and tears welled in her eyes, and she heaved a joyous sigh and cried, "Yes, Otto!". I gently pushed the ring onto her finger and it fitted perfectly, and she lifted her hand and looked at the ring in awe. "Oh, Otto, it's the ring I have always admired! Thank you!". She donned a new air of confidence and swirled around the room like a prima ballerina raising her hand above head and admiring the delicate little ring with pride. It had been some time since I had seen her this happy after the awful experience of recent months. We all hugged and sobbed a little more, and Alexei opened a bottle of champagne and we toasted our future. My parents arrived some time after and we all sat down to a hearty stew cooked so wonderfully by Olezka. Life couldn't be better.

Chapter Twenty

I married my beautiful Svetlana exactly one month later in the cathedral opposite the restaurant and held a small party afterwards in the restaurant surrounded by close friends and family. My parents sat quietly together as Svetlana's cousins danced in circles, drinking, laughing and singing. Alexei made a toast to celebrate our nuptials and Svetlana's mother continued to spoil us with dish after dish of delicious home cooked food. It was a night that I will never forget. That night we closed the bedroom door behind us to shut out the din of the party and I looked at Svetlana and she smiled seductively at me, her eyes lowering and her tongue wetting her lips. She took my hand and led me to the bed where we sat for a moment. "Unzip my dress, Otto." Svetlana asked and I placed the zip clasp between my fingers and slowly pulled it down, my hands shaking slightly, until her dress loosened around her body. I felt my ardour rise as she stood up and the dress fell from her body to the ground. I stared at her beautiful body and gasped. We made love for the first time and after we laid in each other's arms, satisfied and in love.

We settled into married life well at Alexei and Olezka's apartment above the restaurant. Olezka had set aside the spare room for us as our own "married" room. There was a large double bed with a colourful bedspread handmade by Olezka herself, a small set of table and chairs adorned with beautiful lace tablecloth, an armchair and a washbowl with soft towels. Every day Olezka put fresh flowers in a vase by the window and left us treats such as biscuits or chocolates. I felt truly blessed to be part of this kind and caring family. Svetlana continued to work as a waitress at her father's restaurant and I would go down town every night to perform in hotels to the rich suburbians. At the weekend we would still walk down to the river or wander around the shops on the Champs Elysees.

"My children, you need a holiday to celebrate your wedding." exclaimed Alexei sitting at the kitchen table one morning. "I have a plan." and he thrust a newspaper under my nose pointing at a small advert. I peered at it and then looked up at him a little confused. "But what is this, Alexei?" I asked and looked over at Svetlana who was smiling at me. "It's an opportunity, my dear boy," he said. "Read it!" he shouted warmly and sat back with his arms crossed looking rather satisfied. I read the advert and then re-read it. "For Sale. Small village bakery and two-bedroomed apartment in Port de Vacquelin, Normandy. All enquiries to Monsieur Franc." I didn't know what to think but there were many questions. "What is this to do with us, Alexei?" He looked at me a little impatient but I wasn't good at mind reading. "You and Svetlana. You need a future. Port de Vacquelin, it's a beautiful little coastal village. We have a holiday home there and Svetlana knows it very well. Just think about it, Otto. A place to start your family away from the stresses and the strains of Paris. A great business. You could do this, Otto. You should take your parents too. It would be good for them, especially your Papa. He would have no problem finding work either." I was speechless and less than a week later me and Svetlana found ourselves packing our cases and getting into the back of Alexei's car, ready for the four hour journey to Port de Vacquelin for a week's holiday.

It was the first time I had been away from Paris in over two years and I was so excited to be leaving it behind to spend quality time by the sea. Svetlana had chatted endlessly about her childhood holidays, the endless sunny days, the little cottage her father owned handed down from his parents, and the business opportunity, and my parents had shown great interest in a move away from the drudgery and poverty of the city. We looked at each other, nervous but exhilarated by the sheer thought of owning our own bakery. Alexei had offered to buy into our dream too. We arrived late in the afternoon and stood on the doorstep of the little cottage aptly named Bijou. We waved goodbye to Alexei who was staying with a friend in the next village for a few days, and in his own words, "to do some business" but would be back to attend the meeting at the bakery with Monsieur Franc.

Svetlana pulled the keys to the cottage out of her handbag, her hands shaking with excitement. She placed a key in the lock and turned it but it would not move. She turned around and looked at me, a worried expression moving across her face. "Try again, darling." I reassured her so she pushed it a little further in, turned it with some force and it suddenly opened and she fell through the door. She giggled, relieved, and placed her bag on the floor and stood there, breathing in the familiar scent of the cottage. "I love this place, Otto!" she cried and I walked in, placing the suitcases by the stairs then took a look around. The cottage was of a comfortable size with a living room, dining room and kitchen plus three bedrooms and a small courtyard at the back of the property. It smelt of soft musk and sweet lavender, and Svetlana put the kettle on, and I sat back on the settee and fell sound asleep only to be awoken by Svetlana cuddling me, her soft face nestled into my chest and her rose scented hair tickling my face. "I love you, sweet Svetlana" I whispered in her ear and she kissed my cheek delicately. "I love you too, Otto," she replied.

That evening we wandered onto the harbour front, and sat in a small restaurant, eating fresh fish and drinking white wine. Port de Vacquelin was a small coastal village, many fishing boats resided in the harbour, the village's main industry and it was mostly untouched by tourism except for a couple of restaurants and bars here and there. It was peaceful and perfect for a short break. There were few holidaymakers around now and the late Autumn sun fell sharply, cooling the air. Svetlana pulled on her coat, leant over and kissed me softly on the cheek and I longed for her. We would go back to the cottage and the next morning take a walk to the bakery in search of our new beginnings. We simply didn't know where life would take us but we knew that we would always be together.

The next morning we met Alexei and Monsieur Franc outside the bakery. Monsieur Franc unlocked the door and we stepped in. It was bright and airy, and beautifully kept, with all the fixtures and fittings having been preserved. The upstairs apartment was also in perfect condition and we could see the relief on Alexei's face. He shook hands with Monsieur Franc and arranged to visit his office to sign the paperwork. We had done it! We bought a bakery. Svetlana skipped back to the cottage but I wiped my heavily sweated brow, struggling to keep up with her. The stress of the morning was getting to me so we stopped off at a cafe for a well deserved cool drink. Svetlana was always so optimistic and confident these days whereas I always lacked that self assuredness and positivity that my wife naturally oozed. That evening I sat in the lounge, resting my feet on a small footstool and excitedly wrote a letter to my parents.

"Dear Papa and Mama,

Svetlana and I are having a wonderful time in this little idyll by the sea. We have seen the bakery and we are in negotiations to purchase it so we are very happy. You will love it here. The cottage is very quaint, right next to the harbour which is so picturesque. The sea air will do you good, Papa, and there is plenty of work in the area. It will be the perfect new beginning for all of us.

See you very soon,

Love, Otto and Svetlana. xxx"

I sat back and closed my eyes, dreaming of our new start, and looking forward to many happier days with Papa and Mama, and little Lilly as well as my wonderful new wife. It was almost time to leave and we would be returning by train. Alexei had already left a few days later to get back to the restaurant, having already completed his business as a satisfied man.

The restaurant was in darkness when we arrived back in the city except for Mama and Alexei huddled together under the dim light of the oil lamp at the back of the room. What was Mama doing here and where was Papa? I felt unnerved by my mother's abnormal presence and we rushed towards them. I saw her face, pale and wan. "Mama, what is the matter? What has happened?" I sat down beside her and Alexei looked at me sadly. My Mama looked at me, her face terrible and frightened. She hesitated then unexpectedly wailed, "Your papa is dead, Otto. He is dead". I was stunned and stared at her momentarily in shock before holding her in my arms. Svetlana calmly sat next to me in silence holding my hand, and Alexei mouthed an apology and got up out of his seat and disappeared behind us. I swept the hair out of mama's eyes and looked at her. "Mama, what has happened? Tell me what has happened." I knew Papa had been unwell for many weeks, if not months but this was so unexpected. "He collapsed in the street last night Otto. They found him dead - two men on their way home from work. There was nothing anyone could do. It was his heart. Forty six years old and dead. Why...why? They killed him Otto. They killed him. I am so sorry Otto."

Her words played heavy on my mind but I knew what she meant. We felt betrayed all over again; first by my parents' many friends and now death. She weeped a little more and I felt tears starting to flow from my eyes too. I wiped my eyes with the back of my hand, and we wept some more together, unashamedly and without fear. We were united in grief and we held each other tightly for that moment. Then there were no more words to be spoken. Alexei appeared with fresh strong black tea. "Here, you will need this, Otto." he said. I loosened my grip on my mother and took the cup appreciatively, sipping the hot sugary tea slowly. It did feel good. Mama got up and made her apologies, going to bed upstairs, where Olezka had made her up a bed alongside Lilly. My eyes followed her, a vulnerable shadow of a woman. "We will look after your mama for the time being, Otto. You must unpack your bags tomorrow and tell me about your vacation when the moment feels right. Get some sleep now dear boy". On that Alexei turned off the lamp and we all went to bed.

Chapter Twenty-One

The next few weeks passed as an uncomfortable blur. The funeral was held at the cathedral and the wake at the restaurant all within a week of Papa's passing. People came to the apartment day-in, day-out to pay their respects, bring presents and comfort our Mama. Papa wasn't supposed to die; he was supposed to move to Port de Vacquelin with us and start a new life, away from Paris, away from his grief and his ill health. How would we cope without our Papa. We entered the cathedral and took our places at the foot of my Papa's coffin. I stared at it, without thought or word, just in shock I just stared and I thought again of poor Igor, and then looked down at my pale, cold, shrivelled hands. People filed in in silence, in sadness. We sat and prayed, and whilst we waited for the service to commence Mama looked about the cathedral and her eyes fell sharply on the unexpected sight of Grand Duke Sarkozy and his wife. They sat in the furthest pews at the back of the church, stiff and awkward, faces cold, taut and rigid, void of emotion. We had heard that they had returned to the city, living in more modest accommodation in the 16th Arrondissement but what were they doing here? Was it from curiosity, regret or for forgiveness that they had felt compelled to dress in conservative black attire and make the short journey across the city to this place well below their standing? It had seemed ironic that they had come, for when Papa was alive they were nowhere to be seen from the moment he was released from their patronage. He never got over their unkindness. Mama turned back swiftly and cursed them under her breath, her eyes cold and staring. I had never heard her swear before and have not since.

I strode out early one morning, needing assuagement and time alone. The streets were soundless and calm juxtaposed to my life that had moved at an increasing pace. We lived on through our grief to build a new future and Svetlana and I finally moved to Port de Vacquelin three months later with our Mama and Lilly. However Lilly was not happy. Unlike me she had made many new friends at school and had settled well into the Parisian lifestyle. She went to school during the day at the local Russian school recently set up, and some evenings and weekends she worked at the bakery or restaurant, clearing tables or cleaning to earn some extra spending money. Her friends used to come and visit us at least twice a week and Mama enjoyed making them their tea and helping them sew and embroider. She had begged Mama to let her stay, stormed around the apartment, sulking and crying for days but we all agreed that she was too young to stay in Paris at eleven years of age. She would make new friends quickly in Port de Vacquelin and the school was good. We could see a great future for our precious little girl.

Port de Vacquelin was cold and dark when we arrived on that winter's day. The pace of life shocked me at first with few people on the streets and the silence was deafening. I initially struggled to adapt to my new surroundings and ironically yearned for the chaos of the city but Svetlana, seeing my ever increasing perturbation kept me busy in the bakery, cleaning, painting, plumbing and fitting new ovens. It was exciting and nerve wracking at the same time but I missed playing my accordion so I would sit each evening in the bakery, with just a candle for light, and play my music, thinking of my friends back in Paris. At first I wondered if I had made the right decision moving to Port de Vacquelin; I felt as though I was having to start my life all over again. Sometimes some of the locals would gaze through the window for a moment to watch me play, and smile or clap along. Eventually we started allowing them to gather in the main room, on little wooden chairs they would listen to my playing, and they would bring beer and bread and cheese, and sing along, and we would laugh and talk and they would ask many questions about me and Svetlana and our plans for the bakery. As the first Russians to settle permanently in this small community the villagers were generally welcoming, however we created much consternation amongst some of the elders. I could see their faces, the way they looked at us over their newspapers, peering through the windows of their homes at us, or holding their glare just a little too long as they passed us on the street, whispering into their hands, and the comments, oh yes the comments! We ate strange food, wore strange clothes and worshipped an unsuitable God. Yes, we looked different, our countenance harsher and our French broken but we were benign in both resolve and desire.

People shuffled past the bakery every day, sometimes momentarily stopping to take an inquisitive look inside, its front windows glistening and the doorstep always scrubbed to perfection. There was an air of excitement in the village at its reopening and the new Russian owners. Of course Svetlana's family were well known in the village, having had a holiday cottage here with her larger than life grandfather patronising most of the bars in the village for many years. One morning Svetlana came downstairs from the apartment above and announced "We're ready, Otto, to open. We have done it!" I hugged her, eventually settling down with steaming hot mugs of cocoa and a tot of rum to celebrate. That evening we went back home and Mama had made coq au vin and rice. Although it had been crudely pushed on her, she had learned to cook in earnest and was enjoying French cuisine and we were certainly not complaining. We drank rose wine and planned the launch of the bakery. "We will open in exactly one week." Svetlana proclaimed and so we did.

After much leafleting and knocking of doors the day of the opening arrived, with many people filling the small bakery and delighting in the home baked cakes that Svetlana had patiently created the night before. There were many smiles and mirth. We had named our new bakery "La Boulangerie Bijouterie" or Bijou for short after the holiday cottage. Eventually people started to retire and we were finally left to clear up and enjoy our success. "It was a shame that your Papa could not come, Svetlana. He would have loved this." I said whilst I wiped the tables. "Yes, it is a shame but he will reap the rewards soon." she said and laughed heartily. I then thought of my own Papa. I could see him here, sitting quietly at a table drinking tea and conversing with the locals, always slightly reserved and I think slightly intimidated by the outgoing French. He would have been very content in Port de Vacquelin and it would have helped him beat his demons. Sadly it was not to be. And then my memory was thrown back to Igor. What would he be doing now? Following in his father's footsteps as the next Grand Duke probably. I expect he would have given anything to give up that life and live a more simple existence like this one. He too would have loved it here. I thought of the share of the business that Alexei had invested into. Alexei was a shrewd businessman and wouldn't bankroll in something that wasn't viable, surely? I was always full of self doubt but Svetlana's face lit up with optimism and my thoughts were swept aside for that one moment.

We had been open a few weeks when I found myself with a spare afternoon, all my jobs completed. We had spent very little time away from the bakery since moving to Port de

Vacquelin and I thought it was time to go out and explore on foot. I took the cobbled street up the hill and then crossed the road to search for a path across the fields and out into the Normandy countryside. The little village nestled between impressive cliffs and I found myself ascending a steep path that led me out onto the top of a high promontory. The wind was vicious but not disagreeable and I sat on a mound and took out a small box of sandwiches and a flask of tea. I had never seen the sea much before. We had glimpsed it on occasion when we first moved to Port de Vacquelin but not in such enormity. It stretched out, beyond the airspace, a vast expanse of blue and grey with flashes of white. I was mesmerised by its power and beauty. I shut my eyes and breathed in heavily, the scent of flowers and the sweet sea air dulling my senses. "Hello young man" I heard a voice and I opened my eyes, squinting in the sunlight to see an older man peering at me with a dog on an old bit of rope. Without asking he sat down beside me and his dog laid down on the grass panting. "You new here?" he asked and I nodded. "We've just opened a bakery in the village. Bijou. Do you know it?" I was happier these days to speak to people, more relaxed with my social skills. "Ah yes, I know it well." he said and pointed out to sea with his stick. "You see over there? Those small boats?" I was wondering where his conversation was going. "They have gone to be at sea. They owned the bakery for many years. Monsieur and Madame Claude. They were friends of your grandparents." He stood up and wished me well and left with his little dog. I sat a little confused then realised he must've meant Svetlana's grandparents who had bought the cottage Bijou all those years ago. Well, I had learnt something that day. I decided to stay a little longer, not needing to be back at the bakery until tea time. It was silent on the cliff top with only the sound of the whispering grass and the odd seagull squawking and swooping. All uncertainties of living in such a quiet place dissipated in that moment.

We made many good friends in the village. I couldn't believe that there was such an abundance of musicians in such a tiny place; fiddlers, accordions, whistle players, guitarists and singers. We would meet every week in our little cottage, wine being poured and much laughter being shared. People would spill out into the small courtyard at the back of the property on a fine summer's evening, or onto the street at the front. The neighbours would join us, sitting on the floor when there wasn't space, listening and cheering our every note. One evening whilst playing at the cottage my friend Jacques nudged me playfully. "Otto, why don't we put on an impromptu concert in the church? Wouldn't that be fun? Taking our music to the masses!" and he leaned over and helped himself to another bottle of Merlot. Well, I hadn't thought of it, but why not, I thought. I invited some of my old friends from the orchestra in Rue Daru to join us, and there we were, about twenty five of us, sitting, laughing and smiling, playing an eclectic mix of classical, jazz and blues, for a packed church. What an evening and I couldn't help but realise how much I had changed. From those early days in Paris when I was a nervous boy accordionist standing in a restaurant, daunted by my audience, to now. So many things have changed that I was grateful for. I had been forced to grow up very quickly in Paris so that we as a family could survive the harshness that it threw at us and even more so after Papa died, and though I had missed out on my formal education and the chance to be an architect like my Papa I had accomplished so much more in my life; I was a businessman, bricoleur, baker and manager of finances to name but a few. For the first time I was truly grateful for what life had thrown at me.

Chapter Twenty-Two

The upstairs apartment smelled of cinnamon and baked biscuits and Alexei and Olezka sat quietly eating their dinner in the dining room. Alexei looked tired and Olezka held her hand out to him. "Alexei, are you feeling well?" she asked and he looked at her and sighed. "I am always under par nowadays my dear. Perhaps time has come to give up this life and take it easy. I am sixty-six years old." She nodded in agreement. Working every day in the bakery was taking its toll on her kind, loving husband and she wanted it to stop. "We can sell the bakery you know, Alexei and you can pursue all those hobbies. Just imagine it!" she said and he stared at her a bit surprised. "Yes, I suppose we can." he said and they both got up and sat on the sofa listening to some classical music. "I will make plans tomorrow, Olezka. We will be happy." he assured her and kissed her gently on the cheek. The next day Alexei walked to the local estate agents and discussed selling the business and the apartment. "We can market it for you. You should get a good deal, Alexei. It's a lovely business." said the estate agent.

Svetlana and I still hadn't unpacked all our boxes and so I decided to spend some time one weekend going through them. I sat on the floor in the living room and unfolded one of the boxes, excitedly wondering what I would find. I lifted out an old jacket that I hadn't worn for a long time when a small piece of paper fell out of its pocket. I watched as it fell to the floor and I bent down and picked it up, wondering what it could be. "Oh Otto, what are you doing? It's just a scrap of paper, put it in the bin." said Svetlana, jokingly chastising me as she walked into the room. "No, no Svetlana, I must find out what it is." I replied and picked the paper up, carefully unfolding it. I sat back and felt my blood run cold. It was the address of the family I had met on the ship coming over from Odessa. I had wiped the memory of the journey out of my mind for obvious reasons and sadly also the young couple and their daughter. It had been over two years since we had met. I wondered what they were doing now. "What is it, Otto?" asked Svetlana, seeing the look on my face. I told her about the terrible journey and meeting the young family on the ship and sharing bread and cheese. It was the first time that I spoke about that time in my life and I smiled at the memory; how they had cheered me up and stopped my stomach from rumbling. It had been such a hideous time in my life that it had been erased from my memory. "I must write to them, if they still live at this address. I must do it now."

I sat at the table with my fountain pen and some writing paper but couldn't immediately find the words to write but eventually they tumbled onto the paper.

Dear Konstantin and Maria,
Please forgive me for taking so long to write to you. I hope that this letter reaches you after two years. I hope you remember who I am. We met on the ship travelling from Odessa to Constantinople. You kindly shared your food with me.

We travelled from Constantinople to Marseilles then on to Paris. The journey was very traumatic and my Mama fell ill but is better now. Me and my parents and my little sister, Lilly, settled in Paris but then my Papa lost his job so we had to move and we struggled for many months. Sadly my Papa passed away but me and my new wife, Svetlana have moved to Port de Vacquelin where we have opened a bakery. My Mama has moved with us. I hope that you can write back as it would be lovely to hear all your news.

Fondest regards
Otto Savin

The sun was shining through the window and the flowers in the vase on the windowsill, though slightly wilting, still shimmered. I stared at them for a little while then put my pen down, folded the letter and placed it in the envelope before sealing it. Konstantin and Maria Babanin. I didn't remember their little girl's name. I felt a little guilty for forgetting about the family but happy that I was now hopefully back in contact with them. I thought about their lives. What had become of them and if they were happy and thriving. I remember the little girl's happy face in the station at Petrograd and her parents' anxieties played out in front of everyone.

So much has happened since then; those uncertain days when we couldn't have imagined the suffering we would experience due the many unfortunate situations that fell upon us. I now missed my Papa more than ever and a little sorrow again caught me short. When would these feelings of grief leave me? I grabbed a stamp from my wallet and stuck it on the envelope before rushing out the door and posting it at the post office. It had started raining so I ran quickly back to the cottage. "Where have you been, Otto?" my Mama shouted from the kitchen as I stood on the doormat shaking the rain off my coat. "Do you remember the family I met on the ship all those years ago? Well, I've just written to them!". Mama laughed at me, and we sat in the kitchen with a hot cup of tea and some marmalade biscuits. Mama was enjoying her new life, cooking and baking, helping with the house chores and going for walks along the harbour front. She was the most relaxed I had ever seen her, even more so than when we lived in Petrograd. The simpler life certainly suited her, without the need to dress up, to entertain or to manage a household of staff. She looked softer, had put on a bit of weight which suited her, and was more content generally, and it made me incredibly happy after all she had been through in the last few years.

Two weeks later and a letter fell into our postbox. I picked it up and looked at the writing; I didn't recognise it but it was from Constantinople so it could only be from the Babanins. I was so excited and I sat down at the kitchen table, carefully opening the letter with a knife. Mama appeared and sat with me quietly. I unfolded the letter and started to read.

Dear Otto,
How wonderful to hear from you after all these years. We have spoken about you many times since we met on the ship and wondered what you were doing. I am so sorry to hear about your Papa.

We are still living with Maria's parents but it is a big house and we get on very well. Her parents have been very welcoming though we still miss Russia and our friends. We cannot see ourselves going back there anytime soon. Life has been hard for us too but we have tried to make the best of a difficult situation. We have had another child since we saw you. Little Daniel, now nine months old. He is such a good boy. I am working at a restaurant nearby which I love very much, and Maria is still at home with Daniel. Ava is now at school. She is seven years old and so adorable. She still has the little dolly that you gave back to her. She treasures it with all her heart.

By coincidence we are hoping one day to move to Paris. I would like a business and the city seems like a good place. What do you think? Perhaps we will one day meet again? Take care, Otto and please write back.
Yours,
Konstantin

I was happy to hear from Konstantin and eagerly wrote back. We continued to write to each other over the next few months when Konstantin announced that he would be visiting Paris to look for a business opportunity. Moving away from Constantinople would be a big move for him and his family but hopefully a good one. He had always wanted to own his own business.

Alexei posted a "For Sale" advert in the local press, and then rested his elbows on the table, feeling a little lost. Olezka walked into the room, stopped and sighed, seeing her husband's quandary. "You look a little lost, Alexei. Let me get you a drink." He smiled lamentably and crossed his arms, sitting back on the chair. "It's the beginning of the end, Olezka, Do you think we will be okay?" She looked at him reassuringly.``Of course, my dear, Life will always be okay when we have each other." Soon after a letter arrived addressed to Alexei. It was from a Mr K. Babanin. "Olezka, Olezka, come here please!" shouted Alexei to his wife. "We have a potential buyer. A Russian man from Constantinople looking to move to Paris with his family. It sounds perfect." They sat together, excited by the prospect and the chance finally to move away from the business to live the quieter life they had dreamt of. "Babanin, Babanin? Isn't that the same person who Otto has been corresponding with?" Alexei said curiously. It must be, surely, he thought but Otto hadn't mentioned it. "I will ask him later when I ring him."

Of course it was the same person, exclaimed Alexei that evening whilst sitting down to his favourite meal, roast pork and vegetables. Otto had kept it from him in case the deal didn't materialise. Clever Otto, thought Alexei. A few days later Konstantin Babanin was standing on the front door with his wife and two children. It was a cold Sunday and raining hard and they were all soaked. Alexei rushed towards the door, opening it quickly. "Come in, come in my dears!" he exclaimed. "Olezka, make tea, bring cakes!" But Konstantin was embarrassed by his state of dress. "I'm so sorry, sir, we are so very wet having walked across the city from the station." he said, taking his coat off and wiping off the excess rain with his hand.

Alexei grabbed the damp garments and hung them up on the coat stand, then welcomed them all in, sitting them at a table and Olezka brought tea and cakes. "Would you like something stronger maybe, Monsieur Babanin?" enquired Alexei but Konstantin refused politely. "I am sorry but I do not drink." Alexei was a little surprised but was also relieved that he wasn't a drunk. "So, you want to buy my restaurant, do you?" Alexei said, sitting back and staring at Konstantin attentively. "Well, yes I think so, sir" Konstantin replied, stumbling over his words, a little shocked by Alexei's forwardness. Olezka chortled seeing Konstantin's worried look. "Don't worry young man, Alexei is all bark and not bite." They all then laughed together, and with that Alexei showed the Babanin's around the restaurant and apartment upstairs.

"We have a buyer, Otto! It's a dream come true. Konstantin is moving here in two months' time." Otto was happy for his father-in-law and would finally meet the Babanins. "We've done it!" cried Alexei and hugged his wife. "Perhaps we should tell all the children now?" he laughed. That evening he called all his girls one by one. Their response was mixed. "What will you do?, "Where will you live?" but all the girls were happy for them both.

Chapter Twenty-Three
Spring 1925

Though we had always loved children Svetlana and I chose to delay having them ourselves to concentrate on our flourishing business. My Svetlana was an insatiable businesswoman and the bakery was increasingly doing well under her command. Every day it was a busy little haven of good hospitality and excitement, filled with people, locals during the colder months, plus holidaymakers during the summer of which there was an increasing number over the years.

The counter was always full of sweet delights and it was no surprise that I put on a few pounds as the years went on. Svetlana employed a number of local people to help with the baking as well as serving and washing up and I had the idea of extending the business to include a delivery service. Every morning at 6.30am I would watch as a young lad called Eric would pull up on his bicycle outside the bakery before he went off to school, load boxes of bread and cakes into his basket and cycle around the village with his deliveries. He was a sweet tempered boy of about fourteen years old who would whistle and sing to himself, don his cap at every passerby and finally arrive back with us, still smiling. We would always reward his kindness with a steaming mug of cocoa or freshly made lemonade and a croissant after his rounds. We made many good friends in the village, and Mama had found work at the local school, helping the children with their reading. Lilly too was doing well at school and hoping to go to university to study politics and history.

We were truly happy as a family, the business was settled and as time went on our thoughts turned to starting our own family. Clear today as it was then, I remember Svetlana calling me into our bedroom one afternoon as I cleaned the bakery. "Otto, please sit down. I have something to tell you." She called to me. She was animated and her eyes bright with intrepidation and I had no idea at the time what she was about to say then it burst out of her mouth with much eagerness. "I'm pregnant, Otto!" she squealed with excitement. My heart burst with love and joy, and we hugged and kissed. Our lives were complete and we rushed downstairs to share the news with Mama and our friends.

December 1925

The day started as usual, baking, preparing and cleaning tables when Svetlana started with some discomfort. She took off her pinafore, sat herself down and was moaning, her face contorted with pain and I knew immediately what was wrong with her. "We need to get you to the hospital. Baby must be coming." I said and she smiled as I called a cab. I was scared to death. This was our first baby. Less than twelve hours later Svetlana was sitting up in bed holding a beautiful little baby boy who we called Georges Alexei Boris Savin. He was a bundle of joy, dark brown curls, chubby cheeked and he reminded me so much of my little sister, Lilly. A week later Svetlana came home from hospital, and Mama tended to her every need. They were perfectly in harmony, changing nappies, feeding all hours, washing, cleaning and looking after the baby so well. I was busy in the bakery, working long hours but would rush home every evening to see my wonderful family. It was a joyous time, and Alexei and Olezka came often to visit.

"I"ve got in, I've got in!" whooped Lilly as we sat around the table for breakfast one summer morning. She stood up and skipped around the kitchen in the light of the day. Her dreams of heading for university in England had been realised and we sat staring at the letter that had arrived that morning for some time, reading and re-reading it, unbelieving the good news. Lilly had worked hard at her exams and now at eighteen years old was going to England to study politics and history at King's College in Cambridge. "Well done, my dear Lilly! I will miss you so much" said Mama, tearful but proud of her daughter's achievements. "After all you have been through, you have proven that hard work prevails over adversity." and she was right. Lilly had experienced the worst of starts in life, moving to Paris at such a young age and having to adapt to a harsh upbringing, losing dear Papa, then the disruption of moving to Port de Vacquelin. For a long time I had felt guilty for wrenching her away from her beloved schooling and friends in Paris knowing she would probably never see them again, and then making her start again but she was stoic and soon created a new and better life for herself in the seaside village. Of all of us Lilly was the most resilient; always determined to succeed. She was focussed and resolute and the austerity that we had all suffered seemed to have made her even more irrepressible. She had grown into an intelligent, assertive and self-assured young woman showing much interest in politics and democracy, having been inspired by the work of her mother and the other women volunteers at the community centre in Rue Daru. We certainly had high hopes for Lilly.

Five years later and our family grew to two more. Yes, two more! We had the twins, Clarissa and Francois, or Frank as we nicknamed him. It was a bit of a surprise to say the least but as always Svetlana and Mama managed impeccably. Our little family was now complete but happiness turned to sadness because in the winter of that same year we sadly lost our dear Alexei. He had caught a cold having been walking in the Parc Monceau one day, as he did most days. The cold turned into pneumonia and he never tragically recovered. He was seventy-seven years old. A good long life for a hard working Russian. The funeral was attended by hundreds of people, packing into the cathedral and paying their last respects to a fine man. Olezka remained in the apartment but her life became intolerably lonely so she moved in with her daughter, Alexandria and her husband in Bayeux. Bayeux might have been too much of a change for Olezka after having lived in the chaotic capital for so many years but she adapted well to a more subdued way of living with regular trips back to Paris to visit friends and of course Alexei's grave. She was never far from her beloved husband in thought. Olezka lived another three years before passing from dementia. We missed them both dearly and the pain never goes away.

Our son, Georges, grew up to be a hard worker having joined us in the bakery from a young age but then war broke out in Europe in 1939 and life changed yet again. We continued as normal for a little while but always fearing the ever present fear of German occupation, then the German soldiers arrived in 1940. They mercilessly threw our friends from their homes, with families having to make space for their loved ones in their already cramped cottages, and some families moved into the village church for the best part of two years. Mostly we didn't talk to the soldiers, preserving as much self respect as we could hope for but we had no choice but to conform as they ruled us by violence and the gun. We had heard stories of soldiers dragging people from their homes, torturing then killing them for alleged crimes against the state. We were never one hundred percent sure of the reasons some villagers had to endure such cruelty but we didn't want to suffer the same fate.

Chapter Twenty-Four

There was much fear and frustration and we were scared for ourselves and our children. A curfew was in effect from nine in the evening until five in the morning for quite some years, and at night the village went dark like an ominous mist had befallen it. We continued to run the bakery but resources were scarce and our provision was often skeletal, with just the selling of bread on most days. Then in 1943 Georges came of age and we knew what that meant for our family and others alike. Georges and eleven other young men said their goodbyes one cold and wet day and of these twelve, only four returned home. Luckily for us Georges was one of them. He had been forced to work in Germany; hard manual labour, long days and nights, little rest and little sleep or food, living in nothing better than prisoner of war camps, herded together with thousands of other men, at the mercy of disease and starvation. It was cruel beyond belief. He came home to us a starved and ailing man, but he came home. We are still not sure who to thank but someone was looking over our boy during those terrible years.

We lost four years of our life, most days praying that the Allies would save us, save France from the claustrophobia of German occupation. On the morning of June 7th 1944 I had looked out of the front window curtains, irked by a sudden and deafening noise, and seen fighter bombers overhead. Were they British? Were they German? I could not see clearly so I chanced my arm and peeked out of the front door only to be confronted by an angry German soldier who butted my leg with his rifle, ordering me to stay indoors. He pushed me through the door and I fell, grabbing the coat stand, but clumsily hit the floor, scuffing my elbows. Svetlana screamed, closing the door frantically. I was dazed but got to my feet, annoyed and red faced. "How dare he treat me like that!" I shouted at the door and shook with anger, and Svetlana led me to the sofa whereupon she sat me down and made a drink. All the time there was the overhead roar of planes. "Something big is happening, Svetlana. I'm sure that I glimpsed Allied planes. Are they here to save us, to free us?"

My heart was in my mouth and I could feel its beating hard against my shirt. The terror yet fascination grabbed me, and we sat there listening to distant machine guns and rapid fire when Svetlana suddenly stood up. "Your mama, she's at the bakery. She must come home!" she shouted, suddenly remembering and ran for the door. As she rushed past me I spontaneously grabbed her arm to stop her and she pulled at me, her body straining against mine. "Please let me go and find her!" she cried but I pulled her back onto the sofa. "Stay here, Svetlana, you mustn't go out. It's not safe. She will be okay. She can look after herself. We know that." We sat, frightened, holding each other's hands. "Will we survive this, Otto? Should we not have moved to somewhere safer?" whispered Svetlana, fearful and trembling. "It's too late my love. The children are asleep? Please go and check on them." Svetlana ran upstairs and stayed there for many hours. I could envisage her lying on the bed, holding our dear little ones, both only thirteen years old, whilst I sat listening to the radio and trying to read a book. Our children had not had much of a life so far, the last four years under occupation.

The day eventually became night and I drifted upstairs, exhausted from the emotions of the day, never sure what the next moment might bring, machine gun fire close and the constant thud of bombs being dropped. We all stayed in the same bed that night holding each other tight, tossing and turning, the covers barely containing us, each one of us at some stage awakening and wandering, to the bathroom, or crying and shaking, our thoughts often turning to Georges and Mama, tormented by the deafening cacophony. It was a long night but we awoke early as the sun rose and I went downstairs cautiously.

The noises had subsided, just a faint distant gunshot crackle and planes overhead. I dared not go outside fearing more German retribution, so put the kettle on and made a light breakfast. Svetlana and the children soon joined me, little being said, just the sound of breakfast being consumed slowly and thoughtfully. "What do you think has happened, Otto?" uttered Svetlana, looking a little relieved and more composed than the previous evening. "It's gone quiet. Do you think we are saved?" She looked optimistic but I shook my head pessimistically. "Silence could mean either we are saved or more likely that the Allies have retreated or even surrendered." I replied. We sat together for hours, Svetlana playing board games with the children on the floor, and I watched her, fascinated by the way she cared for them, her whole life sitting in front of her. Every so often she hugged one of them tight and kissed them gently on the head. She was the most loving and selfless person I had ever known.

Early afternoon and there was a knock at the door. I paused for a moment and looked at Svetlana who was staring up at me from the floor. "Best go and look, it might be Mama," she said and I nodded. I walked into the hall and stood behind the door. "Who is it please?" I shouted loudly, and unusually an Englishman's voice called back. "Good morning, sir, my name is Corporal Geoffrey Packham of 47 Royal Marine Commando. It is my duty to tell you that we have successfully captured Port de Vacquelin from the German offensive. Please stay in your homes until otherwise notified." Though my English was not good I knew what he said. I fell back against the door, I felt sick and was shaking, shocked yet relieved. "Thank you, thank you, sir." I replied, stammering in my best English. "It is my pleasure, sir." he replied and then I heard his footsteps disappear along the cobbles. Not long after there was a loud bang at the door. "Let me in, it's Mama, please let me in!" I ran to the door, opened it and Mama walked in, her face ashen. She sat on the sofa breathing heavily. She had walked at pace across the square to the cottage despite of the lockdown and the danger. "I got stuck in the bakery. There was pandemonium. German troops on the street, shooting, shouting, then the English soldiers arrived and rounded them up. I hid in the apartment above with Monsieur Deschamps and his family. This morning it was quieter so I baked bread for the villagers. They need to eat. I will go back later and I hope to open the bakery. I met an English soldier who said it may be okay. I think it is safer now." Otto looked at her, proud of his mother baking bread whilst the village was under attack, always thinking of others. Later that day we were allowed to leave our homes. We walked out, with some trepidation and strolled up the cobbled street to the square. The village had suffered, some houses had been bombed and we soon heard that people had died. The church had been hit with both families losing their lives. We mourned for many days the loss of our friends, the sacrifice of freedom and the consequences of war.

It took a long while to rebuild Port de Vacquelin, with both the buildings and the people affected, with about 150 men and women perished due to the war. Men came from every village to help rebuild bombed buildings and the villagers rallied around those who had been dealt the hardest of blows, having lost their loved ones. Our good friend, Mylan Laurent, lost both his parents when a freak British bomb dropped on their cottage on the evening of the seventh of June 1944. Having heard the explosion he had been one of the first on the scene and the terrible memory of what he witnessed haunted him every day. People like Mylan were always welcomed into our bakery. During the day it became a social hub for the community; people dropping in for a coffee, needing that time to talk to release the pain and grief or make new friends, or just to meet old ones. We were grateful for every day of freedom that had been given back to us. We hope that our village would one day flourish again but it would be some years before we saw that truly happen.

Chapter Twenty-Six
June 1949

Mama and I sat in the train carriage, anxious for what we may find back in our old village in Russia. Mama was now seventy-three years old. It had been a long and tiring journey but we pulled into Leningrad station early in the afternoon. "Phhh, Leningrad. How could they?" said Mama, disdainfully. The old pain was etched on her face; she hated the new regime and the persistent honouring of the old leader, Vladimir Lenin, who although having passed for many years now, was still alive and well and sitting uncomfortably in Mama's mind. We arrived by taxi into the village just thirty minutes later. On first appearance it hadn't changed too much; the odd new shop, some new houses and a hotel which Mama and I would be staying at but first we needed to see our old house. We had instructed the driver to drive us directly to Bushin House; Papa had named the house after his grandfather.

We sat in the back of the car, and I rested my hand on Mama's knee and looked at her. "Are you ready to do this, Mama? Are you still happy to?" I was concerned for her welfare. She was frail these days and more so due to the long journey. "Yes, Otto. I need to lay some ghosts to rest my dear." she replied pensively and looked out of the window as we drew near the drive. The long stone wall surrounding the house was still there, though overgrown with weeds and somewhat crumbling. "Is this the house?" enquired the taxi driver and we nodded in silence. He drove part way up the drive then pulled in. Huge dense bushes crept across the driveway and the trees hung low and heavy, in need of a desperate prune. The once beautiful gardens looked neglected and Papa would have been furious I thought and laughed to myself. Even though it was mid summer there was a sudden eerie coldness in the air. Mama shuddered. "Yes, please just stop here sir. We will be fifteen minutes at the most." I said and pulled my collar up before stepping out of the car, Mama following on.

Standing here in the silence there were too many memories to fathom and we looked up at the house. It was a savage sight and worse than I could have imagined, and nothing or no one could have prepared us for such sadness. The house was a shell of its former grandeur, a burnt out skeletal frame, the stonework smashed and the ruined window frames dark and foreboding. We trudged up the driveway, scraping the gravel with our feet as we walked, the only noise was our breath, deep and heavy. I looked around and remembered our last moment here. We had sat huddled together in the car, the chauffeur with his peaked cap and uniform; the last vestiges of our cruel life played out before us and in that moment we were saying goodbye to all we had and all we knew, never knowing if and when we might return. There had never been a worse moment in my life. Not until Paris.

We arrived at the front steps, the front door had long gone and we stepped over fallen masonry, grabbing hold of the walls to steady ourselves, and ended up in the large foyer. "Be careful Mama, we don't know what to expect. There might be artillery." I warned her and she nodded at me before looking around. The old house could still be seen, bits of old wallpaper, smashed panelled doors and broken furniture. The house had been crudely set on fire and probably bombed too. The walls had blown out in places and Mama scoured the old sitting room, picking broken pieces of glass and ceramic, bullets and old Bolshevik uniform. Shadows fell upon the room gloomily. She shook her head with anguish and walked back out to the foyer and started to make her way down the hall to the kitchen but her way was blocked by brickwork. "Be careful Mama, it's very dangerous. You could fall easily." I cautioned her and she stopped and turned back, disappointed that her further venturing had come to an abrupt end. She looked up the sweeping staircase and again was disappointed to see that the stairs were damaged and unclimbable.

We made our way into the former living room. There was nothing recognisable left, not one piece of familiarity. Mama stared up at the ceiling, formerly an ornate mural of the ascension of Christ, modelled on Rembrandt's famous painting. The ceiling had been burnt and the mural destroyed and I felt flagellated by the sheer vandalism. I turned away with shock and caught sight of a glint of something in the rubble. I bent down and there it was something twinkling up at me. "Mama, mama, there's something buried in the stones. Look mama!" I was excited that in between all the damage was something that looked so precious. Mama came rushing over and stood over me trying to see what I could see. "What, Otto, I can't see." she said a little impatiently. I dug in the earth, scraping away at the stones and there appeared a little brown wooden box, covered in dust and broken in places. I lifted it up, blew the dust away, and held it in my hands as carefully as if it were an eggshell. "It's one of my jewellery boxes, Otto. Let me look!" she said excitedly and I passed it to her, whereby she sat down and placed it on her lap, opening it carefully. Inside were a number of diamond rings, gold bracelets and necklaces tangled together. "The looters must've dropped it when leaving. I always kept it in the bedroom." she said happily. She closed it and held it close to her face, smiling and relieved. "My beautiful jewellery. I'm so happy, Otto."

We stood there gathering our senses, shocked to have found something so beautiful in a sea of destruction, getting ready to make our exit, when we suddenly heard a voice shouting at us. "Hello, who is there?" A male voice echoed around the house and we turned around and looked about but could not see anyone. "Hello?" I replied inquisitively and the male voice shouted again. "Hello there, are you okay?" he said and there we saw him standing in the doorway. He was a portly man probably in his mid fifties wearing a dark blue beret and red checked scarf. He looked rather farcical at first sight as he stood waiting for us. We walked towards him tentatively, aware that we could have been accused of trespassing. Who was he, we thought? As we got closer he threw his arms up in the air with surprise making Mama jump. "Madame Savin. I cannot believe it. I'm so pleased to see you!" he shouted with joy, raising his hands even higher, a big smile on his face and at first we did not recognise him then Mama's face brightened. "Anton! Oh my goodness, Anton, it's you. Me dear man!" and she rushed towards him and hugged him tightly and then I remembered. Anton, our tutor, from all those years ago. He was older and greyer but he hadn't changed; still rambunctious, still larger than life.

The three of us held on to each other, as if it was our last ever hug, as if all life mattered on it then we pulled away slowly and Mama wiped the tears from her eyes and I reached for a bottle of water from my bag as she looked pale and faint. Anton looked at us with astonishment. "Why are you here? How are you? Is Monsieur Savin with you?" There were so many questions but they would have to wait, and we explained that we had come back to visit probably for one last time. "Please settle yourselves in at the hotel, and then meet me at 6.30pm at the public house for a meal and we can talk more. I think your Mama needs a rest." he said looking kindly at Mama and then disappeared down the driveway and we waved goodbye. Our time here was finished and so we got back in the taxi and went straight to the hotel for some repose.

"Hello, my dears!" shouted Anton as we entered the public house that evening, and we sat down with a much needed drink. We told him all about our lives, the struggles, the tragedy of losing Papa so young, and the new found hope in Svetlana and Port de Vacquelin. He looked genuinely pleased for us and then he told us of his life. "I stayed here for a little while after you left, working as a school teacher in Petrograd but soon left for Lille as I did not like the new Russia. Of course I have French citizenship so leaving was easier for me, and I went back home. I returned three years ago to take care of my ailing sister, and I still live with her, just around the corner from here. We have a simple and happy life." He took a swig of his beer, grinned then continued. "What happened to our household staff?" Mama asked hesitantly. She frowned slightly but Anton reassured her. "Do not worry. They all got other jobs. Factory work, cleaning, shop work and the like. We all managed. And Stila the dog got a nice home too. There was much poverty and distress though. Food and fuel were sparse in the villages. Some people didn't make it." He gazed into the distance momentarily and lamented. "We lost many elders to the cold."

Mama and I were silenced by this and thought of our own plight in Paris during the cold months. "What happened to our neighbours, the Ivanovs?" Anton bowed his head, and slowly answered. "Oh it was not good news. Two weeks after you left the Bolsheviks arrived in the village. They went to each of the big houses, one by one, including yours, and looted, taking all possessions and valuables. Most of them were then set on fire. Yours was spared for a little while as the soldiers lived in it but then they left and firebombed it, leaving it as you saw it today. Nobody has been there since, just so sad. The Ivanovs? Oh yes. Unfortunately the Ivanovs had delayed their departure as Monsieur

Ivanov wanted to conclude some important work. What was so important about that final deal? We will never know. It was to be his final fatal mistake. The soldiers went in the night and shot them all in their beds." Anton stopped and wiped his forehead with his handkerchief, as he was now sweating quite heavily. "And shockingly, their household staff. It was terrible. We all lost good friends. They took the bodies away, refusing to give them back to the families, and burned them in the forest. They were animals, senseless animals and it was one reason why I wanted to leave so badly." Mama looked shocked, realising it could have so easily been our family, our household. Anton composed himself, changing the subject. "Anyhow, I have a little surprise for you!" he exclaimed. He requested we put on our coats and follow him out of the public house and across the road.

He knocked on the door of a small terraced cottage and the hallway lit up. "Just coming!" shouted a gruff voice and we heard keys rattling in the lock. The door opened and there stood a little old man, white haired, wearing a white vest and scruffy brown trousers, with worn slippers on his feet. "Good evening, Anton, how are you? Please come in." he said, inviting his friend in, then stopped as he saw Mama and myself. He looked at Anton who smiled but he was unsure who these strangers were and we felt the same. "Do you remember these two, Mikhail?" said Anton and there was a pause before Mama exclaimed. "Mikhail, our dear chauffeur. Hello sir!" Mikhail too remembered immediately, and there were many smiles, hugs and kisses. Gone was the formality of our past life, we were all just humans now.

Mikhail was such a gentleman ushering us into his tiny abode, making us tea and listening patiently whilst we told him our lives. Every so often he would nod and smile, and exclaimed how life could be so cruel to all men regardless of their class or status. Mikhail was now eighty-eight years old but still tinkering with cars with his son and grandsons. He had found work as a mechanic after we left for Paris. His wife was asleep upstairs. "She is very old. Just two years younger than me." Mikhail said, winking at Anton and chortling. I remember his dry wit, often joking with me whilst my parents' backs were turned. I had always liked Mikhail. We finished our tea and got up to go when he stopped us. "Please come with me." he said and grabbed his coat and hat and two sets of keys, still wearing just his slippers on his feet.

We walked down the road behind him, turned right into a narrow, unmade lane and then went around the back of the cottages to some old garages. I put my arm around Mama as it was a little chilly now. Mikhail took a torch out of his pocket and unlocked the furthest garage. He pulled the door back and it noisily scraped along the gravel floor and he tutted. He turned the light on and the garage was filled with a harsh yellowish hue which momentarily hurt our eyes. It smelt heavy of oil and grease and was cluttered with tools, bits of machinery and piles of newspapers and rags and then I saw what I thought was the shape of a large vehicle draped with a big dusty old grey sheet taking up most of the space in the centre of the garage. Mikhail put his torch back in his pocket and took the sheet in his hands and gave it a great big tug and in one sweep the sheet fell away and there stood a beautiful old car, shiny and gleaming. At first we didn't recognise it, then Mama fell back slightly and cried in disbelief, "My Gregoriiy's car! Oh Mikhail, you kept the car. Gregoriiy's pride and joy." Mikhail beamed with pride and took the keys out of his pocket, unlocking the doors. "Please allow me." and he donned his peaked cap and jacket that were sitting on the passenger seat, and opened the car door for me and my Mama.

We stepped into the car and sat in the back, in our old familiar places. The smell of leather and the soft, smooth feel of the seats took us both back in time and I sat and peered out of the window, almost as a child, with wanderlust, remembering happier times. Mikhail got in the driver's seat, turned the key and started the engine. Its low delicious roar was soothing to the soul and I closed my eyes and listened to its heart-warming thrum. "Tomorrow, I can take you for a drive to your favourite places if you so wish." he said and Mama stretched out her hand and placed it on his left shoulder delicately. "Yes we would love that, thank you, Mikhail." He lifted his hand and placed it on hers and gently squeezed it. "It would be an honour, Madame Savin." he replied and turned off the engine. He got out of the car and stood for a moment, handing the keys to my Mama. "The car is yours now Madame Savin. We have kept it safe for you. I hoped for this day. I hoped that we would meet again. We have waited a long time for this day." said Mikhail but Mama held her hands up. "No Mikhail, it is now yours, your son and your grandson's. I want you to have it. Gregoriiy would have wanted that too." The old man's eyes filled with tears and he shook my Mama's hand and bowed slightly. "Thank you so much Madame Savin. Thank you so much."

Mikhail was overawed, shaking slightly and I genuinely believed that he thought we would one day return and the car would be returned to its rightful owner. We eventually said our goodbyes and the next morning we rose early to meet Mikhail and Anton outside the cottage for a trip out to the countryside. Most Saturdays, Mama, Papa, Lilly and myself would get in the car and Mikhail or Mr Gagarin as I knew him, would drive us to the countryside, out to the lakes and then up to the viewpoint, where we would eat a picnic made by our cook, Mikhail waiting patiently in the car whilst we ate and chatted, looking at the view and enjoying time together. Those days were precious to us and even if we didn't understand that fully at the time I certainly understood it now.

Our time in our village was over and we had to return to Port de Vacquelin. We were expecting a visit from my little sister, Lilly, and we were very excited having not seen her in a long while. She was now a member of the French parliament, supporting the underprivileged in the city and living in the 15th arrondissement in Paris with some friends. We said our emotional farewells again to Anton and Mikhail and knew that it was possible that we would never see them again but we promised to keep in touch. Three months later Mama passed away. We found her one morning lying on the bed, her clothes neatly laid out next to her. She was in her favourite nightgown with her hair in curlers and her make up impeccably done. She had been getting ready to go out with her friends. She looked so peaceful. The doctor said that she had suffered a sudden and fatal heart attack. She was seventy-three years old and we buried her in the graveyard a week later. She had found her peace, visiting the old house and had settled those demons that had secretly followed her around for all those years.

August 1988

Well my friends we've come a long way, me and you. We never know how life will turn out, do we? I remember sitting in the garden of our beautiful manor house near Petrograd as fifteen year old Otto, taking every moment for certain, thinking that life was mapped out, the dreams, the aspirations, the inevitability then suddenly it was gone. Just like that. Taken forever. We all learned quickly not to take things for granted, didn't we Papa? I am an old man now, eighty-seven years old and weary, ready for the next life with my sweet Svetlana. Ah, how I miss her still. I have been blessed with a beautiful family and a good long life despite those early years and losing my dear Papa. "Ah we've done good Svetlana my darling, we've done good. you and me."

Otto passed away on 27th May 1988 and was buried alongside his dear wife, Svetlana in the small graveyard in Port de Vacquelin. Rest in peace, dear Otto.

Chapter Twenty-Seven
September 2018

"Wow, look at this place, Dahli, it's so pretty!" squealed Rann as they passed the sign for Port de Vacquelin; brightly coloured terraced cottages lined tiny cobbled streets winding their way down to the busy harbour front. It was a beautiful sunny morning and Rann leaned out of the van window and shrieked with excitement "Ooooeeee! I've got a good feeling about this trip!" she said and closed her eyes, relaxed and lost in the moment. They drove alongside the harbour wall, passing the visitors ambling casually, took in the glorious sea views then headed up a road following the campsite directions on the satnav.

The site was larger than Dahli had expected, set in and around a woodland, and incredibly busy, even for mid September. She dropped Rann off at a modern self-catering chalet adjacent to a small lake. It was serene and a little way from the main hubbub of the campsite. Typical Rann she thought; never one for slumming it. Dahli then ventured on to find her own pitch. There it was, large and grassy encircled by a tall hedge for privacy. It was fine for now she thought. Lots of people were milling about and Dahli watched a family go by; a little boy on a push bike excitedly kicking up the dirt, his dad carrying bags of baguettes and other necessary provisions, his little sister in a pretty pink swimsuit holding a bucket and spade and wearing cute little star shaped sunglasses, giggling excitedly, and mum with a bathing towel slung over her shoulder all heading for the swimming pool. Dahli shuddered at the thought of being part of a family. There were children playing football behind her, their ball thumping the tarmac with quite a noise, and an older couple lazing on deckchairs by their motorhome drinking bottles of cider at 10am in the morning and playing loud brash 80's rock music, the man reading the paper and the woman resting underneath a huge yellow sun hat. Dahli grimaced and was starting to wish that she had booked into a smaller, quieter campsite. It was only for a week though she reassured herself, and she would be spending very little time here.

She hooked the van up to the electric and put on her shorts, t-shirt, sun cream and sun hat. She grabbed a bag and locked the van. Rann appeared and they crossed the campsite car park, passed over a small country lane and took the footpath down to the old town. The path ran alongside an expansive field, stunningly golden, the corn moving in synchronicity in the slight breeze. Birds were soaring above and the air was silent. Dahli had forgotten how beautifully peaceful this part of France was. Rann swigged on a bottle of water and sighed. "I couldn't be happier, Dahli " she said and put her arms up to the sky and stretched. Dahli smiled and was so pleased to have her sister here.

After a gentle fifteen minute walk they started to descend down a narrow cobbled street, edged with brightly coloured terraced cottages. They passed an old woman washing her front step. "Bonjour!" she shouted. "Bonjour!" shouted Rann back, proud of her newly found command of the French language. The woman then uttered something back whilst beaming in their direction, and Rann smiled ruefully. "I haven't a clue what she said." giggled Rann and the two girls laughed. The woman huffed and went back to washing her step. Dahli and Rann soon found the harbour front lined with pretty little restaurants, cafes and souvenir shops. People were sitting drinking and eating, chatting indiscriminately or walking along the cobbled sea front, stopping now and again to allow for the slow moving cars that passed by them. Holidaymakers, locals, students and day trippers, everyone was here today, enjoying the hot sunshine and fine sea air. Over at the harbour, weather beaten, brown-skinned fishermen were standing in their brightly coloured boats, adorned in fluorescent oil skins, mending their nets, washing down the decks and shouting over each other. There was a faint smell of fish mixed with garlic in the air.

What a wonderful little place this was, Dahli thought. She left Rann looking at clothes in one of the many shops, and wandered around a back street coming upon a small square. A young man was sitting on a stool in the middle of the square under a tree, playing the guitar accompanied by an older man riffing on an accordion, and a few tourists had gathered to listen. It was typically French and made her heart skip a beat with excitement. She paused for a while, threw them a few coins which was appreciated with a "Merci" from the young man, and then she looked around for somewhere to eat as she was starting to feel hungry.

On the corner of one of the cobbled streets she spied a small bakery cafe brimming with people sitting outside at chairs and tables under a large red awning. The cafe had two huge floor to ceiling windows and on display in one of the windows was a plethora of sweet patisserie. Her stomach rumbled and she licked her lips with anticipation. She crossed the square and strolled into the cafe, looking for a table to sit at. A small, plump young woman wearing a bright blue apron and wiping tables down with a cloth walked over to and beamed at her enthusiastically. "Bonjour, welcome to Le Cafe Savin. Please take a seat just here and Marianne will be over to serve you." she said in her best French but Dahli could tell immediately that the woman was not French by her accent. "Thank you." Dahli replied in English and the woman smiled. "Ah you're English then?" she enquired and the two women laughed. "Yes I am." replied Dahli. "Well, I'm Beulah. I own this cafe with my husband, Eric. Welcome again." said Beulah joyously and she continued to wipe down the tables.

Dahli settled herself into a chair and perused the menu scrawled in chalk on a large board on the wall behind the counter. The cafe was very twee but in a quaint way, with red checked table cloths, black and white tiled floor, vases of flowers on each table and pictures of local scenery on the wall. The air smelled of powdered sugar and strong coffee. Marianne came over and took her order - a cafe au lait, a glass of freshly squeezed orange juice and a croissant with jam and butter. Dahli looked over at Beulah and smiled. She felt a connection with her. She didn't know what it was, but there was something there. Something about Beulah was likeable and comforting. Dahli waited patiently for her order, and began to look around the cafe. Above her head was a large black and white photo. Something about the photo caught her eye. She stood up, leant forward on tiptoes and peered a little closer at the photo, being careful not to overbalance. She steady herself putting her hands on the table, and looked even closer. Before she could do anything else Beulah was standing next to her again. "Let me tell you about that photo..." and she continued on, delighted to have an attentive audience.

The photo was of a young Svetlana and Otto Savin with their son Georges, a toddler in age, standing proudly in front of the bakery cafe. The year was 1929 as scrawled on the back of the photo, said Beulah, and the couple had been owners of Cafe Bijou, now Le Cafe Savin, for two years. They stood there in their finest clothes, obviously a staged photo, looking serious and stiff, their eyes cold and focussed. The cafe had changed much over the years with the addition of outdoor seating, the big red awning and the large feature windows being added more recently but it was obviously this cafe, perched on the end of the street lined by cobbles. Beulah said that her husband had found the photo in a box in the loft along with some old letters addressed to Mr O. Savin and written in Russian which they hadn't yet got around to translating. "The photo had been in an awful state so he got it professionally cleaned, framed and hung. The letters - we just haven't had time to get them looked at yet. Maybe soon." she explained and continued. "According to the locals the Savin family owned this cafe for over sixty years before a local French man bought it and tried to turn it into a bistro, the fool!" laughed Beulah. "It lasted one season before someone saved it from then being turned into a supermarket. There was local uproar at the plans. Seems the locals needed cakes in their lives more than groceries! We took over the lease two years ago."

Dahli thanked Beulah for her information and continued to gaze at the photo. "Do you know any more about the young couple?" asked Dahli inquisitively. "Yes," said Beulah, "Russian, from Paris, having escaped Russia during the Revolution of 1917. I know little more about them. Old Mr Savin only passed last year." "Old Mr Savin?" Dahli asked. "Yes, he lived a quiet life down on the harbour front, in a small cottage with the same name as the cafe, Bijou. He used to come in here once a week, sit in the corner, reading his paper. Kept himself to himself. Nice, quiet man. Otto and Svetlana were his parents who also lived in the same cottage many moons ago. Seems it's been in the family for some generations." "Bijou?" thought Dahli, "That's the same name as the keying. I wonder." Beulah went back to cleaning the tables, happy to have utilised her storytelling skills so exquisitely, and Dahli reached in her bag for the keyring. She took it out and looked at it again. Yes, Bijou.

Dahli suddenly felt a strange closeness to the Savin family and shivered slightly, putting the keyring back in her bag. She looked at her watch. Time to meet Rann, and plan the afternoon. Beulah came over again. "Let me finish my story." "Oh, okay." Dahli sat back, aware of the time and not wanting to be late to meet Rann back on the harbour front. Beulah sensed her slight impatience. "I'll be quick. Francois Savin, or Frank as everyone knew him, passed away last year at the ripe old age of eighty-five but the cottage has sat empty and forlorn since then. No one really knows why. His surviving relative is Christian, his nephew but he lives in Paris, visiting only once a month or so. Busy man. Works as a lecturer at some university or other. The only person visiting more frequently is Juliette, Frank's housekeeper who works at the library a few days of the week. I think she is looking after the house for Christian. Anyway that's the full story now or as full as I can make it! You must be on your way. I hope to see you again." Dahli was starting to think that Beulah really was the gossip of the village but very charming with it.

Chapter Twenty-Eight

Dahli finished her breakfast and the two women bid farewell, Dahli rushing out into the sunshine, passed the cafe patrons and onto the harbour. There was Rann waiting for her, many bags in hand, adjusting her sunhat to block out the fierce sun. They walked along the harbour front admiring the clear blue sea gently lapping up against the harbour wall. People were zigzagging casually across the cobbled road, in and out of shops, stopping for ice cream or sitting down for a bite to eat. At the far end of the harbour a crowd had gathered to buy fresh oysters of different sizes, with sellers busy bagging them up. It was an unusual sight that Dahli was not accustomed to, and she watched with great happiness. She laughed to herself at this antiquated tradition. "So what did you find on your travels Dahli?" Rann interrupted Dahli's thoughts. Dahli shook out of her reverie and told her about the cafe, Beulah and the Savin family. Dahli said she would need to find Juliette the housekeeper to find out more about the Bijou cottage but in the meantime they would continue with their sightseeing and tonight eat in one of the pleasant fish restaurants by the harbour. After all, they were on holiday.

The next day they got in Rann's car and drove to Bayeux as promised. Rann wanted to shop but Dahli was more interested in the history and disappeared off to see the Bayeux Tapestry. Later she sat under a tree by the cathedral waiting for Rann and her plethora of bags. She wondered what she might have bought this time; shoes, clothes, perfume, toiletries. You name it, Rann bought it. "What did she do with them all, and where did she put them all?" Dahli pondered, exasperated at the very thought. Thank God her life was simpler. Dahli then thought back to the Savins and planned to visit the library and find Juliette. That would have to be tomorrow now as Rann probably had more shopping to do.

The next day Dahli ventured out on her own, leaving Rann to sort through her shopping which she knew would take forever. Dahli had found out that the library opened at 10am so she walked down to the town early, meandering through the fields and watching the butterflies playing in the meadow. She really couldn't get enough of this place. Her time here was slowly running out so to find Juliette today was an absolute must. The library was near the cafe, just off the village square. It was an old building, possibly an old church and disappointingly looked closed but then a young man exited from the front door and Dahli felt relieved. She grabbed the door before it closed in front of her and walked in. The library was fairly empty and the woman at the reception was busy sifting through some papers. "Bonjour" she whispered, "Can I help you?" Dahli moved towards the counter and enquired about Juliette. The woman looked suspicious at first but then warmed to her. "Yes of course, she's just in the back. Please give me a minute." She disappeared into the back and soon returned with an older, waif-like woman with short, straight bobbed hair and little round John Lennon glasses. "Hello, can I help you?" said the woman. Dahli looked at her, her pink cheeks and wrinkled nose made her smile. She was your stereotypical librarian, straight out of a storybook. Dahli introduced herself and asked her if she had a few minutes to talk with her.

The two women sat down at a nearby table and Dahli nervously explained her circumstance. She got the keys to the cottage out of her bag and showed them to Juliette. Juliette took them, inspected them closely, looking over the top of her little glasses. She put them down, thanked Dahli and then a huge smile radiated across her face. "So, your mother, was she called Mathilde? Mathilde Sorensson?" In her excitement Dahli had forgotten to mention her mother's name. Dahli replied. "No, Mathilde Rosenberg. Her maiden name was Sorensson though." Juliette smiled. "Ah, I don't believe what I am hearing. You have found Mathilde for us. You have found her! We have been looking for her for a year." The delighted woman shook Dahli's hand avidly. Juliette went on to explain that when Frank Savin died, Christian Savin, his nephew, had been notified by the solicitor that the cottage had been left to a Mathilde Sorensson but after much searching they had not been able to find her anywhere. Christian had never heard of the woman or knew of the connection between her and his uncle Frank. They were completely baffled by this woman.

Dahli was delighted to have solved a mystery. Juliette looked at her watch. "I must get back to duties now, but let me write Christian's number down for you to ring him. He will be so surprised. He's such a sweet man with his adorable wife and two little ones. He lectures in Russian at a university in Paris." she said rather proudly as if Christian was her own flesh and blood. She found a piece of paper and wrote the number down and passed it to Dahli eagerly. Dahli carefully put it in her wallet and promised to ring Christian as soon as possible. The two women hugged, kissed like old friends and said goodbye, and Dahli left the library feeling a little overwhelmed. It seems she may have inherited a cottage in France and a whole lot of back story.

A week later and Dahli was restless to move off the campsite to a smaller, quieter space, especially as she was now planning to stay in Port de Vacquelin a while longer after discovering the truth about the cottage. She wandered down to the campsite restaurant for a bite to eat and noticed a poster with bright green lettering stuck on the wall by the fruit machine. "Open Mic night TONIGHT! 8pm sharp". She thought for a while whilst chewing on a cheeseburger, then decided it would be good for her to blow the cobwebs off her guitar and sign up to play.

That evening the campsite pub was filling up nicely with regular performers, hugging and kissing each other, shaking hands and laughing. Dahli didn't know anyone there and felt slightly uneasy, having not played for a few months in public so she put her guitar case down by a table and headed over to the bar for a drink. She had rehearsed three songs, sitting in the van, strumming gently and singing softly that afternoon so not to attract any unwanted remarks from holidaymakers. She looked at her watch; it was 7.10pm. She was due to meet sister at 7.30pm so plenty of time to get one in, she thought. She slid herself onto a bar stool and put her handbag on the counter, peering over to the optics to see what was on offer. She stood up on the bar stool for a better look when she started to overbalance slightly and fell awkwardly against a man sitting next to her. "Oh, Christ, I'm so sorry." she said pulling herself off him and readjusting the bar stool. The man helped her to her feet and smiled. "Hey no worries." he replied in French. "I'm Joe by the way. Darius Joe McCoffey. Nice to meet you." Dahli was surprised by his familiarity, interested by his accent which obviously wasn't French, and she introduced herself before ordering a Southern Comfort and lemonade. She sipped the drink quickly, ordered another and watched the man as he sat next to her, filling in a crossword in an English newspaper. "Er, three down, I know that one." she quipped and he looked up at her, a little surprised. "Well, spill the beans then." he laughed. "Serendipity." she replied and he entered the word into the crossword.

Joe disappeared off to the toilet and Dahli sat back feeling a little more relaxed. "Is that a glint I see in your eye?" remarked the barman who Dahli had become acquainted with over the last week. "Ha, ha!" replied Dahli sarcastically but the barman had correctly perceived an undeniable attraction that Dahli was struggling to fathom. Did she desire him or was it that he had been polite and she admired that quality in a friend? He was undisputedly good looking, with dark brown curly hair, blue eyes and an affectionate smile. Perhaps this was her serendipity, she thought to herself. Dahli looked at her watch; it was now 7.40pm and Rann was late, which wasn't like her at all. Dahli returned to her table and sat down with her drink, wondering what had become of her sister. She then noticed a couple setting up the musical equipment for the open mic night. They bemused her, bickering and waving their arms about, unquestionably a married pairing, she thought. "No, not there, put them here." the wife shouted at her husband and he begrudgingly moved the speakers. She went back to twiddling knobs and plugging in leads at an alarming rate. He tested the microphone "One two, one two." and adjusted the microphone stand, nodding to himself with satisfaction, his wife still chuntering to herself. He then grabbed a pen and paper and people started introducing themselves to him, and him scrawling with gusto. The barman suddenly appeared behind Dahli. "If you want to play then you'd best go and get your name down now." he advised so Dahli approached the old man and the barman returned to the bar. "Hi, I'd like to play." she said a little hesitantly. "Ok, love, you're down for 8.30pm. Three songs. Name please." he replied without looking up. "Dahli. Thanks." she replied and left him puzzling over the spelling of her name.

Satisfied, Dahli sat back down, sipped her drink and unclipped her guitar case in preparation for her performance when she suddenly heard a loud noise behind her. She looked around and saw her sister falling through the pub door, her bag catapulted to the floor and her legs wobbling from side to side. She squealed with laughter, picked up her bag, steady herself and then lurched towards Dahli. Dahli caught her and sat her down, disturbed by her sister's behaviour but the smell of alcohol betrayed Rann's state; she was drunk. Rann squealed a little more and Dahli was uneasy with the situation, "What have you been doing, Rann?" she asked, slightly annoyed with her sister. "Well, I stopped off at Lou's and she opened a bottle of Champagne for a laugh. Couldn't resist." she slurred and hiccupped. Lou was a young woman that Rann had befriended staying in the chalet next door with her boyfriend. Dahli said no more but hoped that Rann wouldn't spoil her evening and her performance.

8.25pm and Dahli took a quick look over her shoulder to see if Joe was still at the bar in the faint hope that he had stayed long enough to hear her play. She was still vexed by her fascination with him. He was hunched over the newspaper, filling in the crossword and oblivious it seemed to the live music being performed. Dahli sighed because for some reason she really wanted him to listen to her, as if she was performing tonight just for him. "Dahli, you're up." shouted the old man and Dahli stood up, grabbed her guitar and lead and nervously made her way to the stage. The lights were down low, just a small spotlight on the microphone stand and Dahli felt incredibly jittery. She sat down on the high stool which wobbled slightly, and plugged her guitar, giving it a quick strum and adjusted the microphone stand. "Hello, I'm Dahli from the UK." She addressed the noisy crowd and she could hear Rann whooping madly with excitement from the back of the room. "I am going to perform three songs'' and there was a small ripple of applause from a few enthusiastic drinkers at the front. She waited for the audience to quieten but realising this wasn't going to happen she launched into the James Taylor number,"You've Got a Friend". The stunned audience hushed as Dahli sang, her voice soaring sweetly and sonorously; they were astonished. The song came to an end and the crowd exploded in rapture, clapping and whistling. Dahli, taken aback, was more relieved than anything to have got through the song without forgetting the words. Her next song was "Somewhere Over the Rainbow." and she finished off with a song of her own called "Heaven is Waiting". She thanked the audience, jumped off the stool, unplugged her guitar and walked off the stage, with people congratulating her as she passed by them. She beamed with satisfaction and sat down, took another drink and sighed heavily, with relief, laying the guitar back in its case. "That was amazing, Dahli." cried Rann, hugging her sister warmly. Dahli looked over her left shoulder but was sad to see that Joe had already left, his empty glass and newspaper still sitting on the counter. She got up and walked over to the bar and ordered another drink. "Joe gone then?" she said, trying to sound nonchalant. "And what's it to you?" chuckled the barman, winking knowingly. "Yes, he shot off just after you finished. He's on earlies this week at the restaurant. Great singing by the way." "Oh thank you. Restaurant?" acknowledged Dahli. "Yes, he works as a chef at La Petite Grenouille over the road from here. Is that enough information for you?" He joked with her. Dahli laughed and thanked him. The two sisters walked back to their camp pitches after an enjoyable evening, Rann now having sobered up and feeling a little embarrassed by her behaviour. "You're on holiday, Rann." said Dahli. "Chill out and have some fun." Dahli was going to miss her sister who had found the week's holiday a great tonic, made some great friendships but would be heading home in a couple of days.

Chapter Twenty-Nine

The next evening Dahli and Rann strolled down to the harbour front for the last time together. It had been raining slightly and the old smooth cobbles glistened in the pale sunlight. The air was cooler but the streets were still busy with people meandering about, taking their time to take in the sea air. Rann dived into a couple of shops for "one last mad shop" as she called it while Dahli took a seat on the harbour front looking out to the now quite grey sea. In the week that they had been in Port de Vacquelin the weather had turned somewhat more sombre. Dahli zipped up her hoodie and wrapped her arms around her body. A couple walked past her, ice cream cones in hand, and Dahli wondered how they could possibly eat ice cream in this temperature, shivering at the thought. Rann appeared and they walked together to the restaurant where they met with Lou, her boyfriend and another couple who they did not know. The evening was pleasant enough and they made their way back to the campsite. At the entrance the women said their final farewells, hugging tightly and promising to keep in touch. Dahli watched as Rann wandered out of sight with Lou and the others.

Dahli stood there, a little lonely but then suddenly caught the sound of music coming from across the road. She looked across the road and saw the sign, "La Petite Grenouille". Joe's restaurant, she thought. Why had she not seen it before? She crossed the road and stopped as the music got louder. She peered into the restaurant and it was just closing up, a couple of women sweeping the floors and a man closing the blinds down and turning the sign on the front door to "Ferme". He acknowledged Dahli fondly. Dahli instinctively waved, and then listened again. The music was coming from down the side of the restaurant, a distant guitar being strummed and someone singing gently. Although the sign said "Prive " she took the decision to open the gate and walk down the alley beside the restaurant, being careful not to be seen. The music got louder. She could see a young man sitting with his back to her, crossed legged on a big armchair with a guitar straddled across his body. He sang, a beautifully sweet voice accompanied with delicate finger picking. She didn't recognise the song but it was evocative of the Appalachian music she had heard on her travels in America.

The man stopped singing, leant down to pick up a bottle of beer, had a quick swig then turned back to playing. He was oblivious to Dahli's presence. Dahli quickly checked her watch; it was 11.30pm. At least she didn't have to get up in the morning, she thought as she carried on walking then the man who must have heard a noise suddenly stopped playing and turned around. "Shit." thought Dahli. "I've been sussed." "Hello?" he said inquisitively, then recognised Dahli. "Ah Dahli, hello. What are you doing here?" Dahli walked forward and stood next to him. "Sorry, I heard the music and had to come and see what it was. I'm glad I did. You sing so well." Joe smiled and put his guitar down, offered Dahli a chair and a beer and they sat there in the cool air. "Do you actually know what prive means?" said Joe cheekily and laughed. Dahli didn't answer but drank from the bottle, a beer that tasted bitter and not to her liking but she continued so not to seem impolite. "Please continue singing, Joe" said Dahli and so he did. For some time Joe sang, song after song, beer after beer, enjoying the small audience and the gratitude that Dahli showed. It had been some time since Joe had sung to anyone, probably two years when he was in Spain working at a beachfront cafe. Then Joe put his guitar down and they began to talk.

They talked for what seemed like hours. Joe had been born in Limerick to Irish parents who named him Darius after Darius the Great, the Persian leader from 550 BC. Joe explained that his mother had always been a fantasist and his childhood had been one of dragons, trolls, fairies and other fantastic beasts, and life at home had been wonderfully chaotic. He had chosen to change his name to Joe after much teasing at school. He had studied at a catering college in London but had always wanted to spend time abroad. He left London ten years ago and worked his way around parts of Europe, Spain, Portugal, France, Italy and Greece primarily. "I even got married, but that didn't work out!" he laughed but with some sadness in his voice. He was now living in a caravan at the back of the restaurant having been there for six months, working as a sous chef and enjoying every minute.

Dahli spoke of her time travelling, her semi-nomadic lifestyle, working cafes, cleaning and picking fruit. She was even a toilet attendant at one point in a swanky hotel in

Australia. You name it, she had done it just so she could experience travelling. They both laughed at their shared experiences but what now? Joe was keen to gain more experience in restaurants with the dream of running his own someday. Dahli spoke about her cottage and the will. Her future was unclear unlike Joe who seemed very set on making his name in the restaurant industry. "You were married then, Joe?" enquired Dahli. Joe looked a little surprised at Dahli's forthright question. No one had asked him about the marriage for some years so it felt a little odd. "Yes, she was the love of my life. Adrienne. We had a daughter, Genevieve. She'll be three years old now. They live in Paris." he replied ruefully, hanging his head despondently. "They?" said Dahli. "Yes, Adrienne lives with her new partner, Henri, and our daughter in Paris. We got a divorce but we keep in touch, and are on pretty good terms. We just wanted different things out of life. Adrienne wanted to settle down and I wanted to continue travelling. We met at college when we were very young. Typical story really," said Joe. "So you visit them regularly?" asked Dahli. There was a silence and Joe sighed and moved awkwardly in his seat. Dahli suddenly suspected that she had overstepped the mark, said too much, delved too deeply. "Sorry Joe, I didn't mean to pry." she said but Joe looked up. "No, it's okay Dahli" he replied smiling sadly. "I haven't seen them since Genevieve was a baby. I fear now that she may not know me and Henri is her new dad. Just don't seem to have the time...well maybe that's just an excuse? I dunno. I send Adrienne money each month to provide for Genevieve. I would never shirk my responsibilities." He sighed again and crossed his arms defensively. Dahli pressed on. "She will always be your daughter, Joe. Go see them. It's not far to Paris. Spend a day or two getting to know Genevieve. It'll be good for you all." Joe looked at Dahli and nodded in agreement. "Maybe one day soon Dahli, maybe one day soon."

They moved into Joe's caravan out of the cold air and continued to talk and drink well into the night. The conversation was so perfectly natural and eventually Dahli fell asleep on Joe's big bed. Joe covered her up and snuggled up next to her; there was only one bed, so what else was he supposed to do? They slept soundly until the light started to break through the blinds and Joe awoke and crept carefully around Dahli so as not to disturb her. He put the kettle on and as the steam whistled out of the stopper Dahli woke up with a start. "Christ, where am I?" she cried, a little alarmed at her unfamiliar surroundings and then she remembered and felt an electric shock feeling race through her body. "We didn't, did we?" she shouted over to Joe and instinctively looked under the covers. Joe turned around and smiled, amused. "No," said Joe softly. "No we didn't. We have slept fully clothed and I've just got up to make a cuppa." Dahli laughed, slightly embarrassed, and they shared tea and some toast. Dahli left Joe to his daily rituals and walked back across the road to the campsite. She felt warm and happy, content that she had made a good friend in Joe but still a little unsure as to her true feelings towards him. She hoped she would see him again.

Chapter Thirty
Late September 2018

Miranda opened the front door of her house in Didsbury quietly so as not to disturb Steve who would be sleeping upstairs. The kitchen lights were still on unusually. "Hmm, he must've forgotten to switch them off." thought Miranda as she took off her coat and hung it on the hook behind the door in its usual place. She fell into the lounge, absolutely shattered from travelling all day. It was already midnight and she would soon go to bed but she sat on the chair for a moment in silence, just breathing in the familiarity of her beautiful, comforting surroundings. "Damn," she thought as she suddenly remembered that she had left her bag in the car but she started to doze lightly however she was suddenly awoken by a noise coming from the kitchen. She leant forward to see her husband coming in through the door but he was not alone. A tall, dark haired woman dressed in jeans and leather jacket followed him. Miranda felt the cold air sweep into the house as they fell through the door, obviously drunk, giggling and smiling. Steve turned around to face the young woman and he embraced her, kissing her fondly on the lips, and grabbing her body salaciously. They fell against the kitchen work surface clumsily and parted as Steve reached for a couple of wine glasses and a bottle of Merlot sitting in the wine rack.

"Oh God, what do I do now?" thought Miranda horrified as she sloped off the chair onto the floor, on all fours, trying at all costs to avoid being seen by this very distracted couple. She felt sick and hot but kept her eyes firmly fixed on Steve and his amorous friend, appalled but consumed by what she was witnessing. She sidled up the wall and hid out of sight as Steve and his companion walked into the lounge, oblivious to Miranda's presence and sat back on the sofa, switching on the television and glugging back wine in between kissing passionately. Miranda made a dash for the kitchen and disappeared out of sight. "Phew" she thought. She felt herself falter and grabbed the work top, closing her eyes momentarily to compose herself then she stood forthright. She felt like a stranger in her own home. A surge of anger hit her and without thinking she looked around the kitchen, grabbed the opened bottle of wine and in a sudden and unplanned willful act of compulsion she walked up behind the cavorting couple and discharged the rest of the wine over their heads, screaming, "You bastards!"

The woman shrieked and they stood up quickly, frantically wiping down their wet clothes and faces all panicked and aghast. Steve stood there shaking. "But Miranda, you're supposed to be home tomorrow, aren't you?" He looked unsure. Miranda screamed at him, "No you fucking moron!". He had been caught out. Before any more could be said Miranda threw down the bottle in disgust and rushed out of the house, grabbing her coat as she went. She unlocked the car, fell in and without thinking drove off at great speed. She felt small and pathetic, and so utterly betrayed. Tears rolled down her face and she stopped the car further down the road to compose her shaking body. Her mobile phone kept ringing and through her tears she could see that it was Steve. Then the text messages started, "Ring me Miranda. Please ring me!" "Fuck off! Fuck off!" she screamed at the phone, turned it to silent, threw it on the back seat and started the car up again.

It was well past midnight but Miranda just kept driving through the tears, beyond Manchester, beyond the northern counties and on to Portsmouth. She stopped only for petrol at the 24 hours station where she had a quick comfort break and grabbed a sandwich and a drink. The adrenalin rush kept her awake, and she finally arrived at the international ferry port at 4am. The next ferry was 8am so she sat back and waited. It was cold, dark and silent, and she felt unbelievably lonely and like a limb had been ripped from her. All she could hear was her own breathing. Her whole life had just been spun on its head. How could he? How could he? We were a team, strong and supportive; Miranda and Steve; the power couple; always and forever. The thought of a third person in this relationship was unfathomable. "This was something that happened to other women, not me," she thought angrily.

The ferry left on time and Miranda settled back in her small cabin, very aware of the need for sleep, a shower and change of clothes before arriving in France. So many things were rushing through her head; what should she tell the kids? What should she tell her work colleagues? How is she going to keep the business going? She had impulsively just run away without thinking anything through. At least she could work remotely for the foreseeable future, and had a toothbrush and a suitcase of clothes. She rang Dahli and told her what had happened. Miranda hadn't expected any sympathy from her sister as she had never liked or trusted Steve but she needed to hear her voice, her reassuring voice, deep and consoling. Perhaps Dahli was more intuitive than Miranda had given her credit for. The desperate texts and calls continued from Steve but Miranda was in no mood to deal with him just yet, if ever. He deserved to suffer right now. Foolishly he had even called Dahli but she had given him short thrift. This made Miranda chortle. She could just imagine the conversation.

Dahli was waiting for her at the campsite when she arrived back in Port de Vacquelin. The sun was shining and the air scented with summer flowers. Neither of them had any idea what they were but they smelled divine. They hugged and Miranda broke down. Dahli said nothing straightaway but just held her. "It's going to be okay Miranda." reassured Dahli, "You're strong. You'll be okay, I've booked you into an Airbnb for a couple of nights until you know your plans." but all reassuring from her sister could not make her feel any better. She wanted it all to be a bad dream, soon to awaken from. The next few days Miranda settled back into Port life, visiting the local shops, cafe and bakery, walking along the seafront and sunbathing in between working but she knew she would have to face the devastating truth soon. Miranda and Dahli spent a few days together when Miranda had a phone call from her sixteen year old daughter, Sarah in Nantes who invited her to stay with her for a couple of weeks as term had finished. Sarah's sister, Nicky, would also be staying and it would be like a bit of a family reunion. Miranda left Port de Vacquelin to, as she put it, "get her head together and sort her life out." Dahli was pleased that the girls were supporting their mother and selfishly she could now concentrate on sorting our her own life too.

Dahli had postponed calling Christian. There had been many times when she had wanted to but put it off. Was she afraid of saying the wrong thing to him or opening up a new chapter in her life that she was not ready for? Whatever the reason she knew that Christian would be expecting a call from her anytime soon and she couldn't hold off any longer. She sat quietly in the van one morning, opened her wallet and pulled out the piece of paper with his number on it. She punched in the number into her phone and waited for the dial tone. The phone rang and the butterflies jumped around in her stomach. Then the tone went to answerphone. "Hello, This is Christian. Sorry I cannot come to the phone right now. Please leave a message after the tone. Thank you." Dahli pressed the red button and cut the call off but immediately felt stupid and punched in the number again. Again the call went to answerphone and this time she responded. "Hello Christian. This is Dahli Rosenburg. I hope you are expecting a call from me about Bijou cottage. Please give me a call. You now have my number. Thank you. Goodbye." and she again pressed the red button feeling relieved to have made the call. For two days she waited for Christian's call but nothing. Perhaps he hadn't got her number? Perhaps Juliette had given her the wrong number? Perhaps she had dialled incorrectly? Doubts went through her mind so Dahli rang the number again and left another message. This wasn't panning out as expected.

Dahli decided to walk down to the harbour front and go and visit Beulah. They had become good friends over the past few weeks, meeting for drinks and a bit of shopping, talking about their lives and their plans. Beulah was sitting at a table at the back of the cafe folding napkins. The cafe was quieter now as the tourists had started to fade away with the colder weather however there were still a few people sitting outside enjoying the last of the summer's warmth. Dahli wandered in and took a seat next to Beulah who hugged her affectionately and Beulah grabbed a couple of coffees and sat back down. "Any news on Christian, then?" she asked. "Nope, still haven't heard anything. " said Dahli sadly. "A bit of a mystery. I'll give him a few more days then go back and see Juliette. She might have an email or postal address for him." Beulah looked disappointed too. She was hoping to hear about the next part of the mystery but also felt for Dahli.

Eric appeared from behind the counter and said hello then dashed out for provisions. "Do you fancy coming round for dinner tonight, Dahli? We are having coq au vin." continued Beulah. Dahli never turned down a supper invite but she had already arranged to meet Joe tonight. "Uhm... would you mind if I brought a friend? Is that rude to ask?" she asked cautiously. Beulah laughed intrigued. "Friend, you say? Not a man is it? A boyfriend maybe?" "Yes, it's Joe from La Petite Grenouille. I expect you know him? And no, we are not boy and girlfriend." said Dahli firmly to dispel any gossip. Beulah knew everyone, so of course she knew him. "7.30pm sharp. Eric doesn't like being made to wait!" joked Beulah and on that note they said their farewells. Dahli walked out in the fading sunshine and wandered down to the harbour front, sitting on her favourite bench overlooking the fisherman tidying their nets. She took out her phone and rang Joe announcing the slight change in their plans hoping that Joe didn't mind. Joe was delighted as he enjoyed Beulah and Eric's company. Beulah and Eric lived in a modern three bedroomed house on a new housing estate to the west of the village. They had chosen not to live in the small apartment above the cafe and Dahli assumed that they had plans to extend their family.

Beulah poured large glasses of wine, and Joe and Dahli laid back on Beulah's red velvet sofa when Dahli's phone rang. She took it out of her back pocket and looked at the screen. "Oh God, it's Christian!" she stuttered, staring at the ringing phone in her hand. "Well, answer it then!" shouted Beulah from the kitchen, and Dahli swiped the screen, standing up and dashing out of the lounge into the hallway. She closed the door behind her. Beulah came back into the lounge. "Exciting isn't it? At last he is ringing her. Can't wait to find out what's going on." Eric tutted. "You are so nosey Mrs Smythe." They all laughed. Beulah and Eric brought the wine in and sat on the other sofa opposite Joe.

"How's things with you, Joe?" asked Eric, seemingly curious at Joe's ever developing career plans. "You still thinking of setting up your own restaurant?". Joe looked a little sheepish. He had to admit that he had been so busy working that his future plans had stalled. He dreamed of having his own restaurant in Paris and smiled at Eric. "Yes Eric, I will one day have my own restaurant I'm sure but I have been working too hard to think. It's been a hectic season." Eric acknowledged Joe and took a drink of his wine. He offered Joe his financial expertise and Joe thanked him for he was sure that Eric could help him but not now, not at the moment. He sighed. Dahli came back into the room, excited. "I'm going to Paris next Wednesday!!" she announced. "To meet Christian and his wife, Amelie. He has a week off from university." She sat back down and took a great big swig of her wine.

Beulah was visibly relieved at the outcome and Joe smiled with some sorrow as he thought of his daughter in the capital with her mother and "new" father. He shook his head to relieve himself of his angst. The rest of the evening swiftly came to an end, and Joe and Dahli started to walk the twenty minutes back to the campsite. They were slightly drunk and full of great food, laughing and giggling then Dahli suddenly changed the subject. "Joe, why don't you come with me to Paris next week, to see your daughter? I'm going by bus and train. Doesn't take long." Joe suddenly sobered up and said nothing for a while. "How can I, Dahli? I'm working?" he replied but Dahli was insistent. "You can ask work for a day or two off. You've worked your butt off all season." Joe started to feel irritated; he hated being told what to do and Dahli sensed his annoyance. "Just saying, Joe. It's up to you." she continued. Joe shrugged his shoulders and they continued their walk in an uncomfortable silence until they reached the campsite gates. "Good night Dahli, thank you for a lovely evening." Joe said formally. "Yes goodnight Joe." and Joe crossed the road and disappeared up the alleyway to his caravan. Dahli felt sad that Joe had not taken too well to her suggestions. Perhaps he will think differently tomorrow, she thought but then she thought, maybe not. He was a strong willed Irish man after all.

Chapter Thirty-One

Almost a week went by then the night before her trip to meet Christian in Paris, Dahli heard a "tat, tat, tat" at her door and a small gap in the curtain provided her with enough view to see Joe standing there, pacing a little and looking troubled. She got out of bed, wiped her eyes, put on her dressing gown and slippers and unlocked the door. "Oh, hi Joe. You okay?". He looked up at her. "No, no, I'm not Dahli." He jumped in the van at Dahli's invite and sat down, his eyes red raw. Dahli instinctively put the kettle on and sat down next to him and he looked Dahli in the eyes. "It's Genevieve, Dahli. It's Genevieve. She's very poorly. She's got meningitis. I could lose her Dahli, and I don't even know her. My own stupid, selfish idiocy. I could lose her, my beautiful daughter. I remember the day she was born. What was I thinking not seeing her?" He slammed his fist down on the table with frustration and Dahli laid her hands gently on his arms. Joe calmed a little and explained that Genevieve had fallen ill that evening and been rushed to hospital. Adrienne had rung less than an hour ago, and the only person Joe wanted to talk to was Dahli. Kind, caring, calm Dahli he thought. He needed her help and support more than anything. He wanted her to tell him that everything would be okay but of course Dahli couldn't do this and it pained them both. "Do you want to see her, Joe? Can you visit her in the hospital?" Yes, he said. "Then come with me tomorrow morning, Joe," and he nodded silently. Joe stayed a little while then went back to his caravan. The restaurant gave him some time off to be with his daughter so he packed his bags ready for an early start in the morning. Dahli felt relieved that they two of them were talking again. She had missed him.

The next morning they headed to the bus taking them to Bayeux then train into Paris. Dahli was inwardly excited but Joe was subdued and anxious. Adrienne had rung to say that Genevieve had had a comfortable night but was not yet out of critical care. They arrived at St Lazaire train station; Joe had already planned in his head the short trip across the city to see Genevieve so as not to be late. He had bought a small teddy at the station for her, and the lasting impression Dahli had of him was him disappearing with the teddy in his back pocket, his curly brown hair dancing up and down as he walked briskly away. She hoped that his day improved.

Dahli looked at her watch; it was 11.30am and she was due to meet Christian and his wife at 12pm at a local patisserie cafe. She checked Google maps for the directions. Not far, she thought. She strode out of the station into the cool air. The roads were busy with commuters and cars and she felt alive in the city and remembered fondly her trips to Paris when she was a teenager. The year was 1995 and they were a group of excited girls jumping on and off of the Metro, walking arm in arm through the parks and visiting the many museums and galleries, submersing themselves in the history and culture of this great city. Her heart beat a little quicker and she wished her sister was with her, but maybe next time, she thought.

The cafe was brimming with people, eating, drinking and chatting; just a normal day for a cafe in the heart of the capital but for Dahli it was a thrill. She entered the cafe through its ornate iron wrought door and immediately her eyes were drawn to the refrigerator, full of beautifully crafted cakes, placed provocatively at eye level, the aroma of freshly baked bread filling her senses. She looked around the cafe and saw a vacant table and made her way to it hoping she would beat the couple who had just come in to it. She sat down and placed her bag on the floor when a young waitress appeared. "Bonjour, madame." she said. Mademoiselle actually, thought Dahli, but never mind, after all she was an old spinster she laughed to herself. The young waitress placed a beautifully written menu on the table and took her drinks order. Dahli checked her bag to ensure that she had brought with her the keys on the old brass keyring and her passport. She needed some evidence that she was who she said she was and not some fraudster. She checked her watch again - it was 12pm exactly.

Christian and Amelie held hands as they pushed open the big wrought iron door of the patisserie, feeling relaxed and happy. This was Amelie's favourite cafe and she was already looking forward to lunch. Christian was wearing his light blue driving jacket so Dahli recognised him. Dahli had also promised to wear her black leather biker jacket and Christian looked around the busy cafe hoping to catch a glimpse of her. "Black jacket, black jacket." he said to himself repeatedly as his eyes wandered from one table to the next in a blind panic, the cafe being so busy. "I can't see her Amelie. Do you think she is here?" he said a little flustered. Amelie took his arm reassuringly. "I'm sure she is, darling." They stood in the middle of the cafe when Amelie suddenly gasped. She froze and put her hand to mouth. "Oh mon dieu!" she yelled. "What is it?" asked Christian then he also caught sight of Dahli walking towards him, and stopped in his tracks. There she stood; tall, athletic with soft light brown hair, brown eyes, button nose and slightly crooked smile. "Wow, the likeness is uncanny, Christian." said Amelie gathering her emotions. He stood and stared at Dahli for a short moment then composed himself and held his hand out to her, and she was also a little speechless. "Hello my dear Dahli. it's great to meet you." he said, throwing a warm smile at her. "Yes, hello Christian, sorry. Please come and sit down here. The waitress will be over soon to serve us."

They sat down, ordered lunch and drinks, and chatted about the weather and the journey to Paris, each still too afraid to mention their incredible likeness. "Tell me about Bijou and your mother, Dahli. Especially your mother." he said, and Dahli retold the story of the will and the keys, explaining her mother had passed some four months ago and that her inheriting the cottage was a complete mystery. She rummaged in her bag and produced the keyring. "I'm so sorry about your mother, Dahli." Said Christian sympathetically, and then looked down at the keyring. "Oooh, that's old. Look, Amelie, this might have been granddad's." He giggled like a small child. "You must go and look around the cottage, Dahli; Juliette has the keys. Uncle Frank lived there almost his whole life but it's yours now for sure. I will sort the paperwork and get it all made official." Dahli felt emotional. She was about to own a real property. She didn't even live in a house and hadn't done so for some years. A new chapter in her life was about to begin but how did Frank know her mother and why did her and Christian look so alike?

She looked over at Christian, how they were similar in appearance; however he was such a gentle soul, often being guided by Amelie and softly spoken; very unlike herself, the headstrong, somewhat bossy Dahli. She quizzed Christian a little more without hopefully appearing too rude. "How did your uncle know my mother, if he did know her and why would he leave her the cottage in his will? I'm perplexed." Christian shook his head and looked equally mystified, smiling meekly. "We honestly have no idea Dahli. If it wasn't for you turning up in Port de Vacquelin we wouldn't even have found out more about the elusive Mathilde. And what about me and you, Dahli? Why are we so alike? I don't get it." He gazed at her with those soft, slightly sad, inquisitive, brown eyes and Dahli felt an emotional attachment to him which blindsided her.

She put the keys back in her bag and there was a sudden silence as if everyone was gathering their thoughts. "Okay, so what's your date of birth, Christian?" she asked. changing the subject slightly. "Fourth August" he said then they both said in unison, "1980". "Oh Christ!" Dahli exclaimed realising the mounting seriousness of the situation. "We could be related, brother and sister surely, but how?" Dahli felt sick at the thought and Christian explained that it could be possible as he had been adopted by his uncle Frank's twin sister and brother in law when he was a baby back in Russia where they lived in a small village outside of Moscow. He had moved to Paris when he was eighteen to study Russian and then stayed on as a lecturer in Russian culture, meeting Amelie at the university and getting married. They live a quiet life, living in the fifth arrondissement in a small two bedroomed apartment. His parents had died about ten years ago and Christian had then endeavoured to find out more about his biological parents but had drawn a blank on more than one occasion so had temporarily given up on the search. "But I knew my father, Christian." continued Dahli. "I knew when and where I was born. Manchester, UK. There was only me at the birth, honest! I was brought up with my sister, Miranda. Perhaps this is all just a coincidence."

Dahli laughed at the absurdity of the situation and there was then lots of head scratching, when Christian had an idea. "It may be easier to trace the possible relationship between my uncle Frank and your mother. Maybe someone in the village may know more? He lived there all his life I think." he said. Dahli agreed and after some more discussion and more pleasantries it was time for Christian and Amelie to head back home to relieve the babysitter who was caring for their four year and six year olds, Justine and Armand. "Let's sort the house first for you then we can start to try and piece all these relationships together." said Christian kindly. "Yes, great idea. It's been great seeing you both. I hope we can meet again." but Dahli was intrigued to find out more about her mother's relationship and she now had time on her hands. They parted with hugs and kisses, and a quick selfie on Dahli's phone, and Christian and Amelie disappeared from view.

Dahli stepped out of the cafe and into the bright sunlight of the late summer's day. She loved Paris, its sounds and smells, and smiled as she walked along the pavement, passing by a numerous shops and cafes, breathing in the city air. She stopped and sat down on a bench and thought of Joe. He was planning to stay another night in the capital, and she considered the same; perhaps she could meet up with him? She decided to ring him. The phone rang and eventually Joe answered. "Hello Dahli." he sounded out of breath as though he was running. "I'm just on my way to the hotel. Genevieve is going to be okay. I'm so relieved. What are you doing now? I want to see you, my friend". Dahli was delighted to hear Joe sounding more positive and crossed the city to meet him at the hotel he was staying at. That evening the atmosphere was almost celebratory as they downed cocktails and talked endlessly about their day. So much had changed for the better in the last twenty four hours for both of them. Dahli stayed over at the hotel, and they both travelled back to Port de Vacquelin the next day.

Chapter Thirty-Two

Port de Vacquelin was empty when they got back that afternoon. Being late September the tourists had started to drift away, and just a few locals were hanging around the harbour front. Dahli liked the new village; she felt alone and at peace. She headed for a cafe but Joe passed on another drinks session and headed back to his caravan whilst Dahli stayed in the village to contemplate her next move with regards cottage Bijou. She had been in the village now for more than two weeks and couldn't see herself moving back to England just yet but she was desperate to find somewhere else to stay as the campsite would soon be closed for the season. Instinctively she rang Joe. "I'm sorry Joe, I know we've just seen each other for like two days but I really need to find somewhere else to pitch my van. I'm planning to stay a little longer and the campsite is closing soon." Joe paused then said, "Why don't you pitch up next to me? We have electric, water, toilets etc. I'm sure Jean, the owner, wouldn't mind. You'd have to pay something, if that was okay?" Dahli wasn't without money, having now cashed the cheque from her mother. She agreed it was a good idea and left it with Joe to ask Jean if it was a viable option. She wandered back to the campsite, rang her sister to tell her about Christian and the cottage, grabbed some food from the shop and flopped in her van, now dependent on Jean's decision to secure her short term future in Port de Vacquelin. One hour later and Dahli was moving her van from the campsite to the back of the restaurant.

A week later Dahli was sitting in a cafe in the village with Beulah telling her all about her trip to Paris, Christian and Joe but Beulah was distracted. "What's the matter with you today?" asked a concerned Dahli, looking Beulah straight in the eyes but she looked up at the sky and started to cry, wet warm tears rolling down her face. She took a tissue out of her pocket and wiped her face but the tears still flowed. "There is so much of my life I haven't told you about. I try to keep certain things to myself but sometimes I just lose it like today." Dahli had sometimes caught Beulah behind the counter in the bakery staring into space, sad and lost and had often wondered what was distressing her but hadn't felt able to ask her. Dahli put her arm around her friend. "Tell me, Beulah. You can trust me. I might be able to help." So Beulah started from the beginning. "Are you sure? How long have you got?" and she carried on, and Dahli ordered another couple of coffees and cake for it was going to be a long afternoon.

Beulah and Eric's story
September 2007

Beulah was lost. She had taken a wrong turn and found herself in an empty lecture theatre except for a male student sitting on his own behind a desk. She looked across at him but he didn't see her, preoccupied, with his nose stuck firmly in a book. "Excuse me," Beulah said softly but no reply. "Excuse me," she said a little louder, perhaps a little too loud and the student suddenly looked up. "No need to shout!" he yelled at her. Was he joking, she thought. Determined to get to her lecture, she continued. "I'm looking for room E212. I'm late for my first lecture." Without a word, the student closed his book, stood up and strode towards her. He was dark haired, very tall and looked like he needed a good meal. "Follow me, please. You're on the wrong floor. I'll get you there." he said stiffly. Beulah thanked him and followed him like a puppy. What a hero, she thought. Beulah thought it polite to introduce herself and the student seemed surprised by this but smiled anyway. "Well Miss Beulah, I'm Eric Smythe. Yes, an old fashioned name I know. Ha ha and all that." He said belittling himself, and quickened his pace, struggling to keep up with his long stride. "There is now Miss Beulah." Beulah thought him strange but thanked him when they arrived at the right lecture room, and said goodbye. Without a word he waved as he walked away and she thought no more of him.

That evening Beulah had promised to meet with her new friends, Sarah and Jodie from Freshers' held the previous week. They were all studying law, a phenomenal course, intense and demanding yet Beulah was a bright student and had passed her A levels with flying colours. She had left her hometown of Falmouth to join others at King's College London and had her whole life planned out; get a degree, join a great firm of lawyers, meet her perfect partner, get married, live in a nice house and have children. She had always been an organised person, scheduling her whole life so meticulously almost to the point of obsession. So far her plans had come to fruition so she saw no reason why the rest of her life shouldn't follow suit.

The three girls headed to the Students Union; cheap beer and a live band, what could be better. They snuck into the already rammed bar, its wall almost dripping with condensation, and ordered a round of drinks before sitting on the floor by the stage area, laughing loudly and commenting on every male student that walked past. "Too tall, too small, too geeky, too trendy, too thin, too fat." They giggled churlishly. "Oooh aren't we awful?" they shrieked. "Ah you should've seen the one I met today. Proper odd!! Eric Smythe" laughed Beulah, one too many beers taking their effect. Sarah raised their eyebrows. "I know Eric." she said. "He's okay to be honest. One our course, year above. They call him Eric the Bun because he's always baking for the guys on his floor in the hall." They all laughed at the thought of Eric the Bun, a full grown man, making Victoria sponges. "I'll set you up on a date." joked Sarah. Beulah snorted drunkenly and thought nothing more of it.

A week later the three girls were back in the Students Union but this time for the weekly prize quiz night. Completely sober and determined to win, Beulah sat down with her two friends and grabbed a pen and paper. "Are we ready for a fight?" shouted Beulah. "Hold your horses, Beulah, " said Jodie. "We're waiting for three more to join us." and she winked at Sarah. Beulah pulled a quizzical face. "Who?" she said and at that moment three young men were stood next to her, grinning foolishly, pints in hand. "Can we join you ladies?" one of them said in a silly voice and they sat down, one of them grabbing the pen and paper. Beulah grabbed them back indignantly. "Oi that's mine." she proclaimed. "Not so quick, young lady." he said and Beulah looked up and saw a familiar face. It was Eric "the Bun" Smythe. She groaned with annoyance at his childish attitude, and then vaguely remembered Sarah's words from the drunken band night. "Damn!" she said to herself reluctantly. "There was no getting out of this now," she groaned. "I will just have to put up with him for the next few hours."

The quiz got under way and Eric and Beulah astonishingly became the quiz dream team. Heads closely together they continually pushed themselves, deliberating, questioning, analysing and delving deep into the back crevasses of their minds to find that one perfect answer. Their friends watched in awe as they answered question after question correctly, everything from history to pop music. At the end of the quiz they went up together to claim the first prize, with cheers from the audience. Afterwards, the six friends laughed and whooped, and drank heartily until finally it was time to walk home. Eric asked Beulah if he could see her again and of course the answer was yes.

Eight years later Eric and Beulah had graduated with first class degrees and law qualifications, and were living in London, Beulah practising law in a small but successful law firm, and Eric working as a financial director of a large national charity. They had married the year after leaving university, and decided to focus on their fledgling careers. Beulah had almost everything; her degree, her apartment on the banks of the Thames, her perfect husband and her rewarding career. There was only one other thing left now to achieve: children.

Beulah paused and took a cup of coffee. "So what happened, Beulah?" asked Dahli intrigued. "Everything, Dahli, and nothing." replied Beulah as she blubbed a little more. Beulah and Eric agreed to try for children once their careers were cemented and financially they could afford for Beulah to take some time off. Beulah started getting broody, taking folic acid supplements, reading book after book about conception and pregnancy and gushing over baby clothes and accessories in the baby shops in the capital. She had already planned the pregnancy and the first few years after the birth down to a tee. All she needed to do now was get pregnant. Her and Eric had a great sex life so she assumed she would fall pregnant quickly. Surely it was just a matter of time? Every week she would meet with her girlfriends in a local cafe. "So, are you?" They would ask her week after week. "No, not yet." she would reply and giggle. This was a fun game for some time but then as the weeks became months and then a year her friends stopped asking the question and would look at her sympathetically, "Ah it won't be long, Beulah, just keep trying."

Beulah became withdrawn and meet ups with her friends became infrequent. She couldn't face the questioning, the sympathetic voices and the growing number of baby bumps, and Eric became increasingly concerned for her welfare. After many tests and procedures Eric suggested IVF as a last resort. Beulah agreed but after three failed rounds Beulah had to accept that she was never going to get pregnant. She threw herself into her work instead, refusing counselling for her increasing depressive moods to Eric's despair, lost copious amounts of weight from constant worry and her marriage began to break down with constant and bitter arguments. Eric had had enough. "I'm booking a two week holiday in France, Beulah, to mend our relationship and take some pressure off you. This is our last chance." Beulah reluctantly agreed and a week later they found themselves on a ferry, crossing the water to their favourite Normandy resort, Port de Vacquelin. Eric had found a peaceful and luxurious boutique hotel to Beulah's excitement, and was crossing everything that the short break would make Beulah a happier person otherwise he wasn't sure where they were heading.

Dahli stood up and ordered two more coffees. Beulah had wiped her tears so often that her face was red and swollen. She had stopped crying and sat there, feeling pathetic and a little tired. Dahli reappeared with an encouraging smile on her face. "Carry on, if you can Beulah." so Beulah took a deep breath and carried on with her story.

Beulah relaxed as her and Eric ate in the best restaurants, strolled along the harbour front, swam in the cool sea, sunbathed and drank exquisite wines but what had really caught Eric's eye was the "for sale" sign on the local bakery, tucked away in a small square just off the harbour front. The bakery looked sad; post gathering in abundance in the doorway, the shutters broken and the windows dirty. The inside had been stripped off its furniture and the room was bare. He was nervous to mention it to Beulah but he had always dreamed of owning his own bakery. Stepping away from the hectic life of London had cleared his mind of fear and risk, and he fantasised of baking bread and cakes all day long instead of sitting behind a desk in an open office, cramming figures into his brain and listening to the constant banal rhetoric of his associates. One morning whilst Beulah still slept he rang the estate agent and made an appointment to view the bakery. He broke the news to a sleepy Beulah who was so hung over that she agreed to tag along but only if he promised to treat her to champagne and oysters in her favourite fish restaurant that evening. There was always a condition with Beulah, he sighed.

They walked over to the bakery and stood outside in the bright sunshine. Beulah put her hands on the window, peered through the glass, sighing begrudgingly. "What the heck, Eric? Why are we wasting our time here? We could be on the beach." She tutted, drew back from the window and folded her arms in defiance, making Eric anxious. Perhaps she was right, what are we doing here, he thought. Nevertheless the estate agent appeared from around the corner, young and fresh, smartly dressed with not a hair out of place, clipboard in hand and a great big grin on his face. Beulah felt even more irritated but Eric shook the young man's hand enthusiastically. They spent the next half an hour touring the building, with its bakery cum cafe potential plus a small two bedroomed flat upstairs which the previous owners had left in a complete mess, clothes and black bin bags strewn everywhere, the kitchen filthy and the wallpaper torn and walls damaged. Eric thanked the young man and the couple made their way down to a harbour front cafe without a word spoken between them. Eric ordered a couple of large glasses of white wine and a Caesar salad to share.

Beulah suddenly spoke. "Let's do it then Eric." She then went back to drinking her wine without making eye contact. Eric sat back and stared at her gobsmacked. "What did you just say?" he replied. "You heard me first time Mr Smythe. You've always wanted this Eric. You're a baker. You're wasted in an office. Just do it." She carried on drinking, emotionless and still. Eric pulled her towards him, hugged her stiff body, kissed her gently and she relaxed in his arms and cried a little. They then toasted their future life with champagne and oysters.

"And that's the story, Dahli. We bought a bakery cafe and here we are two years later." Dahli smiled but asked tentatively, "But what about children, Beulah?" Beulah looked down and sighed. "Nope, but we have our new life and it's great. We have super friends and a successful business that we love but you know, sometimes I still feel a huge gaping hole in my life and I just lose it, like today. Thank you, Dahli, for listening to me. Maybe we will consider adopting or something. We'll see." She smiled, and Dahli, ensuring that Beulah was okay, gave her apologies but she had to go. She was due to meet Juliette again at the library.

Chapter Thirty-Three

Dahli was excited. Not only was she meeting Juliette again to visit Bijou cottage, her sister was due back in the village and she was hoping in time to accompany her. Juliette was waiting outside the library, wearing her signature round glasses, dressed in a long brown skirt and holding a little brown satchel. Dahli laughed to herself at the sight - a cross between Harry Potter and Miss Tiggywinkle, she thought. They hugged and Dahli checked her watch hoping that Rann would be waiting outside the cottage for them. It was only a short walk to the cottage, located just off the harbour front. They turned a corner and Juliette pointed out Bijou - a small, pale stoned terraced cottage, with blue shutters that needed a good paint and small square sash windows that looked a little unloved. Juliette took the keys out of her bag and stood patiently but there was disappointingly no sign of Rann so Juliette unlocked the front door and pushed it open. A strong smell of mothballs and cigarette smoke was unleashed catching Dahli slightly off guard. "Sorry the cottage might smell a bit off having not been lived in for over a year." apologised Juliette before picking up the post from the doormat and placing it on a small wooden table with the door keys.

It was an old fisherman's cottage, tiny and compact but now well sought after by the second home owners, and one of many in the village. Dahli walked across the narrow threshold and stepped into the hallway of the cottage. To the right a large mirror hung on the wall next to a coat stand with a couple of black overcoats hanging off it and below on the floor three pairs of brown leather shoes. Dahli thought immediately of Frank as it felt as though he was still here with all his belongings untouched. A steep flight of stairs took Dahli's eyes upwards and she leaned over to the left to take a look upstairs. "Just two double bedrooms, a cot room and a bathroom upstairs, Dahli love. It's not a big place." said Juliette disappearing into the living room. She opened the curtains and wiped her finger along a line of grey dust. "Must get on and sort that." she said to herself.

Dahli followed her into the room and looked around. It was small and crammed with furniture; a large worn dark red leather sofa piled high with old man's clothes, a mahogany dining table and chairs covered with a yellow floral tablecloth, a cabinet displaying photos and trinkets, and a gas fire where the old fireplace would've been, surrounded by a dark green tiled mantelpiece displaying a number of what looked like family photos. There was a dusty old television in the corner of the room, and a battered radio perched on the edge of the table. Juliette leaned over the mantelpiece, picked up one of the framed photos and handed it to Dahli. "This is Frank. A recent photo, and see that one there?" she said pointing to another frame. "That's him when he was younger. Maybe 40 or so. He was quite good looking, wasn't he? Tall and handsome." Juliette laughed and Dahli smirked and Dahli walked back into the hallway and went into the kitchen.whilst Juliette started dusting. Oh dear; dark wooden units, dirty and stained, cluttered with pans, plates and tea towels everywhere everywhere. Dahli had never seen so many old tea towels. The room looked out onto a small courtyard.

Disillusioned, Dahli sat down and sighed; this cottage was in need of a lot of work to make it liveable. She noticed there was a key in the back door so she turned it, pushed the door which scraped along the stone floor before eventually opening, and went out into the courtyard. She sat on a rusty old metal chair and took out her tobacco; she desperately needed a smoke. The courtyard caught the sun's rays and she placed her tobacco pouch on a round metal table and started to roll a cigarette when she heard a voice shouting to her. "Hi, Dahli, I'm here!" It was Rann. This lifted Dahli's mood and she rushed to greet her sister. Rann looked relaxed and happy, wearing joggers and a hoodie, her hair tied up in a scrunchy and big sunglasses perched on her head. Gone was the stiff work apparel that had become Rann's signature status symbol, replaced with comfortable wear, matching her new found breezy attitude. "Wow, you look amazing, Rann. The break has done you good!" Dahli said, happy to see her sister looking so content, and the two of them sat in the courtyard, the warmth soothing them, and Rann spoke again, "Dahli, I'm sorry, I'm going back to Didsbury tonight. I'm booked on the late ferry. I need to go and sort things with Steve. I'm not sure what I'm going to do though."

She stood up and paced around the courtyard, a little confused and unsure of herself. Dahli was disappointed that she was leaving but knew what she was saying; Rann had been away from home for the best part of three weeks and her marriage had always been important to her; through thick and thin as she would always say. There had been that moment a few years ago when Rann was convinced Steve was having an affair with a woman at work. All the signs were there; working late, coming home smelling of perfume, leaving his phone off. He had strenuously denied it but Dahli had not been so sure and now she was even less sure after his latest behaviour. Dahli looked at Rann. "You do what you need to, Rann. I'll be here for you whatever happens." Dahli wished Rann would leave Steve and start afresh. She was a strong and financially independent young woman with her whole life ahead of her; why be stuck with a lousy philanderer? She had never liked or trusted Steve but with little evidence to back up her claims. Rann smiled weakly and sat back down. "Well, this place is nice." said Rann changing the subject but Dahli wasn't convinced. It hadn't quite been the cottage she expected. Juliette appeared with a phone up to her ear. She mouthed, "work", and Dahli stood up and passed her, and once upstairs Dahli pushed one of the bedroom doors open and peered in while Rann disappeared into the other room.

The room was in darkness so she put on the light and sat on the bed feeling it give slightly under her weight. The bed and the furnishings were old and worn and the room had a faint smell of urine mixed with men's cologne. It was definitely Frank's bedroom; there was a dressing table covered in bits of used tissue, a half empty glass of water, some razor blades and a can of shaving foam, a comb and a notebook, a black and white photo of a couple and by the bed was a set of drawers, the drawers all slightly open. Dahli looked down at the threadbare beige carpet with dismay, then opened the top drawer slowly and carefully for fear of breaking it. She looked down at the contents - mostly a jumble of clothing - jumpers, shirts and underwear and for some reason she felt compelled to put her hands under the clothes and rummage about. Eventually she pulled out an old photo album and placed it on her lap and felt herself tremble a little with excitement as she opened the front cover.

Rann suddenly appeared at the door. "Come in, come in and sit beside me. I'm trying to find any evidence of our mother's relationship with Frank. We need to find out." said Dahli, comforted by her sister's presence. Dahli turned each page over slowly then every so often she peeled the cellophane away and picked out a photo. Photos of Frank, possibly his friends, his family but who was to really know? Perhaps Christian would or someone in the village? Frank had lived in the village almost all his life, only going away to university for a few years. Surely someone might know him or remember him, thought Dahli. Christian had said that Frank had taught history at the local school for 40 years before retiring to a quiet life.

There were so many photographs so she closed the album and put it on the bed. "Rann, take a look in the drawer please as I think there may be more photos in there." Rann put her hands in the drawer and pulled out the pile of clothes and put them on the bed in a rough pile. Underneath the clothes she found a small cardboard box and three more smaller photograph albums. She took them out also and placed them on the bed next to the clothes. "I've not got time to look through these now, Rann." Dahli said, starting to stand. "I'll take them with me." She started to stand up, holding the albums and the small box but Rann put her arm on her to stop her. Dahli sat back down staring at her sister, wondering why she had stopped her and Rann's eyes filled with tears. "Oh goodness, Rann, whatever is the matter?" Rann wiped her eyes. "Just a moment thinking of our mother. Caught me unaware. She was so young and beautiful, her whole life ahead of her. How happy she would be. I miss her so much, Dahli. I just want her here with us. It's bringing it all back." Dahli hugged her sister, knowing and feeling the pain, pleased to have her to share this discomfort with, pleased they had become friends again. "We have each other, Rann. We can and will get through this." Rann smiled at her and the two got up and said their goodbyes.

A few days later Dahli had some time to sift through the photographs that they had found in Frank's house. She sat herself at the table with a cup of tea and pulled the photograph albums out of her bag onto the table. She looked at them; there were five albums of photos from many places, dusty and musty smelling. She breathed in the familiar smells and gave them a quick wipe over with a duster, opened the front cover of the first one, and started to look through the photos. Years of memories, pictures of Frank and his family, Christmasses, birthdays, holidays at home and abroad, photos of the cottage and miscellaneous parties however after hours of sitting with her shoulders hunched over and with her eyes starting to hurt she found no clues to her mother's relationship with Frank. However it was a joy to be part of Frank's life, she thought, and she was about to close the final photograph album when she suddenly glimpsed a small, faded photo with some familiar faces. She peeled away the cellophane sleeve and looked closely at the photograph. It was slightly blurred but Dahli could clearly make out Frank sat on a wall with four other friends. They looked so happy, arms linked and with huge smiles on their faces.

Next to Frank was a beautiful much younger woman with mousey blonde hair and wearing a Rolling stones t-shirt, a short mini skirt and espadrilles. Her legs were crossed and she leant against Frank. Was it her? Was it their mother? Dahli looked even closer and smiled; yes it was their mother, her smile undeniable. The wall looked recognizable too. Dahli was sure that it was the harbour wall in Port de Vacquelin. The brick work looked familiar and the small turret of the fishermans' cabin was just in view. The sea was its usual perfect blue and calm. She laughed to herself, elated with happiness and relief but what was her mother doing in Port de Vacquelin? She would wander down to the seafront later that day and find the setting of the photograph, sitting in the exact place the photograph was taken, wondering what these five people were doing there, what made them so happy and why her mother was part of them.

Chapter Thirty-Four

Dahli visited Bijou a few times over the next few weeks with Juliette always in tow. Perhaps she didn't trust her to visit on her own, thought Dahli? Juliette would always clean and tidy the cottage, talking to herself whilst she worked and Dahli would sit and make a drink, walking around the cottage to consider what renovations should take place. She had money from her mother and was sure that there would be local builders and painter-decorators who could help her out. It would be an effort but it needed doing. Dahli's next step was to create an advert to put in the local paper to see if anyone knew anything about Frank and her mother. She drafted the advert and rang Rann who amended it slightly over the phone. "Sounds great now, Dahli. Hope you get some information from someone. Good luck!". Dahli emailed the advert and a copy of the photograph that she had found to the local newspaper. Dahli sat at her table late at night one evening, beer in hand, checking her emails but still nothing. It had been three weeks and no response from the newspaper and she was feeling defeated. Then she suddenly had a thought; spam, check your spam. Why hadn't I thought of that before, she reprimanded herself. She clicked on her spam inbox; 231 emails. She painstakingly filtered through them and there it was staring at her.

To: Dahli.Rosenberg@gmail.com
From Info@PortdeVacquelinPost.com
14 October 2018

Dear Miss Rosenberg

Thank you for your recent email with regards Francois Savin. We have had one response from a Madame Fontainebleau of Little Acres Care Home, Rue de Sacre, Port de Vacquelin. Please could you contact the manager, Phillippe Benoit, at the care home for further information.

Thank you and good luck with your search for more information.

Kind regards

Louis Serie

Assistant Editor

Dahli looked at her watch. It was 6pm, surely too late to ring the manager but she picked up her phone and plumbed in the numbers anyway. A voice on the other end of the line spoke and Dahli asked for the manager. "Of course, who can I say is calling please?" Dahli felt relieved and explained her circumstances and waited a little while then a deep. male voice answered. "Hello Dahli, I'm Phillippe Benoit, the manager. We've been waiting to hear from you. We have a Madame Fontainebleau here who would like to speak to you about Francois Savin. She knew him very well. Can you come in on Wednesday at 11.30am?" Dahli agreed to see Madame Fontainebleau, thanked Phillippe and put the telephone down, not knowing what now to expect but in three days time she would know.

She decided to walk to the nursing home, just twenty minutes along the main road, then down a quiet country track. The day was bright though getting much colder now as the seasons headed into Winter, and Dahli decided to put on a warm jacket, her only blouse and a pair of blue jeans. What was appropriate to wear when visiting an old lady in a care home, she asked herself. The walk was pleasant with few cars on the road and she passed by the modern housing estate where Beulah and Eric lived and followed the fields down the country road until she reached the entrance to Little Acres. A large and foreboding entrance enveloped by two huge stone plinths and old iron sign, Dahli could see a long drive with a procession of old oak trees either side of a gravel road, and in the distance an old French mansion. She walked up the drive, the only sound was her shoes trudging through the gravel and the small birds chirping and squawking in the trees. It was perfectly calm and Dahli was lulled into a sense of tranquillity, the ideal mood for her meeting with the old woman. She reached the steps of the house and walked up to the front door. There was a row of buttons, and she pressed the one marked "Manager" and it buzzed loudly. After a few moments a voice spoke to her. "Hello, how can I help you?" Dahli leant forward and put her face near the speaker shouting back in an awkward fashion, "Hello I'm Dahli I have a meeting with Phillippe Benoit." There was a pause then the female voice called back, "Please come in." and the door buzzed for a few seconds then opened automatically and Dahli stepped over the threshold into a large entrance hall. It smelt of a mixture of disinfectant and jasmine, and she stood there for a few moments when a young man dressed casually in grey cargo pants and polo shirt walked towards her. "Hello, Dahli. Welcome to Little Acres. I'm Phillippe Benoit. Please come and sign in." Dahli signed in and grabbed a visitors pass. "Follow me please." he said and they walked down a light, airy corridor framed with paintings of local scenery which impressed Dahli who gratefully discarded her archaic views of care homes being stuffy and smelling of urine.

They passed room after room, each one emitting its own sound, voices talking, televisions blaring and radios playing classical music. Nurses rushed around, some pushing trolleys of pots of tea and biscuits, others holding medication or armfuls of papers. Finally they reached the last room and Phillippe knocked on the door before entering. "Good morning Emille. You have a visitor to see you." shouted Phillippe. Dahli followed him a little hesitantly. "Emille is deaf as a post and has a short memory but is very switched on for an eighty-seven year old." said Phillippe to Dahli quietly. She nodded as if she understood what was being said to her and looked over at a small, frail looking woman sat in a big armchair in the far corner of the room. She was beautifully dressed in a cerise silk blouse and blue trousers with perfectly coiffed hair, large round horn rimmed glasses and pink lipstick. The room was nicely decorated with a large window looking out to the fields beyond, pictures on the wall and an old fashioned dressing table adorned with the old woman's personal objects; framed photos of family members, a number of ceramic dogs and some scented candles.

The old woman smiled, "Please come and sit near me. I cannot hear too well." and Dahli sat on the chair to the left of her, with Phillippe sitting a little further away. "This is Dahli, Emille. You have some information about Francois Savin and Mathilde Sorensson for her. Do you remember telling me the other day?" said Phillippe, and Dahli nodded but the old woman looked confused and narrowed her eyes, trying to recall the memory. There was silence but Dahli persevered. "Hello Emille. I have to come to see you about Francois, Frank Savin. Can you remember him? And also my mother Mathilde Sorensson?" Dahli's tone of voice became a little desperate and she looked at Emille intently. The old woman suddenly smiled warmly, "Ah yes Francois, of course." and Dahli smiled too with relief. "But before that let's have tea and cake. Be a darling, Phillippe, and ask Cara for some refreshments." Dahli sat back a little relaxed and waited for Emille to converse with her but she sat again in silence. They were having some difficulty communicating. "Do you remember my mother, Mathilde? A friend of Frank's?" asked Dahli but again Emille did not speak, and there was another silence but then all at once she spoke, slowly and quietly at first. "I remember Frank. We grew up together, born in the same street, went to the same schools. A quiet boy. Not one to mix with the rest of us but he was likeable enough. We used to go to church together and sing in the choir. His family were musical so I recall. What was it you wanted to know?" and with that Cara arrived with the refreshments.

Phillippe poured the tea and the three of them tucked into sponge cake, however Dahli was nervous of the break in the conversation. Would Emille again forget what they were talking about? They eventually finished eating and Emille continued. "Who did you say? Mathilde? I do not know a Mathilde. Frank was a darling but he had an awful wife. Why were they together?" she said, looking at Phillippe who shrugged his shoulders. "Mathilde? I do not know a Mathilde. I am sorry." Phillippe moved a little closer. "But you said the other day that you knew her, you remembered her?" said Phillippe but Emille looked at him anxiously. "I am sorry I cannot recall the name Mathilde. Was she a friend of Frank's? I only remember his wife. Awful woman." Dahli was aware of the old woman's increasing anxiety. "It's okay Emille. Do not worry yourself. Thank you for letting me know about Frank. Thank you for your time." Dahli felt disappointed. stood up and said her goodbyes to Emille. Phillippe and Dahli left the room. "Did Emille say any more to you about Mathilde?" asked Dahli but Phillippe shook his head. "Sorry Dahli, she just said that she knew her and that was that." Dahli sighed, said farewell to Phillippe and left the old house really none the wiser.

Dahli just wanted to get drunk, and be with Joe. They arranged to meet after the restaurant closed that evening. Joe was waiting for Dahli, beer in hand, understandably concerned for his despondent friend. Dahli felt like she had hit a brick wall. What was she to do now? Another advert maybe in the newspaper in the vain hope that someone else could help her investigations? Joe put some music on and passed a beer to a seated Dahli but she slipped her hand in her pocket and produced a bottle of Jack Daniels. Joe laughed and grabbed a couple of glasses. The amber liquor soothed a subdued Dahli and she began to dance around the caravan, giggling and humming along. "Come on Joe, join in!" she blurted out, grabbing his hand. He put his drink down, stood up and reluctantly started to sway awkwardly. He tried to sit down but Dahli grabbed him again, pulling him towards her. "Nope. No getting out of it." she said, singing louder and louder. She spun around and lost her footing, grabbed Joe and they both fell onto his bed. Dahli found herself lying on top of Joe and they faced each other, the sound of the music suddenly silenced. Without a word she leant forward and kissed him passionately. She withdrew, "Don't stop" he said, his voice deep and they made love urgently and wantonly.

Dahli was woken abruptly by her phone vibrating loudly in her bag. She leant over Joe who was sleeping soundly, and grabbed it. "Hello?" she said a little gruffly. "Hello Dahli. Sorry to wake you. It's Phillippe. Phillippe Benoit. Please can you come up to the nursing home, as soon as you can? Emille is remembering your mother. She is lucid and saying lots of stuff. As soon as you can, Dahli." Dahli pushed her hair away from her face. "Yes, of course. I can come now!". She put the phone down and nudged Joe and he stirred slowly. "What's going on? You okay, Dahli?" He wiped his eyes and yawned. "I have to go. Phillippe has rung from the nursing home. Emille has got her memory back. Woohoo!" She was still a little drunk and excitable. "I'll take my push bike. Got to go." and she launched herself off the bed, pulled on her clothes and started to make her way to the door of the caravan. "Wait." said Joe. "I'll drive you there. I didn't drink quite as much as you so should be okay." Dahli whispered thank you and sat back on the bed smiling. She was happy for two reasons; one, she might get some more information about her mother, and two, she could avoid the delicate subject of last night for a little while longer.

Dahli strapped herself into the car and Joe started the ignition. The old car slowly turned over and Joe gave it a rev before putting it into gear and slowly setting off. Joe wiped the condensation off the front window with his hand. They hardly spoke, Dahli nervous about her second visit to Emille and Joe, a little embarrassed at last night's events. He had always been a little shy with women and Dahli was a force to be reckoned with on the best of days. He wanted to kiss her again and feel her warmth against his body but she seemed a little distant. It had been a long time since he had felt this way about any woman but she was hard to read. Some days she was soft and loving, almost flirtatious and child-like. Then other days she was harsh and abrupt, arrogant and too self assured for his liking. What was she thinking now, he wondered. The answer to this would have to wait until Dahli had been to the nursing home to see Emille. They arrived at the front steps of the home and she jumped out, leaving Joe in the car. "I could be a while, Joe. Do you want to go home and come back later?" she said and Joe nodded. "I'll see you later. Hope it goes well." he replied glumly and drove back down the drive out of sight.

Chapter Thirty-Five

Dahli found herself again walking down the bright corridor, with Phillippe, the atmosphere homely and comforting. "She's been very chatty this morning, and happy, very different to yesterday. This is how dementia goes." said Phillippe wistfully Dahli hadn't yet put a label to Emille's condition and knew little about dementia but was glad of the window of opportunity to see her again. She smiled to herself and they soon arrived at Emille's room. She was on her feet tidying some magazines on her table. "Oh hello. Have we already met? Please come and sit down." she said and took her seat in the big armchair. "Phillippe, the girl looks famished. Please bring some refreshments." and Phillippe disappeared out to the corridor. "Hello Emille. So lovely to see you again. You have news about my mother?" "Phllippe tells me that you visited just the other. I am sorry that I did not remember you from your last visit but I remembering more about your mother now." Emille smiled and placed her hand on her knee and began her story.

"Mathilde was beautiful, inside and out." she said, smiling fondly to herself at the memory. "A girl of about twenty-five if I remember. She lived with us for almost a year whilst she worked at the local school as an English assistant. She was from England, northern parts? We became very close but her life got complicated." Emille stopped talking, stood up and opened the wardrobe, reached down and picked up an old cardboard box then sat back down with the box on her lap. Dahli watched the old woman fascinated by her movements, so elegant, she thought. Emille looked down at the box and placed her hands gently on it before carrying on. "She met Frank at the school. He was teaching history and in a nutshell after a while they fell in love."

Emille looked sorrowful, and she sighed and looked at Dahli, her eyes slightly glazed. "She came home one day and told us she had met a wonderful man but he was married. We warned her to be careful but she was a carefree, single, rather naive girl." Emille laughed slightly. "Eventually she couldn't hold back her passion and they started a secret relationship. He was so much older than her, but no wiser so it seemed." Emille smiled tenderly then frowned. "And nothing could be secret for long in the village and of course the wife found out." Emille's demeanour changed and she sighed, seemingly annoyed by the following events. She explained that Mathilde regretfully broke up with Frank as he would not leave his wife, and she went back to England heartbroken. "I left her at the bus station with just her suitcase, looking incredibly sad. I didn't want her to go but she felt that she had no choice. Her heart had been ripped apart and she wanted nothing more to do with Port de Vacquelin. I thought I would not see her again but then some months later she wrote to me to say that she was pregnant." Emille paused. "With Frank's babies. Yes, babies. Twins, and she had started a relationship with another older man, Ian, and was to marry him. It was all too sudden. She wasn't thinking straight. I just wanted to turn back time for her."

The old woman paused, her face fraught, the memories painful. "But he was cruel. He would only marry her if she gave up one of her babies. You see, it was obvious to all that he didn't really like children but he wanted to be with Mathilde. It was obvious why. She was a pretty young thing, looked great on his arm, and they would pass the child off as their own but she was destitute, Dahli. Cold man. Mathilde had no support from her family so Ian was her way to a better future but with an incredibly heavy price to pay." Dahli couldn't imagine the pain that this would have caused her mother. It certainly explained her frequent bouts of depression when Dahli and Miranda were children, the emotional outbursts and periods when she would lock herself in the bedroom for days at a time. Dahli had witnessed Ian's impatience with her mother, and remembered the arguments and the heavy slamming of doors, and Dahli and Miranda would be looked after by their aunt Jude whilst their mother suffered, time after time. Dahli suddenly felt guilty and ashamed; if only she had known the grief her mother was feeling surely she could've helped her. Then she remembered Christian. He will be completely dumbstruck by all this; how was she to tell him about their mother and father, the newspaper advert and Emille? She hadn't kept him up to date with her investigations. She would have some explaining to do.

Emille took a sharp intake of breath and explained that when Frank found out about Mathilde and the babies he was very remorseful. He now wanted to be with Mathilde, said Emille, but was afraid of his wife and her strict Catholic upbringing, the shame to the family of a separation. He eventually did leave his wife but it was too late as Mathilde was already engaged to Ian and about to be married. "Frank was a coward who lived to regret his actions." smarted Emille, grimacing. She had mixed feelings about Frank. He was a nice, quiet man, but often lacked substance and dithered over his decisions. "However there was some light in the story. Frank's sister and husband were childless and not able to have children, living in Russia. They adopted Mathilde's little boy, I think illegally, and took him back to Russia so he did stay in Frank's life as his uncle, and Mathilde saw him also about once a year during his childhood. Christian never wanted to find out about his real parents and I'll never know why but he was happy and we knew that that meant more to him at that time. It was a real mess though. Dahli. Lives ruined. "

Emille looked tired but Dahli was confused and needed answers. Things started making sense suddenly. Dahli was very different to her father and her sister; they were disciplined and often regimented in their ways while Dahli and her mother were more happy-go-lucky and easy going. Ian had never been kind to Dahli, never hugged or kissed her as a child, or praised her when she, for example, excelled in school. He had always shown favouritism towards Miranda too. It was obvious why now but Dahli was still confused. "Emille, why didn't my mother tell me that I was Frank's daughter, even tell me when I was an adult after Ian died?" Emille just looked at her forlorn. "She was afraid, Dahli. Afraid of her circumstance, afraid of Ian. She knew Christian was being well cared for and that is all that mattered...and you weren't always around to talk to. You were away a lot." Dahli felt slightly attacked and gulped. God no, she thought, was I that distant physically and emotionally? Did her mother say that to Emille? Emille carried on. "Me and your mama kept in touch by letter for many years." and she looked down at the box on her lap and then looked up at Dahli. "They are all here." Dahli was stunned. ""Every letter?" Dahli asked. "Yes, we wrote to each other over a period of thirty plus years. My last letter from your mother was last year just before she got sick. I miss her heart. These are yours now, dear Dahli."

Emille passed the box to Dahli who looked at it in awe. How would her mother feel if she knew that her secret had now been revealed? Perhaps Emille and her mother had made a pact to tell Dahli once she was passed? Dahli struggled with the truth, her hands shaking and her heart racing and she opened the box tentatively, the familiar scent of roses drifting across the room. She sifted through the letters, pausing every so often to open one and read it, her fingers touching every word on the page. She could feel her mother's every emotion and felt tears prick her eyes, and she wiped them away with the back of her hand. Emille put her tiny hand on Dahli's knee and smiled contentedly, knowing that the letters would be treasured forever.

"I am sorry, Dahli, I am very tired. Could we meet again next week please? Please take the letters with you." Dahli acknowledged and thanked her, kissed her gently on each cheek and left the room, few words were said but the couple had shared something so precious only they could ever understand. Dahli went out into the cold air, blinked in the bright sunshine and sat on a bench in the gardens. She was still clutching the cardboard box in her hand then placed it next to her and momentarily sat very still but abruptly burst into tears. She sobbed, the tears rolling down her face and her shoulders heaving. She felt sad and anguished, her whole life oddly turned upside down by an old woman in a care home.

After a moment she collected her emotions and stood up, walking back down the long gravel path and out onto the country road, passing the modern housing estate and back down the main road to the restaurant. She didn't want to see Joe, or anyone. She wanted to be alone to take in the fresh air and gather her thoughts. It was midday and she could see that the restaurant was starting to fill up with lunch guests. Dahli saw Joe behind the bar serving a young woman, animated and happy, chatty and smiling. His life carried on as normal and she felt happy for him and turned around and went back to her van, laid on the bed and soon fell asleep, exhausted from the morning's happenings. After a short cat nap, she awoke much brighter and took the letters from her bag. She decided to read the letters in chronological order, starting with the first one marked April 1980.

39 Moyse Avenue
Walshaw, Manchester

April 2nd 1980

Dear Emille

I am sorry that I have not been in touch earlier but it has been hard here since returning from Port de Vacquelin. I have managed to find a place to live on a council estate; lodging with a nice family, and have secured part time work in the local shop. People have been very welcoming but I feel an enormous sadness still and to make things worse I am pregnant. I have feared telling you because I have been very stupid I know. Yes, it's Frank's babies. Yes babies. I am expecting twins. I gave my love to him and only him, only twice. Do you see him at all? I am very scared right now for my future. I have been seeing a man called Ian however I am not sure if he cares that much for me. We will have to see. Please write back. The babies are due in August, just a few months away. I expect people will start to judge me now that I am starting to show. How did life come to this? Please write to me. I miss you.

Take care Emille,

Love Mathilde xxx

Dahli folded the letter and placed it back in its envelope. She pulled out the next letter and opened it slowly, read it, and then the third and then the fourth.

Didsbury

Manchester

August 7th 1980

Dear Emille

I hope you are well. I finally gave birth three days ago. My mother helped me through the birth but she has gone now. Ian has yet to visit. I am sitting here with my two babies and they are perfect. Ian and I married two weeks ago. Time will come when I have to give up my little boy but I mustn't be sad as he will be going to Russia with Frank's sister and husband. I hope to see him at least once a year when they visit Port de Vacquelin. It is good to be back in touch with Frank but I still miss being with him. Ian and I are living in a nice house near Manchester and he is a solicitor. He is providing for me and my baby well. I will be home from the hospital in a few days. It would be lovely to hear from you. I don't know anyone in the area yet so letters from you are joyous.

Take care my Emille.
Love, your Mathilde xxx

Dahli felt her mother's sadness and emptiness. She sat back and inhaled sharply and screwed up her face in anger at the sudden thought of her father's controlling behaviour. To expect a young mother to separate her babies; how could he be so cruel? He always seems to hold all the cards. She put the letters back in the box and poured herself a large Jack Daniels. She regretted so many things right now; leaving her mother alone whilst she travelled for many years; it must've seemed that she had lost not one but two children over the years. Falling out with Rann; time is precious, why waste it arguing? Not being able to tell everyone earlier about her father's adulterous behaviour. She, too, had been dominated by his narcissistic exploitation of her situation and she felt ashamed. She shivered at the thought of him, and took another sip of the bourbon. Her only thought was to ring Rann. She called her number but it went straight to answerphone. "Ring me please Rann. I need to talk to you." she forced the words out of her mouth, fighting back tears out then put the phone on the table. Moments later it rang and Dahli poured her heart out to her little sister who listened patiently on the other end of the phone. It was comforting and soothing. Dahli slept like a baby, tranquillised by her sister's kind words and four glasses of Bourbon.

Chapter Thirty-Six

The next day Dahli still couldn't face Joe just yet so she went into the village to see Beulah. She hadn't seen her for a while and a timely catch up over cake and coffee was definitely overdue even if it was only for a few minutes during Beulah's lunch hour. She wanted to tell her all about her mother and Frank. She would be so excited to learn about Dahli's link to the photo hanging on the wall. She arrived at the bakery and went in, placed her coat on the back of a chair and her bag on the floor and proceeded to admire the cakes on the counter then looked around and noticed tables hadn't been cleared and plates and cups were piling up. She frowned with concern. "Hello, Dahli, can I help you?" interrupted Marianne looking fraught. "Well, yes, thank you. Is Beulah here today?". Marianne looked a bit downcast suddenly and hesitated. "Beulah is a little unwell today. We think she may have a virus or food poisoning or something." She said, "She keeps being sick. She ate a prawn sandwich yesterday. I'd keep your distance, just for a day or two. " she said quietly so the customers didn't overhear.

Beulah was never sick. "Oh okay, send her my love., won't you?" replied Dahli and grabbed her things and went back out into the daylight when Eric came rushing after her. "I'm so sorry Dahli," he said slightly out of breath, "But could you help us out at the bakery for a few days whilst Beulah gets better? I know you've got experience and we're desperate. She's never ill and I am so worried. Marianne and the two girls manage admirably but another pair of hands would help enormously." He pleaded with her with his eyes and Dahli smiled. "Of course, Eric, I can help as long as you like. Start today?" Eric looked relieved and thanked Dahli and they both went back into the bakery.

After four hours of work Dahli flopped down on the bed in the van when there was a tentative knock on the door. God, who now, she thought. She reluctantly pulled herself off the bed, wiped her eyes, roughly tidied her hair and opened the door. It was Joe. "Oh wow, hello." she said a little rudely. Joe stood back and shook his head. "That's no way to greet a friend." he said, jokingly and smiled warmly. "Sorry Joe didn't mean no harm. Just having a hard time today and I've just done a stint at the bakery as Beulah's sick. Come in, please." The two of them sat over a cup of tea and Dahli explained what she had found out at the nursing home. Joe sat there, eyes wide and unable to speak. He wanted to hold her but she looked so cold so he sat next to her bolt upright. Dahli was hoping Joe would say something to ease her pain but he didn't so she got up. "Sorry Joe, I'm really tired." He understood what she was saying so left her to sleep. Maybe another day they would converse less awkwardly.

The next couple of days passed by and Dahli continued to work at the bakery, serving food, washing up, and helping with the cleaning. She felt content and useful. She visited Beulah upstairs after a few days. "Hi Beulah, how are you?" Beulah coughed and her voice was raspy. "I can't stop puking, Dahli. Eric is taking me to the doctor's later as I may need some antibiotics or something. I feel so tired too." Dahli left hoping that Beulah would soon feel better. Beulah hauled herself off the sofa and slowly put on her coat, whilst Eric grabbed the car keys. They walked down the cobbles hand in hand and Eric carefully helped Beulah into the car. He was so kind and gentle with her, she fragile and exhausted. The doctor's surgery was a short five minute drive away, and they arrived, parked up in the small car park and Beulah followed Eric into the surgery where a cheerful woman was sitting behind the reception desk. "Yes, Beulah Smythe. You are next in." Eric thanked her and they sat down.

It was a small surgery and there were few people waiting. Beulah opened a magazine, looking at the photos, too weak to read the articles and Eric put his arm around and kissed her hair then a doctor arrived in the waiting area. "Mrs Beulah Smythe, please." They followed him into a small room and sat down on two old wooden chairs. It had been some time since Beulah had been in a doctor's room. It smelt strangely of a mixture of furniture polish and aftershave, and she looked around the room in a haze. "How can I help you, Mrs Smythe?" The doctor asked and smiled sympathetically. Beulah came back to her senses, inhaled deeply and explained how ill she felt, the vomiting and exhaustion. The doctor paused for a moment and looked at her. "Well I would rule out food poisoning as you are still vomiting. It could be a virus but can I ask, could you be pregnant by any chance?" Beulah looked at him terrified. Just the mention of the word "pregnant" took her breath away and brought back terrible memories, the IVF and the constant failure and disappointment. "Well, yes but I have tried for eight years with no success." Beulah felt dreadfully sick but the doctor pressed on. "I can do a blood test and we will soon know. Just a few hours." He smiled kindly and drew some blood from Beulah who was feeling faint and queasy.

Eric and Beulah left the surgery and went home, only to return a few hours later. They were quiet and sober in their thoughts, were called and followed the doctor silently into his room. "Hello, Mr and Mrs Smythe. I have your blood test results." Beulah looked at him, disappointment already written across her face. She had been here so many times before. Eric squeezed her hand tightly and the doctor continued. "I can confirm that you are pregnant. You are about four weeks gone." Beulah couldn't speak, stunned. She sat back and instantly burst into tears and the doctor looked astonished at her sudden outburst, passing her a tissue. "Sorry it's been very hard these last few years on us and to hear this is just incredible." said Eric, putting his arm around his wife. Beulah managed to compose herself and whispered thank you, and the doctor passed her a leaflet and requested she make some future appointments. They thanked him and left the surgery still in shock.

Back at the bakery Dahli had arrived already, cake in hand, reading a book that she had picked up from the newsagents next door, waiting for her afternoon shift to start. Beulah and Eric appeared at the door. "Hi Dahli, please come up in a while." said Eric and Dahli nodded with a mouthful of cake. Dahli hadn't thought anything more and Eric had given nothing away. She sat for another fifteen minutes, finishing off the chapter of her book, wiped her mouth with a napkin and headed upstairs to see her friend. Beulah was sitting on the sofa, cup of water in hand, looking emotional and tired. "Hi Beulah." said Dahli cheerfully trying to lift her friend's spirit a little and without further ado Beulah announced that she was pregnant and she again burst into tears. Dahli rushed over to her and hugged her. She couldn't believe what she was hearing. "How far gone? Wow, really? This is incredible." Her words barbled out of her mouth and she felt so happy for her friend. Beulah managed to smile in between bouts of nausea and the two women sat together elated.

Chapter Thirty-Seven
Early December 2019

Dahli was still working at the bakery whilst Beulah recuperated from her ongoing morning sickness which was laying her low. One cold November morning she took her early morning coffee at the bakery before starting her shift and Joe appeared at the bakery door. "Dahli, are you there? Ah yes, can you let me in for moment please?" He looked a little stressed and Dahli dived towards the door and unlocked it, pulling the door open for Joe. "Hi Joe. How's you?" she said casually and Joe sat down at her table. "I have something to tell you, Dahli." said Joe and Dahli looked quizzical. She picked up her coffee cup and watched Joe over its rim, worried that he didn't look his usual cheerful self. "I have some news for you Dahli, and I'm sorry that we haven't seen each other for what seems like ages." he stopped for a moment then blinked furiously and nervously. "I'm leaving, Dahli. I have been offered a fantastic opportunity in the city to work under a celebrated chef in an up and coming restaurant. It means one step closer to my dream of owning my own restaurant. It also means that I'll be nearer Genevieve which will be fantastic."

Joe was so happy but Dahli didn't respond, no congratulations or well done, or pat on the back so he stopped and looked down, avoiding eye contact with her. He was sad to be leaving her behind, the one woman who had captured his heart, the one woman who he trusted, the one woman who he felt so natural and relaxed with. He would miss her. Dahli put her cup down and rested her elbows on the table. "Well I'm so pleased for you Joe. It's what you've always wanted. When do you leave?" She looked nonplussed and her words dispassionate. Joe lifted his head slowly and looked at Dahli. "I leave at the weekend. They want me to start on Monday." he said, feeling dejected. He wanted her to say she would miss him; to cry and scream and beg him not to go, but no, she just sat there unfazed. "Okay, thanks for letting me know Joe. I hope it goes well." she said, rising from her chair. "Sorry, I've got to get the bakery opened and get on." and with that Joe left the building, relieved to have told Dahli but upset that she had shown no interest in him or his dreams.

Dahli sighed and watched as Joe left the bakery. She was again letting friendship and maybe even love walk out of her life. The one chance to be happy. Why did she always push men away? She remembered Gabe. He had loved her some years before, he was perfect in every way and they had been together for two blissful years but when he asked her to marry him, she pushed him away and eventually he left her, disillusioned with her non commitment. She had regretted her decision but was unable to commit and live with someone permanently. What was she so frightened of? Was it because of what happened to her when she was fourteen? The abortion, the shock, the shame, the loneliness. It had taken its toll and never been completely resolved, or at all. Or was it just that she was too young, too immature to take on a serious relationship. But at thirty-three years old perhaps she wasn't too young? She wished that she could think and feel differently. She shook her head and grabbed an apron, roughly wrapping it around her waist and tying it in a tight knot. She was so cross with herself but there was no going back, again.

Nine months passed and Joe settled into Paris. He was working in a delightful little restaurant in Rue Xavier Privas, a narrow street lined with cheerful and welcoming bistros, serving up some of the city's finest dining experiences. Nothing could have prepared him for this time in his life and it was just the stimulation he needed to set him on the path to owning his own restaurant. For Dahli life carried on without him. She missed him every day but they kept in touch, with the odd phone call or text. She was still working at the bakery, Beulah having found work was too much with the morning sickness carrying on into the third trimester of her pregnancy. It hadn't gone away and the doctor had said that she was just unlucky. Dahli wasn't worried as she was enjoying working with Eric and Marianne and the girls, and had even been promoted to bread baking.

Two weeks before the birth Dahli got a desperate call from Beulah. "Hi Dahli, sorry but Eric's aunt has just died suddenly and he's got to go to Scotland for the funeral. He'll be away for a few days, can you manage?" Dahli reassured an anxious Beulah. Dahli had now got used to running the bakery some days almost single handedly whilst the Smythes careered from one disaster to another, Beulah's sickness not improving and Eric struggling with the new daily routine of caring for his wife and running a small business. Eric left for Scotland looking glum but as he said, "duty calls." He was due back in a few days, just a flying visit. It was one week before Christmas and Dahli was baking mince pies and putting up some Christmas decorations when she heard a scream from upstairs. She rushed up the stairs to find Beulah sitting on the end of the bed looking at her feet. "My waters have just broken, Dahli! It's too early! I am not due for another two weeks!" she cried, looking down at a puddle of water., her face etched with fear. Beulah had been anxious throughout her pregnancy and now she was doubly fretting. "Don't worry, Beulah. It means your baby is on its way soon, the next couple of days. Babies often come early. Eric will be home soon. Put your feet up and I will clear up and make you a hot drink." Beulah looked at her and smiled, relieved to have Dahli in the same building and here to reassure her. That evening Dahli said goodbye to Beulah, ensuring she was comfortable. "If you need me for anything, please ring me, anytime Beulah " she said as she rushed downstairs. Dahli was tired from a long day at the bakery and was looking forward to a good night's sleep.

The next morning the phone rang and Dahli rolled over and checked the time on her clock. Christ, it's only 6.30am, she thought, who's ringing me at this time, then she remembered Beulah. "Hi Dahli, I think my contractions have started." said a frightened Beulah. Please can you come here as soon as you can. I'm scared." Dahli got up, quickly dressed , ran outside and jumped in the driver's seat of her van, driving at speed down the hill to the bakery. There she found a pale Beulah sitting on the sofa, clenching her stomach in some discomfort. "It's okay, Beulah, I'll drive you to the hospital." reassured Dahli. "Yes, I've already rung them and they are expecting us." Beulah said, smiling weakly. The nearest hospital was in Bayeux, a short fifteen minute drive and it was still early, only 6.45am. Dahli bundled Beulah carefully into the camper van, rang Eric to tell him the news who made immediate plans to come straight home, and started the drive to the hospital. Beulah was obviously in much discomfort by now and sobbing uncontrollably. "Take some deep breaths." Dahli said to her, a little irritated at her emotional state. Why does she have to be so dramatic, she thought. She took some big slow breaths and started to relax slightly but then five minutes into the drive she screamed an enormous scream. Dahli looked at her, "What is it, Beulah?" she asked, alarmed at Beulah's increasingly agitated state. "The baby's head. I can feel the baby's head. The baby is almost here and I can't hold it back. We won't get there in time." bellowed Beulah. Christ, thought Dahli and pulled over in a layby. She carefully helped Beulah onto the bed at the back of the van and called emergency services.

Beulah lay there helpless, panting quickly in between contractions and cradling the baby's head in her hands. "Hello, my friend is in the late stages of pregnancy. She can see the baby's head. We're in a camper van just outside Port de Vacquelin, We were on our way to the hospital. Please come quick!" and Dahli felt panic rising slightly. Stay calm, stay calm and breathe, she told herself. "Stay on the line, Dahli " said the woman calmly on the other end of the line. "And I will talk you through what to do whilst you wait for the ambulance. Please try not to worry as I am here with you all the way and the ambulance is only about five minutes away." Dahli put the phone on loudspeaker whilst Beulah screamed louder with every contraction and at that very moment there was a loud knock on the glass and a young man peered into the van. "Is everything okay?" he mouthed through the glass, having heard the commotion and concerned for their welfare and Dahli turned around. "No, my friend is having a baby right now!" she shouted back impatiently, a little annoyed to have been distracted. The young man shouted back through the glass. "I'm a trainee doctor, let me in so I can help." and Dahli jumped up and pushed open the back door. "Thanks so much mate" she said not wanting to alarm Beulah by showing any emotions but she was incredibly relieved to not be dealing with this on her own, and the young man sat beside her whilst the operator continued to speak instructions to them.

"Right Beulah, on the next contraction push hard down into your bottom and then keep pushing Beulah. That's great. You're doing great." she said, and Dahli watched as this little bundle of life appeared in front of her eyes. First the head, then the shoulders then with one big push the baby flopped out and she grabbed its soft warm body in her hands and just stared. "Wow, Beulah, you have a baby. You've done it!" Dahli was stunned and then the baby opened its mouth and wailed and Dahli held it up to Beulah who couldn't quite take in what she had just accomplished, and put her head back, a little dazed and exhausted. The young man took the baby from Dahli carefully and checked it over before wrapping it in a towel. "You have a beautiful baby girl, Beulah. Congratulations!" he shouted and passed the baby girl to Beulah who wept with joy and smiled, the pain and stress of the last few hours dissipating completely. Dahli was still stunned, sitting on the edge of the bed holding a wet towel and staring at Beulah and the baby. "Are you okay?" asked the young man, concerned. Dahli looked at him. "Oh yes." she said. "Sorry, I can't believe what's just happened." She had never seen or held something so precious and had never felt love like it. She sat back on the bed, emotionally and physically drained and there was a wailing of sirens. "The cavalry has arrived!" exclaimed the young man jokingly and with that a young woman jumped in the van, a huge medical bag slung over her shoulder, and smiled. "Well done to all of you. You've done an incredible job!" She was quick to help Beulah get cleaned up, cut the umbilical cord and gingerly helped her out of the van into the ambulance.

"Eric, oh God, Eric. Can you ring him please, Dahli?" shouted Beulah from the back of the ambulance. "Of course, Beulah." and with that the ambulance disappeared leaving Dahli and the young man standing by the back of the van. "I'm Jacques by the way." said the young man and they both laughed. "Thank you so much for your help. Let me take your number, Jacques and we can meet properly to toast the baby." Jacques smiled, agreed readily and turned back to the track where he had appeared from. Dahli stepped back inside the van and sat on the bed. "Oh god." she exclaimed to herself, looking down at the wet mess. "Looks like I will need a new mattress." and giggled to herself with happiness. She picked up her phone and rang Eric's number. He answered immediately. "What's the news, Dahli. How is she? How are they?" he said frantically and Dahli inhaled slowly. "Everything is perfect, Eric and you have a gorgeous baby daughter. Congratulations." Eric shrieked with delight and Dahli broke down in tears. "It was so incredible Eric." she sobbed. "I delivered your baby. It was amazing." Eric shrieked a little more and Dahli explained the circumstances. "I will be home by this afternoon. I can't wait to see them. Got to go now as we are boarding. See you very soon and thank you, Dahli. You're a star." Eric put the phone down and Dahli jumped in the driver's seat and drove the ten minutes to Bayeux hospital.

Beulah held her little bundle of joy in her arms and cooed at her, and Dahli quietly took a seat on the chair by the bed holding a cup of coffee and eating a Mars Bar when Eric appeared at the door and stopped momentarily. He could not believe what he was seeing. "Wow." he said. "Just wow. Oh Beulah, well done. I'm so sorry I couldn't be here for you." but Beulah wasn't angry and she looked at him, her eyes full of love and joy and they sat together looking at the baby and holding hands, Beulah resting her head on his chest. Dahli decided it was time to leave the happy couple and give them some quiet time together. "Goodbye you two. You three! I am off now." Beulah held Dahli in her arms and squeezed her tight. "What would I have done without you, Dahli? You are truly the most wonderful person. Thank you." Dahli looked at her. No one had ever spoken to her so tenderly and she was taken aback. She thanked her and left the room, tears again welling in her eyes.

Chapter Thirty-Eight

Christian was busy in the office at the university when his phone rang in his pocket. It was Dahli. "Hi Dahli, how are you?" he asked politely. He was surprised when she announced that she had found out news about her mother and Frank, after all they agreed when they met in the cafe Paris not to investigate any further until the cottage handover was agreed. "Sorry, Christian, I couldn't wait. Had time on my hands and all that." she said apologetically but he wasn't angry, rather the opposite, he was excited by her news. "My wife and I have some time off next week by coincidence. Can we come and visit you, and maybe go and visit Emille?" She was taken aback but agreed, already looking forward to seeing him and his wife again. Three days later Christian and Amelie arrived in Port de Vacquelin, deciding to stay at a budget hotel in the centre of the village. They arranged to meet Dahli at the nursing home that afternoon, and there she was, standing on the steps of the large old house, waving madly at them. They parked up and hugged their friend. "Good to see you. Shall we?" said Christian, as polite as ever, and into the home they went together. Phillippe was standing in the entrance hall and Dahli thought him a little awkward. "Hello, please can you just come into my office for a moment." he said, and Dahli knew something wasn't right.

They followed Phillippe into his office, and he asked them to sit down and he leaned on the edge of his desk, crossing his arms. "I am really sorry to tell you that Emille sadly passed away yesterday evening." he announced. "I have been trying to contact you, left messages." "Oh Christ!" Dahli uttered in annoyance. "I bloody well forgot to take it off silent." Then she sat there and started to take in what was being said. Phillippe was white as a sheet. "She was like family to us, having been here so long. We found her sitting in her chair. She looked so peaceful. We are going to miss her so much." He wiped his eyes and Dahli just stared at him, not knowing how to feel, numb from the news. "Oh how awful. Poor Emille. Poor you." she said and looked at Christian sadly. He held her hand and smiled back at her and after a moment Dahli started to stand up but Phillippe beckoned her to sit back down. "She left something for you. It's almost as if she knew her time had come." he said wistfully, and opened the bottom drawer of his desk and took out a small white plastic box and passed it to Dahli. She looked at him. "What's this,

Phillippe?" She held the box in her hand and started to open it. "I'm sorry Dahli, none of us know." replied Phillippe. She put her hand in the box and pulled out a small envelope and then a little red velvet box. The little box immediately fascinated her and she opened it tentatively and in front of her she saw a delicate vintage gold ring, inlaid with tiny rubies and diamonds. She took the ring out of its box and held it closer to her face. She couldn't believe how stunning it was. She put it back in its box and proceeded to open the envelope, taking out a small card. She read it aloud.

My dearest Dahli,
I want you to have this in case I don't see you again. The ring has a special meaning. Frank, your father, was to give it to your mother as an engagement ring but of course she was already betrothed to Ian by the time Frank left his wife. He sent it to her anyway but she sent it back to me, as any memory of Frank was at that time too upsetting for her.

Now that we have found each other it makes sense for you to keep it. I have never told anyone about the ring.
Love as always,
Emille Fontainebleau

Dahli put the card back inside the envelope, thanked Phillippe and said no more of it. The three of them left the house, Dahli asking Phillippe to notify of her the funeral arrangements, and they made their way back down to the harbour front for a bite to eat and to meet Juliette who was bursting with happiness to learn of Frank's love affair with Mathilde. Christian, Dahli and Amelie spent two more wonderful days together, finalising the plans for the handover of the cottage and chatting about Frank and Mathilde. "I am so shocked to hear all the news, Dahli. My father was Frank. Wow, you couldn't make it up. God I wish he would have told me. We spent so many happy days together and thinking about it, we were so similar in many ways. Quiet. tall, studious. Why didn't he tell me?" Christian was sorrowful. He felt regret and some anger at Frank for not telling him and Dahli empathised. "So we are twins, Christian." Dahli said, lightening the mood with a smile. He smiled at her. "Yes, we are. I'm very pleased that you are in my life. Dahli. I feel complete. Strangely for the first time in my life I feel as if I have a history and we can build a future together, the new Savins". Dahli looked at him and laughed. "Yes, we are the new Savins." she replied. "Will you consider changing your name, Dahli. To Savin maybe?" asked Amelie and Dahli was rather taken aback. She hadn't even consider it, but yes it was a possibility. She was certainly not a Rosenburg and never had been and she felt more akin to the Savins.

Later that evening Christian and Amelie visited Bijou for one last time before it was handed over to Dahli. Christian walked around the cottage in silence on his own then sat back in the living room and sighed. "I am saying goodbye to an important part of my life, with even more meaning now. We will get the cottage cleared in good time. What will you do with it now, Dahli?." Dahli had never been good at forward planning and now she had no choice but to consider her options. She couldn't currently see herself living here but wasn't sure if she wanted to sell it. "I really don't know what I will do just yet but you are always welcome here" she replied frowning slightly, gritting her teeth and Christian smiled at her fondly, "Well I wish you well whatever you decide to do. We will be back in a couple of weeks." Dahli looked at her watch. "Oh, God, is that the time? I have to go. I have a gig at the campsite up the road." She then stopped and thought for a moment. "Why don't you two come with me? It's a great night, cheap beer, cheap food." Amelie nodded excitedly, and Christian looked surprised. "You have a gig? You play?" he said surprised, and Dahli explained that she sang and played the guitar. He was amazed. "You wouldn't know this but our grandfather, Otto, was the most wonderful accordion player and singer. He played in the posh hotels in Paris. He used to play to me when I was a child. You must have inherited his talent." Dahli beamed at Christian and they all got in the car and drove up to the campsite. The next day Amelie and Christian said their goodbyes and went back to Paris.

Dahli sat in her van, alone and downcast. She took the little velvet ring box that Emille had given her out of her pocket and placed it on the table, staring at it momentarily before lifting the lid. She pulled at the ring gently but as she did the box came apart.. "Damn!" she thought, fumbling to put the box back together when she noticed a piece of brown, slightly tatty folded paper sitting neatly in the bottom of it. She unfolded it and looked at it inquisitively. There in front of her was some text, written in faded blue ink, in what looked like Russian. Well that sort of made sense, she thought, knowing that Frank's family were from Russia. She took a photo of the piece of paper, and sent it immediately to Christian whose second language was Russian. "See if you can decipher this for me." she wrote on a text to him, and waited only ten minutes before her phone beeped at her. She opened the text excitedly and read it aloud to herself.

November 16 1919
My sweet Svetlana,
Thank you for agreeing to be my wife.
This ring will bind us in love forever and a day.
Yours as always,
Otto xxxx

Then she saw the rest of the text message from Christian. "Hi Dahli. Where did you find this? In the box? This is incredible. Here's the translation. Otto and Svetlana were my grandparents. I met them once a year until I was seven years old. Wonderful people. My grandmother died in 1984 from cancer. She was sprightly right up to the few weeks before she died. My, our mean our, grandfather must have returned the ring to its original box when my grandmother passed away then Frank, I mean my father, must have inherited it. How romantic and sad at the same time. I will tell you more about them when we speak." Dahli took the ring and tried to push it onto her finger but it was far too small. Svetlana must have been very dainty, she thought and placed it back in the box and on the shelf above the bed. The next day she spent her lunchtime browsing and eventually purchasing a delicate gold chain so she could wear the ring around her neck.

Chapter Thirty-Nine

Didsbury

Miranda had not yet slept in her own bed. She was still angry with Steve and could not yet forgive him. She wondered if she ever would, however she was willing to talk, and talking they had been doing much of but getting nowhere. "Do you think we should go for couples' counselling?" said Rann one evening whilst Steve was making dinner. She was keen to make the marriage work but he answered dismissively without looking at her. "Don't be silly, Miranda." he said. What good would that do? We don't need other people's interference, do we? We're okay, aren't we? Just come here and kiss me". Miranda stepped away from him just before he grabbed her waist, the vision of him and another woman falling through the door kissing still vividly etched solidly in her mind. She wasn't in the mood for another argument which there had been many of recently, so went and sat in the other room.

Dinner was conducted in semi silence once again, and the next day she made a tumultuous and life changing decision, and packed her bags and booked a ferry back to Port de Vacquelin. She had had enough of being used, of being manipulated and being cheated on. She thought back to a few years ago when he was acting out of character and all the signs of adultery were there. "Are you sure he's not cheating on you, Miranda?" her friend had asked out of concern one night. She'd bitten her head off and then lost yet another decent friend. Steve had managed to drive a wedge between herself and many of her friends and she was not only sickened by Steve's romancing of other women but was now also very lonely. Finally she had had enough. She left Steve a note to say their relationship was over. feeling no remorse whilst writing it, and then she left it on the kitchen table and departed the house. "The solicitors can sort the rest of it," she thought to herself whilst putting on her favourite music in the car, "You can do this, Miranda!" she thought to herself and smiled.

Waiting back at Port de Vacquelin was her sister. Rann would be staying at Bijou now that the paperwork had been signed and the cottage handed over whilst Dahli continued to stay in her camper van at the restaurant. She was looking forward to helping her get it back to its glorious self, redecorating, painting, and buying new furniture. "Oh, how exciting" she thought. Dahli had no interest in renovations but Rann was an expert so Dahli was leaving the renovations in her capable hands. The house in Didsbury had been completely restyled by Rann, bringing in designers, builders and decorators to do the work. The house had been perfect in Rann's mind but she wasn't sure who would be able to help her in Port de Vacquelin. Dahli had no plans to vacate the camper van so Rann would be living there on her own for the time being. She would be able to work from the cottage and had plans to leave England for good and be based in France, just before Brexit kicked in. She was hoping that Dahli would not mind. The two of them had become much closer since she delivered the letter to her, and she hoped that this would be the beginning of a new chapter in their lives. She liked being at Bijou and hoped that Dahli would let her stay longer.

The two women celebrated Christmas 2018 together at the cottage. For the first time in many years the village had been promised a cold snap over the seasonal period and to their surprise they woke up to a freshly laid thick layer of crisp white snow. Dahli donned her boots and warm coat and dashed out the front door, holding a piping hot mug of mulled wine and wearing a Santa hat and Rann followed, laughing and sliding in her wellingtons along the path. There were many villagers out on the harbour front; families walking hand in hand, having snowball fights and skidding on the snow, and a few tourists down for the holiday season. The cafes and restaurants were closed but a young man was standing on the harbour front selling hot chestnuts and coffee, pleased to be making some money over the quiet season. Dahli and Rann grabbed a bag of chestnuts and a coffee and walked along the front, sitting in the fishermans' hut, and taking in the sights. It was good to have a few days off before setting to work again. They had planned to pop in briefly to see Eric and Beulah and the new baby to take presents then sit down to a Christmas dinner together before retiring to the settee, drinking copious amounts of wine and eating boxes of chocolates. They would toast their mother together and remember all the happy Christmas Days they had spent together in Didsbury as children. There had been some good times amongst all the bad, and Dahli was keen to hold on to these memories.

A week later and Christmas seemed like a distant memory. Dahli had returned to the bakery and Rann was just finishing off securing some contract work via a Teams call when there was a knock at the door. She closed the call, got up from the kitchen table where she was working, and sauntered over to let whoever it was in, glass of wine in hand; after all, it was lunchtime and her online work colleagues would never know. She was expecting a man called Enrique who would help her choose some colours for the hallway and hopefully paint the whole cottage for her and Dahli. She opened the door and he smiled. "Bonjour Madame White. I'm Enrique, your painter-decorator." Miranda stood there and just gawped at him. Wow, she thought, he's gorgeous. He was young, maybe twenty-five, tall, blonde and blue eyed, very surfer-like, she thought. She pulled herself together. "Oh, sorry, yes please come in." she stuttered and he followed her into the kitchen and she wished she had put a little more makeup on. For two hours they looked at colour charts and talked about the plans for the cottage. He showed much enthusiasm but eventually he had to leave. "Goodbye Madame White and see you on Monday to start the work?" She agreed and bade him goodbye before sitting down, feeling flushed. Wow, she thought again, and he's going to be in my house for two weeks? Wow.

Monday soon came around and Enrique started work in the cottage. Every lunchtime they sat in the small courtyard or in the kitchen, Enrique with his small box of sandwiches and Miranda with various different salads that she superbly concocted each day to impress him. "Do you always eat salad, Miranda?" asked Enrique one day. "Oh yes, always healthy food." she said enthusiastically, hoping that a little white lie wouldn't do any harm. He looked at her, eyebrows raised, then she laughed. "Ok, so not always!" she admitted, sighed and he laughed at her. For two weeks their conversations were so easy. Enrique lived in the next village, lodging with his brother and sister-in-law whilst saving for his own house. He had been recommended by the plumber but sadly the two weeks flew by and then the work was completed. "Goodbye Miranda." he said and he shook her hand before getting in his van and driving away. Miranda felt unquestionably sad to see him go. She went to the fridge and grabbed an ice cold beer to cheer herself up.

Three days later Miranda was just going to the shops when Enrique's little van pulled up outside the front door. She assumed he had forgotten something and went out the front of the cottage to talk to him. "You, okay, Enrique? Is anything the matter?" she asked. "Please can we go inside for a minute, Miranda. I need to talk to you." he responded and she felt quite nervous. He followed her indoors and they sat at the kitchen table as they had for those two wonderful weeks. "Miranda, can I ask you a question?" He asked, and before she could reply he continued. "Would you like to go out with me tomorrow evening, to a lovely little fish restaurant up the coast? It's my favourite and I am sure that you would like it too." She sat there blushing and completely gobsmacked. "Really, you want to take me out?" she said confused, and then realised she may have sounded a little rude. He smiled, surprised by her response. "Well, yes, of course. I want to take you out, Miranda. You are great company and also very beautiful. " She opened her eyes wide in amazement. "Wow, yes, Enrique. Tomorrow? Yes, that would be lovely."

She felt sick in her stomach from nerves. Miranda hadn't been on a date since she was sixteen when she first met Steve. Back then it had been a trip to the cinema followed by takeaway fish and chips and a can of coke from Tony's chip shop. Steve had had little experience with girls and he was awkward and shy. Miranda grimaced remembering the first kiss and how Steve had slobbered over her face like a wet fish. It had been ungainly and a little sickening. She looked at Enrique and imagined their first kiss, if and when it happened, to be very different. "I will pick you up at 7pm, Miranda. It is a casual restaurant so you can wear jeans or whatever you feel comfortable in." His English was broken but sincere and he left her on the doorstep, waving at him like a giddy child.

Miranda rang Dahli and told her her news, and Dahli screamed like a banshee and teased her. "Yahoo, Rann, you're in love with your painter. Enrique and Rann, Rann and Enrique!". Rann berated her jokingly and put the phone down with her heart pounding. The next evening Enrique picked Miranda up and they drove the fifteen minutes to Pais-En-Bois, a delightful seaside village, similar to Port de Vacquelin but smaller. There were only four restaurants in the village and Enrique's favourite restaurant was heaving but they had been reserved a quiet table in the corner. "Bonjour, monsieur. I hope you are well. Here is the menu. We have the two or three course plat du jour or the specials board." Enrique ordered wine and Miranda browsed the menu excitedly. Tonight was going to be very special, she thought. The meal was delicious and they talked endlessly and effortlessly. Miranda couldn't believe how happy and comfortable she could be with a man again, and so soon after leaving England and Steve.

They got back in the car and Enrique drove the short journey back to Port de Vacquelin. He pulled up outside and they looked at each other before Miranda opened the car door. "Goodbye, Enrique and thank you for a lovely evening." She kissed him on the cheek and stood up but then stopped still and had a thought. "Would you like to come in for a drink?" she said, then realised what she had just said may have sounded a little forward. "Just a drink, Enrique." She quickly corrected herself and smiled. "Yes I would love to, Miranda." and they went into the house and sat in the living room with glasses of wine. Miranda put on some chilled music and they snuggled up together, Miranda leaning into Enrique who kissed her lovingly on the top of the head. She closed her eyes when Enrique cupped her cheeks in his hand, gently pulled her towards him and kissed her on the mouth. She gasped, feeling the emotion and passion through her whole body. They parted and Enrique put his arm around her. One thing led to another and the night ended with them going upstairs to Miranda's bedroom.

The next morning Miranda woke before Enrique grabbing her dressing gown, roughly tying it around her waist and sat in the kitchen, toast in hand. Enrique appeared and grabbed the toast off her, pulling a silly face and laughing. She giggled and went to grab it back when he pushed her down on the kitchen table, loosening her dressing gown then caressing her body with his hands and kissing her. "Oh, Miranda you are heavenly." he groaned, aroused by her beauty but suddenly there was a knock at the door. "Damn!" said Miranda, quickly jumping up off the table and tying her dressing gown. "No, leave it," whispered Enrique, pulling at her gown and she was tempted to but whoever it was persistent, knocking again and louder this time. "Sorry Enrique." said Miranda and he pulled back from her and ran upstairs whilst she answered the door. Miranda opened the door and there stood a little old man with a white cap on his head and wearing a boiler suit. "Hello, are you Mrs Smythe?" he asked. "Well yes I am, can I help you?" she replied. "Yes, I am Monsieur Lavigne. I have a 10am appointment to inspect your boiler?" he said, seeming a little unsure of himself. Damn, thought Miranda, she had totally forgotten about the appointment. "Yes, sorry, please come in. The boiler is in the kitchen at the back of the cottage. Please go and take a look whilst I get dressed. I will put the kettle on as soon as possible."

She was flustered and embarrassed by her lack of her usual poise and her clothes. Still undressed at 10am, what was she thinking? The little old man wandered into the kitchen and started to get his tools out of his bag. Meanwhile Miranda could hear Enrique upstairs; his footsteps were heavy on the wooden floor in the bedroom. She ran upstairs and grabbed him, pushing him back into the bedroom. They fell on the bed and he kissed her passionately again. "No, no you must go Enrique!" she cried, trying to resist him. She didn't feel comfortable being with Enrique with someone else in the house. He stood up and smiled. "I will see you again, then? " he asked and she nodded. "I'll ring you!" she replied and literally pushed him downstairs and out the front door. She closed the door and leant back against it, relieved. She suddenly remembered that she had offered tea to the boiler man so went back into the kitchen to find he had already made himself a drink. She was surprised by his forwardness but also pleased, meaning that she could go back upstairs, shower and get dressed.

Miranda enjoyed many more dates with Enrique over the next few months but had yet to meet his family so one day she found herself in his village so decided to pop in and see him. She knew he was not working as it was a Sunday and she felt she knew him well enough now to be able to turn up unannounced. She parked her car outside his brother's house and wandered up the front path, ringing the doorbell. There was a pause before the door was opened by a young woman. "Hello, can I help you?" Miranda assumed it was his brother's wife. "Hello. Yes, I wondered if Enrique was here. I'm Miranda." she replied. The young woman looked a little puzzled, not recognising Miranda but smiled. "Please, come in. I'll just get him. He's just out in the garden with Simon. Are you a friend of Enrique's" she enquired and Miranda felt a little uncomfortable. Had he not mentioned her to his family? She waited dutifully, twiddling her hair and looking at her shoes. Who was Simon too, she wondered? Perhaps it was his brother. She decided to walk through to the kitchen whilst she waited, and in the garden she could see Enrique sitting with a young man, his arm draped around him. Oh god, they weren't just friends, she thought.

Her blood ran cold. She turned around and went back to her car, driving away before anyone could stop her. Was she being silly? She didn't know. She arrived back home, threw the keys on the coffee table and sat back on the sofa, fretting for a short while before picking up the phone and ringing Enrique's number. He answered. "Hello, Miranda." he said but she didn't answer straight away. "Be honest with me Enrique, are you seeing a man?" There was no answer for a while then he spoke slowly. "Yes, he's my husband. We have an open relationship. I can still see you." Miranda could not believe what she was hearing. Enrique's idea of a relationship was unusual to say the least. "No, Enrique. I won't be with someone who is also with someone else. Goodbye." she said, putting the phone down. Unlike Steve's betrayal, she didn't scream or cry. She felt indifferent. The relationship had been a bit of fun, lots of sex and a good excuse to let her hair down. He had made her feel young and sexy again. She got up and grabbed another beer from the fridge before putting on the television and watching a good horror movie. She rang Dahli who said, "Better luck next time and try not to pick the married gay!" and they both laughed like crazy.

Chapter Forty

Dahli was aware that she hadn't spoken to Joe for a few weeks but she had attended Emille's funeral and was keeping away from social activities, feeling regrettably blue but she couldn't get him out of her head. One evening she found herself perched on the end of the bed really not sure what to do about him. They were conversing more and more now and gone were the texts and the short messages, replaced with hour long telephone calls late at night and Zoom calls. She felt close to him again and really wanted to see him but she was working long hours in the bakery and Joe the same in the restaurant. She decided to put him out of her mind and reached for the box of letters that Emille had left her on her passing. She placed it in front of her and carefully opened it. Her heart skipped a beat when she saw the letters again, beautifully preserved. There were so many of them but being short on time, she decided to just read the final one tucked away at the bottom of the box. She delved into the box and took the letter out and unfolded it.

Didsbury
October 2017

Dear Emille,

Thank you for your letter and I am pleased that you are recovering well from your hip replacement and enjoying life at Little Acres. I have not been so good recently and this may be one of the last letters for the moment. The cancer has started to spread to my liver and lungs, and the consultant is not sure that my body can take much more chemo or radiotherapy. My days are disappearing before me, Emille!

I have felt much regret these last months. Regret for Dahli and Christian. Should I have told them about their father, about each other? I really don't know but I hope that one day they will find each other perhaps through the keys to Bijou that I will leave in my will to my darling Dahli. Perhaps they will find you too? I would like to think so. You would love Dahli. She is so spirited and reminds me of myself when I was much younger before the pregnancy, before Ian. There are so many things in my life that I wish I had done differently. If only I hadn't met Ian. I mustn't feel like this, must I, Emille?

I have had some lighter days with Miranda and Steve, who are looking after me whilst juggling their own lives. We went for a lovely afternoon tea at Betty's tea shop in York the other day. It was rather posh. They are so kind. I hope to see Dahli again but she has been away for so long and I always miss her.

Take care, Emille. Miss you and love you as always.
Regards
Mathilde xxx

Dahli put the letter back in its envelope and lit another cigarette. This was the final letter between the two women, the end of an era and their friendship. Dahli felt a certain sadness and empathy for Emille who would have known that she was losing her friend; an undeniably resilient and long lasting relationship through the decades. It was now apparent, reading through the letters, that Mathilde had visited Frank sometime just before his death and had handed over the keys to Bijou, though Dahli was uncertain when. She thought long and hard, trying to work out when the meeting must have taken place. Did her mother go abroad sometime? She couldn't fathom out when however Rann would surely know. She wished that she had known about Frank and Christian sooner though what has been, has been, she thought. She couldn't dwell on it and must now concentrate on building a relationship with dear Christian and Amelie. He seems such a sensitive soul, heavily reliant on Amelie in many ways. Being adopted must be difficult, thought Dahli.

She curled up in bed, after making a mug of cocoa and fell fast asleep. The next day was a beautiful April day and she had planned a visit that afternoon to see Beulah so she took her coat, wrapped up well and made the short walk down to the bakery. The Spring bulbs were starting to peep their heads above the soil, with a splash of colour here and there. Eric and Beulah's baby girl was now three months old. They had named her Isobella Dahli Thomasina Smythe. A bit of a mouthful thought Dahli but was pleased when they called her Izzy for short. She felt honoured too to have a child named after her.

Beulah was sitting as usual in her favourite armchair, breastfeeding Izzy, looking content. She was such a good mum and although always exhausted, motherhood suited her. Eric, too, was happier and calmer; Dahli was managing the bakery well and everything was running smoothly. "Hey Dahli, how are you? Please come in and help yourself to a drink." said Beulah. Dahli looked at Izzy and felt a warmth come over her. She felt a strange yearning that she had never experienced before. Izzy melted her heart and she just wanted to hold her close and gaze into her dark brown eyes. "Do you want a cuddle, Dahli?" asked Beulah, noticing her affection for her daughter, and Dahli sat down beside them both and cradled the tiny bundle in her arms. So this is how it feels to be a mother, she thought. She could not believe how she was feeling. She had always dismissed babies and children as someone else's complication but now she sat there almost wishing that she could have had her own child or even children. She sighed, believing that it was too late now at thirty nine years old.

The two of them chatted endlessly, laughing and joking, with Dahli telling Beulah about Joe. "Well you must go and see him. You just seem to be acting like passing ships. About time you dropped anchor and went aboard!" and Beulah laughed heartily. Dahli was again not so sure. Why would Joe now want a relationship, after all he was concentrating on becoming a restaurateur? Surely a relationship would be too much of a distraction for him? She so wanted to see him in the flesh but maybe they had just been a drunken one night stand. Dahli was keen to change the subject, and noticed a pile of old envelopes sitting higgledy piggledy on the coffee table. She looked at them and Beulah noticed. "Ah, do you remember those, Dahli? The letters that we found with the old photo in the loft. Eric got them out and we wondered if Christian would be interested in translating them for us? I think they would be of interest to him as it was his grandfather." "Well I can only ask him. Sure he would be." Dahli replied.

Joe was feeling hot and overwhelmed. Working in a busy Parisian restaurant was very different to the slower pace of Port de Vacquelin. His shift was almost over and the head chef came over to him unexpectedly and he smiled nervously, "Joe please sit down here. You are doing well, Joe. The food you are creating is very good and especially the Normandy specialities. We are very pleased with you. Keep up the good work!" the chef shouted and then went back to cooking and bawling instructions to the sous chefs. Joe felt a glow, a certain pride and beamed. The night was finally over and he wandered slowly back to his accommodation. The owner of the restaurant had fixed him up with a modest one bedroomed apartment above the confectionary shop next door. It was small but comfortable, with a glimpse of the Eiffel Tower from the front window if you leaned far over to the right and stood on your tiptoes. He had been there for over a month and settling well into a hectic lifestyle. The hours were long but he was learning quickly. He would have his restaurant yet, he thought. He thought of Dahli and hoped that they could soon meet.

As the months passed it turned from spring to summer and the days were starting to get warmer and longer. Dahli opened the door of her van stretching in the warmth of the morning. She reached for her cigarette tin and stepped down, leaning against the door to steady herself. She had a bit of a muzzy head from drinking a little too much with her sister the night before. They were semi celebrating Rann's new found love for life and men, Rann having had a series of short relationships since Enrique, and it had been a riotous night at the karaoke over in the campsite. Dahli lit a cigarette and sat, idling away a few hours before she needed to go shopping in the village. She had nothing in but didn't want to spend all day shopping on her day off. She hated shopping, be it for food or clothes. She had denounced consumerism many years ago leaving it all behind to live in her van. She was enjoying her new life in Port de Vacquelin; it seemed to suit her lifestyle, quiet and uncomplicated.

She smiled and breathed in slowly and deeply, calming her senses and relaxing her body. She wondered how Rann was. She had drunk plenty and staggered back down to the cottage. She hoped for the best for her sister. She had suffered an arduous few months, separating from Steve, leaving her home in Didsbury and having to consider some huge life decisions but Dahli was confident that Rann would survive and thrive. She checked her phone. She had a free weekend coming up and wanted to see if Joe wanted to meet up. She sent him a text and got a positive response. "Paris, here I come then!" she said to herself and started packing the van ready for the journey in a few days.

Chapter Forty-One

Paris was full of excitement; the streets were busy, people shopping, sightseeing, sitting in street cafes and picnicking in the many parks. Dahli felt alive, and although she loved the tranquillity of Port de Vacquelin she also loved the craziness of Paris. She wondered if she could ever live in such a place or was the quieter life more suited to her demeanour these days? She wasn't sure. She wasn't sure of anything at the moment. She stepped down from the van and Joe came up behind her and grabbed her waist. "Hello!" he shouted eagerly and she turned around and kissed him on the cheek. They were pleased to see each other after such a long time and not seeing each other had made them grow unexpectedly closer. That evening they wandered into the city, Joe keen to take Dahli to some of his favourite restaurants and clubs and for Dahli to have the whole Paris foodie experience. They stopped off at a couple of cafes for a few drinks before heading to a French restaurant, recommended originally by Joe's head chef and often frequented by Joe on his nights off.

The restaurant was brimming with people and noisy, not quite what Dahli expected, having pictured a small, quaint side street restaurant being more Joe's style. "You'll love the food here. I have been talking to the head chef about taking some lessons with him. He makes the most inventive and creative French and European cuisine that you have seen or tasted. It's art on a plate." though Dahli was most surprised when the food arrived. Teeny portions of something green, something yellow and something red and just about enough to feed a flea. She hoped that it would taste better than it looked and hoped Joe wasn't planning on serving this sort of food up in his restaurant. The wine flowed though and Joe and Dahli enjoyed each other's company despite the food, their closeness brinking on the edge of something more fulfilling, maybe something more substantial. They often held each other's gaze throughout the evening and Dahli giggled endlessly like a child. At the end of the evening Joe took Dahli's hand and kissed it affectionately. "Thank you Senorita, for a beautiful evening." Dahli looked at Joe then instantly kissed him on the mouth, long and seductively. He responded and they eventually ended up making love in Joe's apartment.

The next morning Dahli had to leave to go back to Port de Vacquelin. They had again crossed the friendship barrier but again Dahli had other things to do. Early that morning they had made love one more time but Dahli had dressed quickly and said a brief goodbye, promising to keep in touch. "Au revoir, my fuck buddy!" she had thrown at him as she left, waving goodbye. "Is that all she thinks of me, a fuck buddy!?" Joe was incensed, and Dahli immediately kicked herself for what she said. "Damn!" she thought as she flew down the stairs and back to the van. The drive back to Port de Vaacquelin was uncomfortable. Had she just offended and then lost Joe for a second time? When will she ever learn? She found him insatiable but was struggling to commit any sort of relationship with him. Over the coming months their relationship started to teeter out, the long phone calls almost reduced to a few minutes and the Zoom calls non-existent, Joe still reeling from Dahli's comments and Dahli unable to find a way to resolve the situation. She threw herself into work and tried to put the thought of Joe to one side but she just couldn't.

Dahli had kept in constant touch with her brother, Christian however their communication had lapsed for a while so she decided to ring him one evening. The phone went to answer phone and she rang again a few days later but again no reply. She was just about to start her shift at the bakery one morning when she got a call from Amelie. "Hi Amelie, how are you?" she said but Amelie sounded stressed. "Hi Dahli. Have you been trying to reach Christian? I have news for you. He's not here." She stopped for a moment and Dahli felt a touch concerned. "Is everything okay?" she asked. "Well, sort of, Yes and no. Christian has left to go to Moscow for three months... on a wellbeing retreat. He's done it before. You see, Dahli. Christian is a sensitive person. Doesn't deal with strong emotions well. He's had difficulty dealing with the news about his mother, Frank and you. Life has thrown so much at him, being adopted and all that. He just needed to go and find some peace, some answers."

Dahli was shocked. He seemed to be coping so well, cheerful on the phone in recent months, sounded so together and upbeat. "Gosh, I'm really surprised and shocked to hear this. Are you okay, Amelie?" There was a pause. "No, not really." she admitted. "I wondered if I could come to Port de Vacquelin. I need a break. My mother will have the children for a week starting next Monday. Would that be okay?" Dahli smiled. "Of course it is! We would be happy to see you, Amelie. We can talk more then." Amelie hung up and Dahli felt very guilty. She hadn't known anything about Christian's character, hadn't considered his sensitivities, wading in with her big size nines, recklessly throwing all that information about her mother and Frank at him and then expecting him to absorb it all. She had been tactless to say the least. She wanted to talk to him but wait, no, wait to see Amelie first.

Amelie arrived in Port de Vacquelin looking harassed. She met Dahli and Rann at Bijou and flung herself on the sofa. "Wine?" shouted Dahli from the kitchen and Amelie laughed before answering, "Oh yes!" She had had an emotional few months since Dahli arrived in France. The disclosures had rocked her family's secure, stable life and Christian had suffered constant wakeless nights and bad dreams. He had booked into the retreat located in a forest just outside of Moscow as a last resort to clear his head of the demons that were encroaching on his daily life, and as Amelie later told Dahli, "It was either that or the nut house." Amelie sat drinking her wine, her usual colourful personality dulled and worry etched on her forehead. She had booked into a hotel up the road but Rann offered her a place to stay at the cottage. "Why don't you stay here, nice and cosy, we will look after you for the week. You need a rest." Amelie looked meekly at her, and agreed it was a great idea. "Can I ask, is Christian contactable at all?" Dahli chipped in. Amelie shook her head. "Only in emergencies. They take their phones off them when they first get there. It's pretty punitive. I talk to him every third day though. It's been hard on the children. They are too young to understand. Can anyone understand this though? Even I'm struggling." She said wistfully. Dahli could see her pain. "Why don't we go to our favourite restaurant on the harbour front? Let's chill out, and eat and drink!!" chirped Dahli, Amelie smiled excitedly. "Oh, that sounds like the perfect tonic. Thank you."

The restaurant was quiet and the three women ordered a bottle of wine and perused the menu. Whilst Amelie was choosing her meal, Dahli mentioned the letters. "Amelie, we were hoping that Christian would translate the letters for Eric and Beulah." Amelie shook her head and said it would not be possible at this time however Christian had colleagues that she was sure could assist. That evening Dahli gave Amelie the letters in the vain hope that they would be translated and not forgotten about. She was concerned for Amelie's mental state as well as her obviously physically weakened body. The week away had done her good but her troubles were far from over. The next few days were more restful for Amelie and the break had helped and then she left for Paris with a slightly brighter outlook and thanked Dahli and Rann for their hospitality though Dahli was still feeling unsure about her involvement in Christian's downfall.

Chapter Forty-Two

Amelie arrived back home that evening, and walked through the doorway into their small apartment. It was cold and dark, and silent. She hated the silence. She missed her husband more than life itself, and she missed having her children with her. She sat down and started to unpack her suitcase. At the bottom were the letters. She took one and opened it; a beautifully written letter but Amelie couldn't read Russian so she returned it to its envelope. She knew exactly who would be able to translate the letters; Raphael. He was a young postgraduate Russian language student who Christian had much admiration for. She would visit him in the morning with the letters. She rang Christian and he gave her permission to share the letters with Raphael and wished Amelie well.. It was a relief. The next morning she left the apartment at 10am and walked the short distance to the university. It was a beautiful Gothic building, architecturally ornate and well preserved. About 15,000 students from across the world studied here and Christian loved his work and his environment. She walked through the impressive stone archway and into a large courtyard which she slowly crossed, admiring its splendour. Students were crowding, dawdling and conversing. What it must be like to be so carefree, Amelie thought, remembering that she had to pick the children up from their grandma's at 5pm sharp. They would be overexcited, hyperactive and full of chocolate no doubt but so loved by their grandparents who had helped Amelie out during this difficult time.

Raphael sat behind his desk, typing furiously then squinting at the text on his laptop. Amelie tapped gently on the door and he looked up, then smiled warmly when he saw her, "Welcome, Amelie, how can I help you?" he asked, standing and holding out his hand. They shook hands and sat together. "As you know Christian is taking some time off for his health." Amelie said. "But I have some letters that I would like translating that I have come to possess. They are letters between Christian's grandfather and another man who we do not know. They date back to 1920. I was hoping that maybe you could translate them for me? I will pay you of course.!". Raphael was very pleased to have been asked. "Of course, and no need to pay me. I will come around your apartment, say tomorrow evening?" Amelie looked at him a little surprised but agreed to meet him. She had never had another man in the apartment without Christian present and it would feel strange but she trusted Raphael and his presence made her feel happy. He was a good looking and charming young man and maybe she had a little crush on him though she tried to push her feelings to the back of her mind.

The next evening Raphael arrived with a bottle of wine in hand. He was a relaxed and confident young man and Amelie felt a little excited at his presence. "I bring wine for you, Amelie. I hope you do not mind." She nodded and welcomed him into her home whereupon he sat on the sofa and smiled at her. She poured some wine and placed a bowl of nibbles on the table before passing him the letters. He thanked her and then watched her as she sat down beside him. The letters intrigued him immediately as they were so old. "Wow, from 1920. One hundred years old and well kept." He looked at the front of the envelopes. "They are from Constantinople, or Istanbul as we know it now."

He opened the envelope and started to read the first letter. He smiled. "They are from a Mr Konstantin Babanin. Let me read the first letter, Amelie." Raphael began to read the letter and Amelie's face lit up. For the next few hours they drank wine and Raphael read letter after letter. They couldn't believe the detail, the story of Dahli and Christian's grandfather's early life was played out before them; his life in Petrograd, the move to Paris, the poverty and tragedies, his meeting Svetlana and the move to Port de Vacquelin. Christian would be so happy, thought Amelie. Then also the Babanin's new life in Paris. She couldn't wait to tell Christian about the letters, if she only could get to talk to him properly. Phone calls to the retreat were restricted to only five minutes every few days. It was punishing on her but she was enjoying relaxing with Raphael and the wine was helping to relieve the stress that she had been feeling. There were a total of fifty-three letters from Konstantin which suddenly stopped in 1940 and after this time they were all from Konstantin's wife.

Paris, June 1940

Dear Otto and Svetlana,
I hope this letter finds you both well. I have some sad news for you. Unfortunately I

received a telegram to say that dear Konstantin had been killed in action on May 6th. As you can imagine it has been a terrible time since receiving this news. They have yet to find his body but they expect he was blown up in a grenade attack on the battlefield. They found his ID tag laying on the ground. We will miss him terribly. What a travesty but it was always the risk he took. We take comfort in knowing that he died for his country.

We hope that we can see you sometime soon. It is hard in Paris with the food shortages and the shutdowns each night. We are okay but I know people who are struggling. We have managed to keep the restaurant open most evenings and there is still some normality. I have no plans to give up the restaurant. We are happy here, despite all things.

Love as always

Maria, Ava and Daniel

Amelie wasn't sure if it was the effects of the wine or the emotion present in each and every letter but she found herself crying inconsolably at Konstantin's untimely death. Raphael put his arm around her. "It's okay, Amelie. It's hard. We feel we know Konstantin and now he is dead." She wiped her eyes and pulled away feeling a little uncomfortable being so close to him. "Sorry, Raphael, I'm being silly." He smiled at her warmly and she suddenly moved in close and kissed him on the lips. He responded and they kissed for a long time before she pulled away, shocked and flustered. "Gosh, I'm so sorry. I don't know what came over me." she cried. "I've never done anything like this before." He laughed. "We maybe both needed that, Amelie. Don't worry. It's okay." he said and stood up ready to leave. He caught Amelie as she wobbled slightly on rising. They both giggled, both a little drunk. Raphael kissed her lightly on both cheeks and said his goodbyes. "I will translate all the letters and send you a transcription. Christian will be most pleased." He smiled and left, Amelie watching him from the window as he walked down the street. She felt alive inside from the passionate embrace and then thought of her husband and winced.

A week later and the transcription arrived via email. Amelie was taken aback thinking of the amount of time that Raphael must've spent transcribing each and every letter. She started to write an email thanking him for his time. She signed the email off, re-read it then spontaneously decided to add another sentence. "If you would like to go for a meal sometime, please let me know, as a thank you." She re-read the sentence then paused. She angst over whether or not she should be inviting him out for dinner. On reflection she chose to delete the sentence and in effect end their relationship. It seemed wrong to be dining with another man when her husband was recuperating from his mental discomforts. She sat back and thought of Raphael; gorgeous, sexy, intelligent and young. She was sure that he would have encouraged their friendship but she was married and had to stop it. She felt disappointed. She cursed and pressed "send". "Goodbye Raphael, and thank you." she whispered to herself and then sent the transcriptions immediately to Dahli.

Beulah had set a date to return to the bakery; exactly one year after she gave birth she would be back at work and she was feeling a little nervous. She would no longer need the services of her friend, Dahli however didn't mind. She was happy to have Beulah back where she belonged and she had no plans except to possibly return to England, either to just visit friends or permanently. She fancied travelling again in the camper van but who really knew. Dahli had always been a free spirit. The day of Beulah's return arrived and Dahli and the girls had decked the bakery out with a sign saying "Welcome back, Beulah!", balloons and lots of cakes and many of the village had come to see her. Beulah walked carefully downstairs blindfolded by Eric, giggling like a teenager, then he pulled it off and everyone shouted, "Welcome back, Beulah!" and on seeing the decorations she burst into tears, overwhelmed by such kindness. Glasses of non alcoholic fizz, after all it was 8.30am in the morning, and orange juice was passed around and much cake was consumed. "Come on everyone, let's get back to work!" shouted Beulah after a while, and everyone laughed and Izzy giggled and smiled in her arms. Izzy was now to be cared for by a part time nanny and attend a local nursery but with plenty of visits to the bakery throughout the day.

The bakery started to empty and Marianne and the two young girls started laying the tables, placing the menus carefully in their plastic holders and filling small vases with freshly cut flowers. The coffee machine bubbled away and a number of people stayed for drinks and croissants chattering happily. Beulah stood back against the counter and put on her apron, ready for the day. She smiled to herself and went back to wiping tables and making coffee. She was back at her favourite place. Rann had arrived a little late and sat down, flustered and red in the face. "I'm so sorry, Beulah. I had an emergency work meeting. Welcome back." She quipped and ordered some breakfast. Dahli sat down with her as she took off her coat. Rann was still living in the cottage and had been in charge of its complete renovation and redecoration. It had taken some time and was finished in just under a year. "Dahli, what are you going to do now your work here has finished?" asked Rann, convinced that she would want to move into Bijou now that the renovation was completed. "I don't know, Rann. Maybe I will go back to the UK, either temporarily or permanently. What about you?" Rann swished the coffee grains around in her cup. "Well, I need a permanent base, Dahli. Would you, possibly, consider selling Bijou to me? I want to stay in Port de Vacquelin. It feels like home."

She was hesitant in her words and she looked at Dahli who suddenly was wide eyed and a little surprised. The moment had caught her off guard. "Gosh, Rann, I really haven't given it any thought. I mean, it's possible. I don't know." Dahli scowled and Rann, seeing her sister confused, continued. "Look, you don't need to make any hasty decisions but if you want to, I would happily buy it. I'll keep renting it for the time being, if that's okay with you?" She smiled warmly and Dahli also smiled, comforted by her sister's agreeable words and she was pleased that there was no reason for her to make any snap decisions. Dahli finished her coffee and walked out into the bright sunshine. She felt as if a huge part of her life had just finished, working at the bakery, the completion of the cottage, and her probable relationship with Joe. She felt that everyone around had their lives mapped out, they had a future, but again Dahli didn't feel that way about her own life. Though not too worried, she was starting to feel a little distant from her family and friends and every time she had felt like this in the past she had up sticks and moved on. How often could she keep running away? She was nearly forty years old. Surely she should be settling somewhere. She sighed and wandered down to the harbour front, sat on a bench and watched the fishermen mending their nets. It was peaceful, the air was clean and the sun was trying to force its way through wispy clouds. Port de Vacquelin had stolen her heart and she would miss its tranquillity if she decided to move back to England.

Chapter Forty-Three

Christian came back home after three months in Moscow. Amelie made a huge effort to welcome him back but he had changed however she hoped that it would be a temporary change in his character but as the weeks progressed he became more and more elusive. He started to spend more time away in his office at work, or up in the bedroom, reading or on his laptop. Amelie had to say something. She couldn't let her marriage, the one that had been tried and tested to its limits recently, just fritter away. She suddenly thought of Raphael and fantasised about a life with him, the fun, the laughs. She shook herself free of the thought and called upstairs to Christian. "Christian, please can you come down. I need to talk to you." He appeared, looking drawn and tired, his eyes bloodshot. "Yes, Amelie." he said and they sat in the kitchen. "Christian, we can't go on like this. You have become a stranger to me. You spend most of your time when you are not at work, in the bedroom, doing your things. I need a marriage." Amelie sounded frustrated and her voice broke. Christian looked at her sheepishly. "I will make an effort for you." he replied but she was angry. "No, you shouldn't have to make an effort. You should want to be with me." She retorted, folding her arms and frowning. He looked away from her then down at the table. "I don't think I can, Amelie. I don't think I can have a relationship with you or anyone."

Amelie was shocked and upset. She stood up and pointed at Christian defiantly. "Well if that's how you feel then get out of the house. Just go." she screamed at him. "I have had to put up with so much crap over the last few months. You'll never know how hard it has been. Having to carry on, look after the kids, keep life normal going whilst you swanned around in some fancy retreat. I've had enough of this, of you!" Without saying anything, Christian got up and went back upstairs. Amelie sat on the settee, adrenalin surging around body. She could hear him moving around upstairs and then he appeared by her side with suitcase in hand. "Goodbye Amelie, I am going to stay in a hotel for a week or so, then make arrangements. I'm sorry Amelie, I truly am." He walked out the front door in silence and started to walk down the stairs. Amelie got up quickly and picked up a cushion and threw it at him in disgust. "Good riddance!" she shouted after him but he just ignored her and carried on walking.

Amelie went back inside, sat down and burst into tears. What was she going to tell the children, her parents, her friends? She was so angry, reeling from her husband's actions. How dare he, she thought. She poured a glass of wine and sat and put the television on, trying to blot out the vexation that she felt. On impulse she decided to email Raphael. She opened her laptop and clicked on her emails. She clicked "Compose" and addressed an email.

Dear Raphael,
To say thank you, could I take you out for a meal this week?
Thank you
Amelie.

She pressed send and sat back and waited. She knew that Raphael was often at his computer at work and she hoped that he would respond quickly. She felt nervous and exhilarated and the thought of a relationship with Raphael quickened her pulse. She tried to put Christian to the back of her mind but he was still there, nagging at her sensibility. "No!" she thought. "Christian doesn't deserve me!" A minute later an email notification pinged at her. Raphael had responded.

Dear Amelie
Thank you for your email. I am not sure that we should meet again. I would be afraid that I couldn't stop myself kissing you, and you are married to my colleague, Christian. Let's leave it at that if that's okay.
Kind regards
Raphael

Amelie felt rejected and shocked by the reality check. She had been sure that he would say yes. She wanted to write back and tell Raphael that her marriage was over and that he could kiss her over and over, and that they were free to do as they pleased but she knew they weren't. She suddenly felt lonely and vulnerable, wanting some comfort and love.

She was still married, in a complicated situation. She reluctantly emailed back.

Dear Raphael
Thank you. I enjoyed our time together.
All the best
Amelie

Again she shut the relationship down. She felt so foolish but also somehow relieved. She had just avoided a messy situation. She needed to pick the children up from nursery soon so she closed her laptop, popped on her coat and headed out the door.

Christian unpacked his small suitcase and sat on a wooden chair in his hotel room. He felt the sadness of the quietness that surrounded him and closed his eyes, breathing in sharply. He had learnt to meditate on the retreat which had given him much comfort during the frequent panic attacks that he had experienced and he focussed on his breathing, deepening each intake of air, calming his swirling emotions. He was interrupted by his phone ringing and he looked at its screen, it was Amelie. "Amelie, hello." he said, his voice deadpan. "Christian, please come home. This isn't over. We can work it out." She said, her voice despairing. He wanted to, he wanted her, he wanted his children but was afraid. "I don't know Amelie, I'm not ready for the turbulence of home life. I need space to find a place for myself in this world. I'm afraid and vulnerable. That's why I hide away." He started to cry on the phone. "I'm coming to get you. Where are you?" she said and Christian told her the address and within twenty minutes she was waiting for him in the reception with the children. He walked slowly down the stairs and on seeing his family waiting for him, he rushed over, dropped his suitcase and hugged them all tightly. "I love you all." he shouted to them. After some time they walked to the car and went back to the apartment. Later that evening after the children were put to bed Amelie sat with her husband. "We need to have some help, Christian, Perhaps some counselling or therapy. I know of someone who Justine used. It might help?" He nodded slowly and agreed.

"Joe, please see me after the shift in the office," the head chef called to him one evening, and Joe felt nervous once again to be alone in the company of this celebrated man and later that evening he found himself sitting opposite him, a glass of water in hand, nervously tapping his knee with his fingers. The chef leaned in and spoke. "You have done it, Joe. You have passed the tests and shown true grit in our industry. You want your restaurant? You go and get it my son. You can of course stay here but I suggest you grab the opportunity to lease a decent little restaurant in the eighth arrondissement. Good clientele, popular and profitable. Here are the details, Joe. Good luck!" Joe looked at him slightly astonished though he knew was nearly there, nearly ready. He looked down at the piece of paper that the chef had placed on the table next to him. There was a small colour photograph of a restaurant called "Bijou ", some details and the rental price. Not bad, he thought. For some time he had been deliberating the cost of running his own place and Eric had been instrumental in advising him.

It was workable, he thought but there was only one thing that curbed his enthusiasm. Dahli. He had already been offered the opportunity to take over La Petite Grenouille in Port de Vacquelin as Jean was moving to Spain to run a beach bar and in his words, "For more sand, sea and sex!" He could go back to Port de Vacquelin and be with Dahli, be with her properly if she wanted that but he still didn't know. They had spent a wonderfully romantic weekend together but had avoided talking about their future, just casually saying goodbye and promising to stay in touch. Back to the phone and Zoom calls. Come on, Joe, do something about it, he chastised himself. He had one week to make a decision. This was going to be hard.

Joe's first thought was to ring Dahli and tell her the news. She was ecstatic and wished him well but Dahli was brooding, in more ways than one. She was hopelessly pining for Joe and still unnerved by her strong feelings for little Izzy. These feelings were new to her, controlling and almost disturbing. Should she tell Joe how she felt about him? It was a risk, a big risk but she thought, "Fuck it!" and Dahli decided to drive to Paris without telling him, impetuous in her ways as always. Late next morning she arrived in Paris, parked outside Joe's apartment and strapped her bum bag around her waist. She rang the buzzer and Joe answered. "Hi Joe, it's Dahli." There was a silence then Joe spoke. "Oh my God, hi Dahli. What the f...? What are you doing here? I'll let you in. Push the door." The door buzzed and opened and Dahli pushed it with force and ran up the stairs to Joe's. He was standing at the open door, smiling and Dahli grabbed her breath, mouthed hello and pulled off her bum bag. They went into the apartment and Dahli sat on the settee, making herself at home. "Tea, Dahli?" shouted Joe from the kitchen and Dahli laughed, then replied. "I am parched, Joe. Cheers! Sorry to arrive unannounced. I had a free few days." She tried to sound relaxed but she felt skittish.

A moment later they were perched on the settee together, drinking tea. "Dahli, I need to tell you something. It's really important."Joe said, "Look, I want to move back to Port de Vacquelin. I want to be with you, Dahli, or at least near you, as friends. I can take over the Grenouille and we can be together. We're good together. Oh hell, Dahli, I wish I knew how you felt." Joe thumped the end of the settee with his fist with frustration, and Dahli leant back on the settee and frowned. "But Joe, what about the Bijou? What about your dreams? No, I won't have it." She was promptly angry and she knew now was her final chance to say how she really felt about him.

She put her tea cup down and inhaled sharply. "Joe, you have to lease Bijou. You've spent a whole year training, working damned hard. No, this is your time." and then she stopped and drew breath. She stood up and walked over to the window, staring out at the city aspect. The sun was shining and the buildings gleamed in the warm golden rays. She wondered at the view, its magnificence and its bravery and then put her hand on the window as if to reach out to the city for help, whilst turning around. "Joe, I can't let you do this." she whispered then she slowly faced him and stared, her face ashen. "And I won't let you do this... alone." She smiled at him. "I want to stay in Paris, be with you and support your dreams. Let's see if we can make it work together." She gasped, surprised at her own words and her body crumpled slightly, the energy zapped from her body and Joe raced towards her, picked her up and swung her around, kissing her on the lips. He set her down and they continued to kiss. "You have made me so happy, Dahli. Really? Wow." They sat on the settee and Joe put his arm around her, anticipation pulsating through his body. "We're really doing this, Dahli." and with that they went back out into the sunshine and wandered through the streets, grabbed something to eat and talked about what was to come.

Chapter Forty-Four

January 2020

The new year was incredible for Dahli and Joe and there wasn't a moment to waste; there had been too many already. Joe's dream to own a restaurant was almost complete and the little restaurant in the eighth arrondissement had come through. Dahli was yet to set eyes on the restaurant having spent the last few weeks going back and forth to Port de Vacquelin to tie up loose ends and say goodbye to Beulah, Rann and her friends. It was a bittersweet ending to a wonderful time in the most beautiful of places and she promised to return as often as possible. There they were standing on the kerbside outside the bakery, snow lightly falling, and for one last time she stood and hugged her sister and Beulah, and they cried too many tears. "I will miss you Dahli, but you are doing the right thing." said Rann. "Joe is just the most amazing person and you will be very happy together. Thank you for selling Bijou to me too. It's been a dream come true." They hugged again and Dahli thanked her little sister. "Please come and visit me soon! I can't bear to be away from you." said Dahli and stepped up into the van almost reluctantly. Beulah, Eric and Izzy stood with Rann on the curb, waving like crazy and with the little girl blowing kisses. Rann couldn't believe that her sister was finally settling down. Crazy to think, she thought and Dahli, although incredibly sore leaving Rann, couldn't wait to be working alongside Joe, and being close to Christian and Amelie. She was excited that she finally had a future and something to plan for.

Rann had her decree nisi through from Steve and could start her life again. Finally she felt wholesome, no longer living in a state of emotional limbo. She had given up men for the time being, hoping to create a life not dependent on the male species and that evening Nicky and Sarah arrived for a week's holiday. Nicky was still at agricultural college and Sarah finished at finishing school in Nantes and living back in Didsbury with their father. Rann was pleased for Sarah, having secured work but had initially felt upset that she had decided to move back with her father but on reflection and the cost of renting, it had been a good decision for her. She could save for her own property or whatever she was planning to do with her future life. Nicky, who was still estranged from her father, was still to forgive him for his adultery. She saw everything in black and white but she may understand one day that life isn't like that, thought Miranda. Not long after Steve and Rann parted, the woman who she had seen falling through our door and kissing her husband moved in with him.. She was still there. People hurt each other. People make mistakes. Steve and Rann were on better terms these days and she had gotten past the pain and the grief and grown to accept that they were no longer compatible. Their time together had been wonderful but she had now admitted that they had grown apart. They had both moved on.

Although Rann had set up a very successful and lucrative business, she hoped that her girls would go out into the world and experience what it had to offer, rather than settle down at a young age with marriage and work like she had. However Sarah had news that would cause some upset and consternation, upending the dreams that Rann had for her children. The three of them had been shopping in Bayeux one morning, taking advantage of the good weather, and arrived back at the cottage late afternoon. Sarah sat on the sofa looking slightly unnerved and asked her mother to come and sit with her. "Mum, I have something I need to tell you," said Sarah nervously. She glanced at Nicky who looked worried for her. "Yes, my dear, what is the matter?" Rann said carrying on making the tea and casually arranging some chocolate biscuits on a plate. "Please mum, come and sit down." Sarah continued more insistently and held Rann's arm gently, leading her to the sitting room. Rann suddenly felt concerned by her daughter's unusual behaviour. "Mum, I'm sorry." said Sarah then for an instance just stared blankly at her mum, unsure how to say the words. "What is it, dear?" said Rann, trying to coax the words out of her daughter and Sarah carried on reticently. "I'm pregnant, mum. I'm so sorry." and she lifted her jumper and showed her little baby bump before burying her head in Rann's shoulder and sobbing. Rann felt faint. Her daughter, eighteen years old, was expecting a child. Aaaargh, she thought. She held Sarah in her arms and wiped her tears. "It will be okay, Sarah. You'll make it work." said Rann, trying to comfort her distraught daughter, but she knew that it could mean many sacrifices for her daughter at such a young age. Where would she live? How would she support herself? What about all those career dreams she talked about?

They drank coffee and talked all afternoon. The father was her ex-boyfriend, who, in her own words, "was a bit of a git. Immature to say the least." They laughed and Sarah was relieved to have told her mother. "Will you stay with your father, Sarah?" asked Rann. Sarah shook her head. "Yes and no mum...Dad and Janey are being wonderful and have said I can stay but I plan to travel once the baby is old enough. I have been saving and Dad has given me some money. I want a camper van and see the world." Rann laughed to herself; how wrong could she be about limitations; Sarah had always been a chip off Dahli's shoulder. They were similar in so many ways; courageous, outgoing, untroubled by what others thought of them. "Wow, Sarah, I wish you well. You must come and stay here you know and go and visit your aunty. We would all love to see you." Sarah nodded eagerly. Nothing would stop her and why should it.

March 2020

Just when everything was going to plan the world got sick and Paris locked down. It was March 17th 2020 and Dahli and Joe sat back on their settee exasperated and hugely concerned. "What do we do now, Dahli? We've got a restaurant and staff but no opening date. Worst still, we have no income." Joe said, worried sick. "We can apply for funding from the French government and we will soon have the funds from the sale of Bijou." said Dahli. and this would help carry them through what was looking like a tough few months. Dahli had never before shared anything of her own, had never needed to but for Joe she was willing to sacrifice some of her inheritance because she believed in him and in his business. They soldiered on through lockdown after lockdown, the restaurant finally opening but soon closing again. It was frustrating for Dahli and Joe especially as it was their first business. Finally after almost two years of uncertainty the restaurant opened permanently. It was a relief for the couple and at last they could define their future.

The restaurant was nestled between the men's Turkish barbers and an artisan butchers, opposite the imposing cathedral, opening nightly for French and in particular Normandy specialities; oysters, ciders, mutton, a Normandy version of haggis and apple tart with

Calvados. Joe's reputation as a young and vibrant chef was growing and people came from all over the city, the country and even the world to taste his delights. The restaurant, though small, was contemporary and casual, in muted tones, with chic furniture and eco-friendly practices, offering a memorable dining experience and on a regular basis restaurant owners tried to lure Joe away with the promise of high pay and prestige but he was not tempted. He loved his restaurant and his life with Dahli. "Maybe one day, Dahli but not now." he would say each time.

It was a few months later when Dahli and Joe went to bed as normal. Life was stressful and both were finding it hard to sleep but tonight was different. They both fell sound asleep however Dahli was woken abruptly by a presence in the bedroom. She sat bolt upright and stared into the darkness and there at the end of the bed emerged a little girl dressed in a long white nightgown. She was slender and pale with beautiful dark brown hair, and she sat with legs slightly crossed, smiling at Dahli. Dahli was afraid, her heart beating in her mouth, frozen to the spot but the young girl just sat there, still and quiet, smiling. Then in an instance she rose from the bed and floated away, disappearing into the ether.

"Dahli, Dahli, are you okay? You were screaming." Dahli felt sick, her heart pounding, frightened. "Oh my God, Joe.. I'm sorry. I saw a young girl sitting on the edge of the bed. She was just there. It was frightening." Dahli pointed at the end of the bed and couldn't believe what she had seen. "She was there, as clear as day, as real as you lying there. A young girl in a white nightie. Then she stood up and just disappeared into thin air. It was really strange." Dahli fell back and sighed. Joe caressed her face and got her a glass of water. "Let's go back to sleep. It's only 3am. We've got another busy day ahead." Joe fell back to sleep but Dahli lay there in the darkness, agitated.

The next night Dahli was again visited by the young girl. She again sat on the end of the bed and this time Dahli watched her, less afraid, her long dark hair folded around the top of her nightgown and she had the sweetest smile. "Hello. Who are you?" asked Dahli softly but the girl again rose and disappeared. The apparition reoccurred a few more times over the next few weeks then just came to an end. "I must find out who she is, Joe. It's bugging me. She is obviously friendly, with the most engaging smile." She said and Joe kissed her gently. "You sure you weren't dreaming, Dahli? You've been under a lot of stress recently." he replied and Dahli was a little irritated that he hadn't believed her. "I did see her, Joe. She was real. A real ghost thing or whatever." He nodded and went back to chopping his carrots. She knew that it sounded fanciful but she believed that she had seen someone who maybe had once lived in the apartment above the baker and she needed to find out somehow.

Chapter Forty-Five

Amelie and Christian were early. Dahli saw them peering through the big glass windows at the front of the restaurant. She walked hurriedly towards them, mouthing "hello" and before unlocking and opening the door. "Hi there." she said, waving them through the door. "We are just finishing off. Please make yourself at home. I'll be with you in a mo." She pointed at a table in the corner of the restaurant and dashed off to the kitchen to help Joe pour some wine. "They're early, Joe. Damn!" she said exasperated. Joe calmed her down and said not to worry. It was just before midday and the restaurant would soon be opening. Amelie and Christian had not been seen for some months due to their ongoing personal relationship issues. They had got back together but were open to close friends and family about their marriage counselling sessions. Dahli had noticed that they both looked pale and tired. "I hope we never get like them." she had said to Joe one evening but he hadn't replied, just smiled. Joe was ever the realist. "At least they are getting help, Dahli. Trying to save their marriage. It must be very hard." He was also ever the empath.

Dahli finished off her jobs in the kitchen and dashed out with wine and glasses in hand. She beamed at the couple who were sitting quietly in the corner, "How are you both? Dahli chirped then realised it might not have been the best opening question. Christian grimaced slightly and looked at Amelie for reassurance. "Yes, we're doing okay. You think that's okay to say, Amelie?" he said looking at his wife. Amelie nodded. "Yes, Dahli we're doing okay." The conversation felt stilted with obvious newly acquired therapy techniques being employed. Dahli sat down and poured wine with gusto trying to hide her anxiety, and then Joe arrived to lighten the mood. "Hi all, you hungry?" The restaurant had started to fill up but Joe and Dahli had taken a couple of hours off to spend time with Christian and Amelie who they hadn't seen for some months. The first course was oysters, followed by sea bass and sauteed prawns and finished with Normandy apple pie. "That was delicious, well done both of you." Amelie exclaimed. "But before I forget I have something for you, Dahli" and with that she reached into her bag and brought out a bundle of old letters tied with a bit of shoelace. "Ah, Otto's letters!" shouted Dahli and grabbed them off Amelie. "Thank you!" Amelie felt a little reluctant to hand them over, as if doing so meant the final conclusion of her relationship with Raphael. It had ended months before and he had now left Paris to further study in Milan but she missed him still.

It had been a good couple of hours finally catching up but Dahli noticed that Christian had frequently been distracted by something most of the evening, looking around the restaurant. "You okay there, Christian?" she finally asked him and he looked at her seriously. "Dahli, did you know?" Dahli looked confused. "Know what?" she asked him, leaning in slightly. "This restaurant? You didn't know?" he replied. Dahli laughed nervously, worried that she was part of some weird joke that she wasn't understanding. "What are you talking about Christian? Please explain." He breathed in sharply and raised his eyebrows, his face looking surprised. "Oh my goodness. I can't believe this. Dahli, this restaurant was where Otto and Svetlana met. Svetlana's parents were the owners in the early 1900s. They lived upstairs for quite some years. I can't believe this, and you really didn't know?"

Dahli was gobsmacked. She had absolutely no idea. They both sat in silence for a moment then laughed. "Well, I never, Christian. You couldn't make it up." said Dahli, then she thought of the little girl who had sat on the end of her bed. "So what did Svetlana look like as a child, do you know?" she asked Christian then she remembered the photograph hanging in a frame in the bakery in Port de Vacquelin. Svetlana had been young in the photo, maybe only in her early twenties and though it was black and white, Dahli remembers her long hair and piercing eyes. "There are few photos of Svetlana from her childhood but I knew her in her eighties before she got sick," said Christian. "But she was a striking woman, almost beautiful I would say, with her glossy, long grey hair and wonderful smile." Dahli truly believed that it had been Svetlana sitting on the edge of her bed each night, maybe wishing her well, giving them her blessing. She smiled to herself, content that she now knew.

Christian and Dahli walked out of the restaurant and down to Square Marigny park and then onto the Champs Elysees gardens. It was a chilly and dark evening with only a few people taking a stroll in the pleasant surroundings, and they linked arms, resting for a while before hurrying their pace eventually reaching the river. They leant over the wall breathing in the rich air, gazing at the river, wide and deep, pacifying their active minds and they watched little boats as they chugged up and down, their engines giving off a low thrum and their lights twinkling. "You know I was so close to throwing myself in there," said Christian wistfully. Dahli was stunned by his words that came out of the blue but she put her arm around him and hugged him gently. "Well we are all glad you didn't, Christian." He laughed awkwardly and they wandered further, eventually sitting on a bench talking about Otto and his family, the restaurant, the letters and Dahli felt it time to tell Christian about her meeting Svetlana. "You know that I have seen Svetlana. She came to me several times in the night recently. As a young girl sitting on the end of our bed, smiling." said Dahli, a little worried that Christian might think her crazy just as she thought Joe had, but he just smiled. "She must have been wishing you well, Dahli. You are very lucky." he replied and Dahli felt comforted by his words. "We are here for you now, always, Christian." said Dahli."And likewise, Dahli " replied Christian. It was a profound moment in their new lives together, brother and sister together.

Chapter Forty-Six
January 2022

Dahli sat on the toilet looking at the plastic stick. She felt panic rising as she waited. She closed her eyes then opened them, still no result, then she closed them again, and reopened them and there it was, as clear as day, a blue cross. "I'm pregnant." she whispered to herself. "I'm pregnant." she said again but this time louder and then finally she shouted the words at the top of her voice, tears rolling down her cheeks, clenching the plastic stick in her hand. She ran out of the bathroom and raced into the lounge where Joe was sitting watching television. She flung herself down beside him and shouted "I'm pregnant!" at him whilst sobbing, and he looked at her stunned. "What the f?" he cried then he looked down and saw the plastic stick, pulling it from her firm grip and surveying the results for himself. "Oh my god, Dahli, we're having a baby!" and he put his hands on the top of his head in disbelief, then reached out and hugged the blubbering mess next to him tightly. "Well done, you! We're going to be a family".

Rann arrived for a week's holiday. The recent months had passed far too quickly and it had been the longest the two women had been apart for some years. Rann had brought Sarah and the baby with her. They sauntered through the apartment door and Rann fell onto the sofa and laid her head back, looking exhausted and Dahli felt concerned but didn't say something thinking it might just have been the journey, however Rann continued to look peakish. "Are you okay, Rann?" Dahli asked her one afternoon whilst Sarah changed her baby in the other room. Rann was unusually quiet then spoke, blushing slightly. "I've been diagnosed with early menopause and I'm hating it. Unbelievably there's a support group in Port de Vacquelin and they've been wonderful but I'm still having some off days. I feel old and a bit spent." Dahli looked at her sympathetically. Rann continued. "I can't believe that I can't have any more children. Not that I wanted any more children, oh, I don't know, Dahli, maybe I didn't until this. It's so final." Rann shrugged her shoulders, resigned to her situation and Dahli touched her growing stomach discreetly and felt a little guilty. "You can always talk to me about it, Rann. I know I'm not yet going through it yet but I'm your sister… and you can still drink wine unlike me!" They both laughed.

These were happy times for the two women whose lives had changed inexplicably over the past few years. The years of anger and distrust had been replaced by the simple delights of shopping for baby clothes in the city and eating great food and gossiping about good times. They had also met up with Joe's ex-girlfriend, Adrienne and her daughter, Genevieve. Adrienne and Dahli had become good friends since Joe and Dahli moved to the city, with a shared passion for travel and food, and Joe had started seeing his daughter a few times a week, often taking her to nursery or days out at the zoo or the many parks in the city. "We must meet up again soon, Dahli. I miss you so much. I have even thought about selling Bijou and moving to Paris. Maybe in the future." Rann cried and Dahli hugged her closely. "You do what makes you happy, Rann. It would be lovely to have Aunty Rann nearby though!" said Dahli, laughing. The thought of losing Bijou made Dahli sad though, that fading memory and link to her mother but Rann must do what she felt was right.

Twilight was hitting Paris and Dahli had a few hours to spare so Joe persuaded her to take some time for herself. She walked up to the Champs Elysees and onto Winston Churchill Avenue to admire the wonderful Grand Palais and its vast glass roof, then on to Avenue Montaigne to gaze into the chic couture shops of Chanel, Prada and Gucci. Most of the shops were still open for an hour or two with their frontages still brightly lit and people wandering the streets clutching bags of clothes and other precious items. No matter what time of day or year Paris was always buzzing and Dahli loved it. She ended by walking down to the river, strolling aimlessly, feeling the air pressing on her face and the wind blowing through her hair and for the first time she felt completely at peace with life. She momentarily thought back to her childhood and smiled, remembering that those deep rooted experiences weren't going to haunt her anymore. For most of her life she had abandoned any thought of feeling included, and creating sustained relationships. Feelings of gratification were often brief and she had pushed so many people away over the years; Rann, Gabe, her mother to name but a few but now she had found out the true meaning of family with Rann and Christian, fallen in love with Joe, made some forever friendships in Eric and Beulah, was now pregnant with her first child and was co-running a successful business.

It had all been such a whirlwind, exhausting but exhilarating, and all initiated by a set of keys. "Thanks mum." she said to herself. "You were right. You said go seek the truth and be happy. Who would ever have known I could be this fulfilled and I have you to thank for this." She felt tears rolling down her face as she thought of her mother, and she heaved a big sob. The pain of losing her was still there. She took a bottle of Diet Coke out of her pocket, took a big swig, then screwed the lid back on and looked up to the sky. It was starting to rain lightly and she hurried her way back to the restaurant. Early the next day Joe and Dahli took a short stroll along the embankment, Joe putting his arm around Dahli, protective of his pregnant girlfriend. They arrived back at the restaurant later and Dahli paused for a moment, resting her hands on the glass and looking through the window. "You okay, Dahli?" said Joe, seeing her face but Dahli just turned slowly to him and smiled. "I'm home, Joe." she replied, almost in disbelief. "I've finally come home." and they kissed, smiled at each other, and went through the door.

THE END

Printed in Dunstable, United Kingdom